Bent Creek

Marlene Mitchell

BEARHEAD PUBLISHING
- BhP -
Louisville, Kentucky

Bent Creek

To Betty Jo,
Here's to happiness,
health and humor —
Warmest Regards
Marlene Mitchell

BEARHEAD PUBLISHING
- BhP -
Louisville, Kentucky
www.bearheadpublishing.com/marlene.html

Bent Creek
by Marlene Mitchell

Cover Design by Bearhead Publishing
Cover Concept by Marlene Mitchell

First Printing - January 2010

ISBN: 978-0-9824373-6-0
1 2 3 4 5 6 7 8 9

Disclaimer
This book is a work of fiction. The characters, names, places, and incidents are used fictitiously and are a product of the author's imagination. Any resemblance of actual persons, living or dead, is entirely coincidental.

.Proudly printed in the United States of America.

Dedication

To my niece, Diane Gibbear and my nephew, Richard Borders. Two special people that I would love even if we weren't related.

Other Novels
by Marlene Mitchell

Yard Sale - Everything Must Go

Return to Ternberry

The Chester County Boys

The Women of Magnolia

Circle of Prey

A Little Bit of History

In the heart of Appalachia, just a few miles before you cross the Tennessee border, there used to be a small town called Bent Creek, Kentucky. Bent Creek was nestled in the shadow of Big Black Mountain where the tall pines and cascading streams meandered through the foothills and hollows. It was a coal-mining town that started way back in the eighteen hundreds in a rugged swathe of America. It wasn't much of a town, just two rows of old wooden buildings on a line of railroad tracks leading to the Five Star Mine. If you blink, you would probably pass right on through.

When the mine first opened for business, the mountain men and farmers who lived in the valleys and hollows grabbed their picks and went to work in the underground caverns. They toiled everyday at the backbreaking work of digging the black gold that would keep most of the country running. Each day the rail cars would pull into the newly formed town to carry the coal to the cities far away from Bent Creek— to places that the miners who dug the coal would never see and most never knew about.

To the poor people living in the foothills of Black Mountain the mine and the company store was pretty much their life. They were the poorest of the poor, their lives shackled to the mine for their meager existence.

In the spring of 1928 the laborers at the Five Star Mining Company went on strike. The working conditions in the

1

mine had become deplorable. Each time the miners descended into the shafts they knew that there was a good chance they would not be going home that night. In the two previous years, eleven miners had died and scores injured when the ceilings of the underground caverns collapsed.

For the first time in over a hundred years the noise from the mine was silent when the miners put down their picks and filed out of the tunnels. There were no morning whistles and the constant pounding of the jackhammers digging into the earth had stopped. The trains passed right on through Bent Creek without stopping to pick up their usual load of coal.

At first the miners were not concerned about the strike. They assumed that it would be short lived and their demands met. The country was still climbing out of a great depression and talk of war loomed on the horizon. The mining company officials said they were only holding on by the fringe and their profit margin was shrinking. They could not afford to fix every mineshaft in the area.

As the strike continued into the summer and then lingered on into fall the families living in the backwoods just south of Bent Creek knew they were in dire trouble with the winter quickly approaching. Some moved away, seeking out relatives to help them. Others just packed up their cars and wagons and took off to anywhere they could find work. Even though the mines in Lynch, Kentucky, just twenty miles away from Bent Creek were prospering there was no work to be had for the strikers. The unspoken word among the managers at the Lynch mines was that they were not to hire those men that were responsible for closing the Bent Creek mines. After only one year there were less than twenty families living in the hollows around the dying town.

The mining company store had closed when the supplies were depleted. Mabry's one-room store with few items to purchase and the livery stable were the only two places left in Bent Creek to buy staples. Unlike the company store that traded pay vouchers for merchandise, Mabry's only took cash or bartered for needed products. When all the eggs and chickens and pigs were traded for staples the only way to survive was to go back to hunting for wildlife to stave off starvation. Others took to trapping for animal pelts and making illegal moonshine back in the hills beyond the eyes of the law.

After the mine closed the only reminder that it ever existed was the few miles of rusty track and a faded sign in front of the entrance that read "No Trespassing." Bent Creek had been a small red line that led to a blue dot on the map of Kentucky. Now time had erased its existence.

On the porch of Mabry's store three old men sit in rockers telling stories about the old days. "Life ain't never been no picnic in the holler and it's a whole lot worse since the mine closed. In the spring the rain swells all them thar cricks and at times you can't even git to yer house. The water comes down off them mountains faster than you kin run. Everythang is turned to mud. Then summer comes and everythang is damp and hot and if'n you stand still long nuf that mildew will creep right up yer leg. Then you got them ticks and skeeters that won't leave you be. If'n you make it through fall without dyin from the chill ya got the winter on yer back. The cold jest gets in yer bones and more sickness sets in. I lost a couply toes a few yars back. Froze right off. Food is always on yer mind. Food, tobaccy and a good old slug of moonshine."

"Now if'n ya ast me whar Bent Creek is, I'd have to ponder on that fer a minute. Ya go down this heah road fer a spell then through the kivered bridge. Turn by the old gristmill

and ya'll be thar in no time. Don't go pokin' round in them hollers lessen ya got kin or friends livin' thar. Ya good jest git shot. They don't cotton ta strangers nosen in thar business."

Chapter One

Roy Riley was a coal miner, just like his father and grandfather. It had been a way of life for his family for almost a hundred years. Uneducated and poor, they accepted their fate. Go to work in the mines or starve.

Most of the Riley men had married young and had large families. The same was true of Roy. He took Ida Mae Edel for his wife when he was eighteen years old. In less than six years, six children were born to a woman who was barely out of her teens.

When they married, Roy and Ida Mae moved in with his parents, Abe and Cladda. Cladda and Ida Mae worked from the moment Roy and Abe left for the mine until they came home in the evening. There was wash to be done, a garden to be weeded and always food to be cooked. It was tough work for a young girl. When Ida Mae began popping out a baby every year, Abe said that Roy and Ida Mae had to move. Getting the neighbors together, a house was built about a mile down the road from Abe's cabin. It was far from Ida Mae's dream house—just a square box made out of rough wood with four rooms and a front porch. A privy was built around back along with a chicken coop. Friends and neighbors donated what they could. They were given a rough-hewn kitchen table with two benches, a couple of iron beds and a wood stove. With homemade quilts and bedding, some old pots and pans, a few mismatched dishes and three forks, Ida Mae set up housekeeping for her family.

Just like all the young people who lived in the hills and worked in the mines they dreamed of one day having enough money to live comfortably. They soon realized their future was sealed and the twenty-two dollars a week Roy made in the mine could barely support their growing family. Each week there was not even enough money left over to buy a box of nails or a roll of tarpaper to fix the leaky roof.

Even though Ida Mae discovered early on that Roy had a lazy streak running through him she never gave up hoping that someday he would get up off the porch and work on the house or at least cut wood. It never happened. After working all day in the mine, Roy said he didn't expect to have to do anything else, but drink a few swills of moonshine and play his banjo.

The first child born to Roy and Ida Mae was named William Roy, although everyone called him Willie. He was born just nine months and four days after Roy and Ida Mae married. The next year Ida Mae gave birth to Paul Ronald and then came Benjamin Willis. It was the birth of the twins the following year that wracked havoc on her body. She suffered in labor for almost two days before Rachael Joy and Jesse Roy were born. Lack of good nourishment and the loss of blood, kept her in bed for almost a week, getting up just long enough to feed and change the babies. Ida Mae knew that having more children would surely take her life. She prayed long and hard to the Lord that she would have no more babies, but it happened again.

When Emma Jane was born two years later, Ida Mae lay close to death for almost a week. Unable to find help for her, Roy went to one of the crew bosses at the mine named Jimmy and asked for his help. Jimmy and his wife came to the Riley house. A few minutes later, Roy carried Ida Mae, wrapped in a blanket out to Jimmy's car. The children were told that she was going to the hospital, but would be home soon. Grandma Cladda stayed with the children while Roy was working in the mines. Ida Mae returned two weeks later still looking pale and drawn. That was the last of the babies for the Riley family.

Chapter Two

Most of the Riley kids were not much different from the rest of those living in the backwoods hollows. Just a bunch of rowdy, ragtag kids who occasionally went to school, played outside, helped with the chores and tried to make sure they got enough to eat.

Willie was a funny, cheerful little kid. He followed Roy around like a hound dog puppy. Willie thought his pa was the smartest man he knew, which of course made Roy feel real proud. Willie would do most anything Roy asked him to do, including the chores that Ida Mae said Roy should be doing. Willie didn't mind. As long as he could sit with his pa each evening and whittle or learn to play the banjo, he was happy.

Paul, the second oldest of the Riley children delighted in taunting and teasing the younger children until they cried. He would devise ways to get out of doing chores or find ways to make the others do them for him. Ida Mae said that Paul had a mean streak running through his body and he was always the one to get the switch to his backside first.

Ben, just eleven months younger, was just the opposite. He was soft spoken and kind and the target of Paul's constant teasing. He was by far the most obedient of the Riley children.

Jesse was the quiet one. He stuttered terribly as a young child and seldom spoke. He had a hard time figuring out most things. His father said that he thought Jesse was a little dense in the head.

Then there was Rachael, Jesse's twin sister. Rachael was full of ambition and ideas. She was the one who could figure out most of the problems in the household. Rachael was the only one who could read and write well enough to take care of her father's paperwork. Strong-willed and defiant, Rachael was sure she was never meant to live in Harlan County and from early on she knew that someday, she would leave for good.

Rachael was also put in charge of taking care of Emma Jane while her mother was busy with the household chores. Rachael was Emma Jane's protector. Emma Jane was afraid of everything; lightning, thunder, darkness, empty rooms, animals, creepy bugs, the outhouse, and fear that her father would someday die in the coalmine. Being the youngest, Emma Jane's life was a maze of weaving and dodging to stay out of harms way. The phrase, "the chickens are coming, the chickens are coming" sent cold chills up her spine. She would throw the mash—bucket and all, over the fence and run. The big red rooster with his dark, beady eyes and sharp spurs was her nemesis. He watched her and waited for an opening to fly at her face. Her momma said it was just her imagination and that rooster only did that because he was scared when she screamed but she knew that rooster—and he was her mortal enemy. She begged Rachael to help her feed the chickens.

The goats wanted to eat the clothes right off Emma Jane's body and the pigs would lower their heads and made their foreboding grunts when she came around. Yet Rachael was always right beside her with a sturdy stick ready to take them all on.

It was not unusual that an occasional black snake would be found curled up on the porch or in the winter the house would take on new inhabitants. The field mice would skitter across the floor looking for any little crumb that had been overlooked. Emma Jane would scream until Rachael chased them out the door or whacked them with a stick.

Rachael was different from the other Riley children, in many other ways, too. She was a dreamer. Having mud ball fights and chasing each other was not something she was interested in. She would find a place to sit all alone and pretend she was somewhere else. Combing her long, brown hair and talking to herself convinced the other children that she was touched. Rachael's imagination was her only companion. It was Ben who came to her rescue when the taunting became too much even for her. Yet, Rachael refused to accept her lot in life from early on. She always knew that someday, somehow she would leave Bent Creek and never come back.

Somewhere around the age of seven or eight she began to realize just how poor she really was. With never enough to eat and homemade clothes to wear she began to take notice of everything around her. Life began to sour around the edges when she got her first glimpse of a Sears-Roebuck catalog. All the clothes and toys jumped out of the pages at her. There was not one feed sack dress in the whole book. She did not even have the five cents it would take to buy a blue ribbon for her hair. She wondered what it would be like to wear shoes that fit and had no holes in them.

Embarrassment began to set in when the mine superintendent brought his family to Bent Creek on Christmas Eve to deliver gift baskets. Rachael watched the smirk on his daughter's face as Rachael tried to eat her first banana without peeling it. Rachael looked at the girl's clothes—the wool, brown coat with not a button missing and her boots made of soft leather. The word envy was now another part of Rachael's world.

Rachael had a way of challenging what people said, even going so far as to confront her daddy. With the Sears-Roebuck catalog laying open on the kitchen table, she shared the precious book with Emma Jane. The girls would ooh and aah over the book. When her father pointed his dirty finger at her and told her to get all the fancy ideas out of her head and just accept her lot in life she really didn't want to believe him. "It is what it is, Girl, so you might as well git used to it."

Rachael stood up, her hands on her hips and said, "And what is it really? Thars a whole world outside of Bent Creek and by gosh, I intend to see some of it." That remark earned her a slap across her face.

Rachael liked going to school, which really seemed odd to most of the children. It was only a one-room schoolhouse with a raw, wooden floor and a wood stove for heat in the winter. The smaller children were placed at two square tables, while four rows of desks held the rest of the students. Usually most of the rows were empty. Rachael always sat in front so that when her teacher, Mr. Childs conducted the lessons, she wouldn't miss anything. She was a star pupil and the only one to cry when the school closed.

If it weren't for the occasional visit from the state truant officer most of the children in the hollow would never go to school. Missing school for weeks at a time they would only return to the classroom when they were forced to. The majority of the boys quit by the time they were fourteen to go to work.

Her vision of her world was altered when she read books about the big cities across the country. When she read about Florida she decided that is where she wanted to live. The information in her schoolbooks fortified her notion that there was something big and wonderful out there, and it wasn't Bent Creek.

In fourth grade when she read her writing essay aloud before the class, they snickered and giggled. Who was this stupid girl who thought she would move to Florida and grow oranges in her back yard and pick seashells off the beach? On the way home from school Sammy Joe and some of the other boys from school chased her and yelled after her, "Yer plumb out of yer head, Rachael Riley."

She stopped and faced them. "I'm not crazy! Yer crazy, Sammy Joe Montgomery. You and yer bunch of back-woods hillbillies who can't see further than the tip of your noses. You ain't got no couth. I reckon ya'll grow up and work in the mines jest like yer fathers. Ya'll either be dead or have a case of black lung by the time yer thirty and probably have a bunch of snot nose kids. This dirty town will be yer home till you die." For a moment there was silence and then they began to laugh.

"Go on run home, Rachael Roach," Sammy Joe yelled.

"You too, Monkey ears," she yelled back.

Rachael didn't want to grow old never leaving Bent Creek. She didn't want to be a hollow-eyed woman with a sad face like her mother and settle for a man with coal embedded under his fingernails and no teeth like her father. That is not what she wanted for herself. She wanted to be anywhere except in Harlan County, Kentucky. She wanted to live in Florida.

At dinner that evening, Paul told his father about Rachael's paper and that all of the kids were making fun of her. Roy put down his spoon and looked at his daughter, "That true, Rachael? You making up that stupid stuff again?"

"It's not stupid. Why does everybody think it's stupid? I read it in a book. People can leave here, you know. They have before and maybe some of them went to Florida."

"Yeah, and some come back in worse shape than when they left. You best be writin' bout something you know fer sure," her father answered.

"What about you, Momma, wouldn't you like to go to Florida? It's warm all the time. We could make necklaces out of shells."

"You hush, Rachael. Don't argy with yer daddy. Eat yer supper and stop that crazy talk."

Later that evening Rachael sat on the porch with her mother mending socks. "I'm not crazy, Momma. I know ya'll think I am, but I'm not. Haven't you ever wanted something better fer yourself? Wouldn't it be fun to put on a nice dress and go into Lynch? Maybe have dinner in one of those fancy restaurants like Wendy's and then go to the picture show. That's what I'm gonna do when I grow up."

"I suppose at one time I thought about it," Ida Mae said, breaking the thread with her teeth. "But then I got married and I had more to think about than picture shows. I had to worry about keepin' you kids fed and prayin' you didn't get sick. I reckon all them idees left my head. I jest don't want you ta be sad when those things don't happen, Rachael. You jest got to trust in the Lord to make things right fer you. If'n it twern't fer goin ta church every Sunday and readin' mah bible every night I'd be a lost soul."

"Don't seem like the Lord is answerin' many of yer prayers, Momma, I guess I'm gonna make them happen myself. You jest wait and see."

When the announcement was made that the school was closing and the students would be reassigned to a school in Lynch everyone knew that the children from Bent Creek had just finished the little education they had. None of the families in the hollow were going to travel over twenty miles twice a day to take their kids to school even if they did have to argue with the truant officer.

After Mr. Childs made the announcement on a Friday afternoon, his remark was met with a war whoop from the boys. Laughing and clapping the children tumbled out the door and headed for home, all except one. Rachael sat at her desk with her head down and cried. "I jest can't believe that the government don't care if we git an education. We jest don't count, do we, Mr. Childs?"

"I don't know if that's true, Rachael. It's just that the county can't afford to pay my salary and keep the school open when half the time the children aren't here anyway. You're a bright girl and my best student and I am sorry that this had to happen to you. Do you think there is anyway your family can let you go to school in Lynch?"

"Shoot, no. They ain't gonna let me go anywhere cept outside to hang up clothes."

Mr. Childs sat down on the desk next to her. "I'm sorry to hear that but I hope you keep up with your studies. Life really doesn't much care what happens to us, Rachael. We have to make it happen on our own. You remember that. Now I have to lock up. You best better run on home."

She didn't run. She walked as slow as she could and cried all the way.

After the school closed one day became just like the next. It was always work, work, and more work. There was never time for fun. She was always being told what to do, getting reprimanded or even worse—getting hit for doing her chores wrong. The way she was treated didn't make Rachael feel too good about her parents. She wondered if they really loved her. It was quite evident that her father was partial to the boys and Emma Jane was clearly her mother's favorite. Emma Jane liked to hang on her momma and follow her around.

Rachael tried to believe that her favorite pecan pie her mother made on Sundays or the apples she let the children eat off the tree was her way of showing love. There were no hugs or kisses or special moments to share with her parents. At times when her mother sat mending the already tattered clothing she had to wear, Rachael could see the far away look in her eyes. She was afraid to ask her mother what she was dreaming about. Yet in the winter when the wind blew through the cracks in the cabin and the temperature dipped below freezing, her mother would rise at night and put large stones on the only wood stove in the house. Wrapping them in old material she would place them on her children's feet to keep their toes warm. Sometimes she would stroke Rachael's hair, but no words came from her mouth.

When they were alone Rachael's curiosity was a sense of irritation to her mother. She didn't like answering questions about herself. All Rachael knew about her family is that her mother was an orphan at an early age and was raised by an elderly aunt. Everyone said that Grandpa Abe, her father's paw was a crazy old man. Rachael worried that she took after him when people called her crazy.

Sometimes at night, when the house was dark and everyone was in bed, Rachael would lie awake staring out the window. She wondered what her momma was thinkin'. Was she worried about her children or still wrapped up in her own woes. Thinkin' she shouldn't have gotten married so young and had so many babies. Thinkin' maybe she should be nicer to her kids and maybe sing with them or play games. Maybe even hug them once in a while and tell them she loved them. That's what you should do when you have kids. And her daddy... was he frettin' about how he was going to feed all his youngins or how they were gonna get to school or if they would be able to have shoes to wear when winter came. He should be thinkin' about those things instead of sittin' around doin' nothin'. No, they were probably both jest tired and not thinkin' much about anything.

Chapter Three

      The years passed, one just like the other, eating away at Rachael's life. Willie, Paul and Ben went to work in the mines as each one turned fifteen. At fourteen, Rachael took a part-time job in Bent Creek working at the Sampler Dry Goods Store. She swept the floors and kept the bolts of material in order. At times she waited on the customers. Even though it was almost a two-mile walk to the store, she did not care. Every Friday she was handed an envelope that contained her three dollar paycheck. She would hand it to her father and he would give her back fifty cents to spend. She wished she could keep more, but she was glad that she could help the family. She wondered why he never told her thanks.

      With the added income from the four children working, life was better for the family. Ida Mae could buy more flour and sugar to make biscuits and Emma Jane and Rachael each got a store-bought coat and a real blanket for their beds. The mining company agreed to let the miners' run electric lines from the coalmine to the hollow. The Riley's' had lights! No more foul smelling kerosene lamps or candles on the table. They had lights! And the most wonderful thing that happened was when Rachael's father brought home a radio. It became the center of the house. Each night the programs would start at six o'clock. Everyone would gather around the brown box and listen to country music programs and serial stories. Rachael was enthralled by the radio. She couldn't get enough of the outside world, but promptly at eight the radio and the lights were turned off and everyone had to go to bed.

When the last of the spring rains passed and the warm summer days lingered on until eight o' clock, Rachael's parents would gather with some of the other folks who lived in the hollow for a front-porch party. Most of the junk would be cleared from the yard and candles set out to keep the bugs away. The women would make pies and fresh berries covered in sugar and the men would bring the moonshine. The music came from all sources—a set of spoons, a washboard and a prized fiddle owned by one of the men from the mine. Daddy played the banjo with one string missing that he had gotten from his father. The children would run around the yard playing games. It was a short time that took the edge off of everyday living. The liquor flowed as easy as the music and after a few rounds of foot stompin', Rachael's daddy would grab Ida Mae by the arm and pull her out into the yard, which had become a makeshift dance floor. He would swing her around until the pins would fall out of her hair and the stands of dark-brown hair would twirl with each turn. Her momma would laugh out loud, something she rarely did.

Breathless, her face aglow with a rosy tint, they would return to the porch and sit next to each other. Rachael liked to see her mother happy.

"She ain't a bad dancer fer an old woman, is she Rachael?" her father asked as Ida Mae began to blush.

"Why do you call her an old woman, Daddy, she ain't but in her early thirties. Old women are fifty years old or more. Look at her. Momma is real purty with her hair down."

Roy turned Ida Mae's face to him. "Dawg gone, yer right. She's jest as purty as the day I married her. I reckon that's why we had so many of you youngins'. It's still hard to keep my hands off her."

"Roy Riley, you stop that," Ida Mae said. "Don't be tellin' Rachael bout things she don't need ta know yet.

"I reckon she does," Roy said. She's done past her thirteenth birthday. Time to find her a husband." He roared with laughter, knowing that such talk was always a sore subject with Rachael.

ॐ   ॐ   ॐ

Within a few months with everyone working, Roy was able to buy an old truck. It was the first vehicle he ever owned. He sat behind the wheel of the beat up old truck and grinned from ear to ear. The stuffing was coming out of the seats and the floorboards were rusted, but it had an engine and it could get them to town three times faster than the old mule.

Each morning on the way to the mine, Rachael would jump into the back of the truck, along with Benjamin and Paul. Her father would drop her off in front of the store. Life was the best it had ever been for the Riley family, yet Rachael knew it had to be a lot better for her to stay in Kentucky. The reality of living in a coal-mining town was always with her. Black lung, cave-ins and premature death were always in the conversations of the coal-mining families. Life could change in an instant when the breadwinner of the family was killed in the mines or died from a related illness. It could happen to the Riley's just as well.

Working in the store on a Friday morning, Rachael wiped the sweat from her brow as she unpacked bolts of material and put them on the high shelves. The sound of the sirens interrupted her thoughts. Running to the door she saw thick, black smoke trailing across the sky. Something had gone wrong at the mine. Most everyone stopped what they were doing when the chilling whine of the sirens blared. Men, women and children ran past the store, across the tracks and down the steep grade to the entrance of the mine. Rachael pulled the door shut behind her and hurried along with the others toward the mine. As the crowd gathered there seemed to be an ominous silence. Another burst of soot and smoke began to escape through the air chambers on the outside of the mine. It was a sign that there was a fire deep below the earth. An hour later, word was passed through the crowd that three men were killed inside one of the shafts as they tried to escape the fire. The cries and wails of those related to the miners hurt everyone deeply.

Ida Mae and Rachael were there each time the sirens went off. Waiting just like the others to make sure that their family members were safe. When the men began to appear at the mouth of the tunnel, the wives and children were given a reprieve one more time. Once again the men in the Riley family were saved from the black death. This time the mine took three lives.

Three months later a cave-in killed one of Grandpa Abe's brothers and just a few months later the siren sounded again. This time all of the Riley boys filed out of the mine opening, but there was no sign of Roy. Paul said that his father was working in tunnel sixteen which was further into the mine. It was one of the longest tunnels in the mine. Ben and Paul said when they heard the rumbling and when the siren went off they ran out of the mine as fast as they could. Ida Mae kept asking the men filing out of the tunnel if they had seen her husband. There were only somber-faced men shaking their heads. Afternoon turned to night and night to morning and there was still no word on the fourteen miners still below ground. Someone brought soup and handed a bowl to Ida Mae. She pushed it away. She sat silently on the side of the hill, wrapped in a blanket.

A few hours later word came that the shaft in tunnel sixteen had been cleared and the men were coming up. Everyone stood up, inching closer to the rim of the mine. They watched as the men filed out—coughing and wheezing, their faces black as night. Someone handed the men wet cloths so they could wipe off their faces and be identified. As each man removed his mask of soot there were cries of joy from his family. Roy was the ninth man to come out. Ida Mae ran down the hill and hugged him almost knocking him off of his feet. His hands and knees were bleeding and he couldn't talk. Paul picked him up like a rag doll and carried him to the truck and placed him on a blanket. Ida Mae held his hand all the way home.

After washing in the outside tub, Roy changed his clothes and laid down across the bed. Now was not the time to talk. Ida Mae rubbed salve on his hands and knees and bandaged them with white strips of cloth. She brought him soup and black coffee, but he was too exhausted to eat. He rolled over and spent the night coughing up the soot that was lodge in his lungs.

In the morning the family gathered around him as he sat on the porch eating oatmeal. His voice was hoarse and raspy but he feigned a smile as each of his children filed out the door and sat down beside him.

"It was bad, real bad," he said, shaking his head. "Coal been a fallin' all morning from the ceilin', hittin' our helmets like hail on a tin roof. We kept askin' the pit boss if we wuz safe and he kept sayin' we had nothin to worry about. Bout noon we started to hear the rumblin' a long ways down in the tunnel. Ya heer them sounds all the time, but when it started gettin' louder and louder we knew we wuz in trouble. Then the soot got thick as black molasses and the lamps started goen out. We couldn't see nothin' at tall. The lead man told us to clip our lines onto each other and hold on to the reins of the mules and follow him out of the tunnel. We could hear the rumble gettin' louder and it was pourin' coal. It was catchin' up with us. Then all hell broke loose and the walls just started comin' down in big chunks. We was followin' one behind the other, holdin' tight to that rope and then the line stopped and got real taunt. The mules went crazy and tried to break loose. They were bawlin' and hee-hawin' all down the line, so we jest unhitched them and let them run on ahead afore they stomped us to death. We could hear the men at the end of the line screamin' as they was covered with piles of coal. The lead man yelled to unhook the line, but old Boswork who was behind me didn't want to leave them men. He kept pullin' and pullin' but he couldn't get them out. All them at the front of the line was lettin' go of the rope, so he unclipped his line and we moved forward. When we reached the line of rail carts the coal comin' off the ceilin' was fillin' them cars up faster than ten men shovelin' all at once."

Roy stopped and began coughing. He wanted to tell his story. He wanted his family to know why some of the men were left behind. "I member we crawled next to them carts on our hands and knees fer what seemed like hours an hours. Them rails would lead us out if'n' we was lucky. I'd told myself that when it finally happened to me and I was caught down there in a cave-in or a fire I wouldn't be afraid. But, I was wrong. I kept thinkin' bout my family and that I didn't want to die. I jest kept movin' till we could see the light of the shaft." Roy stopped and began to sob. Long, anguish sobs that wracked his whole body. "Them was my friends that got left behind. Them was good men who didn't deserve to die jest because them mine owners won't spend the money to shore up them tunnels. Good men died today and it could've been me."

He wiped his nose on his sleeve and ate his oatmeal. He was given two days off with pay. By the next Monday he had to swallow his fear and once again go below ground.

The families in Bent Creek were in a panic wondering who would be next. This had been the worst year ever. Three weeks later the unthinkable happened. Another cave-in claimed two more lives. Sammy Joe's father, Jed Montgomery and Rachael's brother, Willie Riley were caught in a mineshaft elevator and buried under tons of large chunks of coal. Even as the other miners frantically dug with their bare hands to find the men, it was obvious that no one could have survived.

Funerals come quick in the summertime in the hollow. The intense heat and no refrigeration usually resulted in burials the very next day after someone died. It was the same for Willie and Jed. Standing on the grassy knoll covered in white crosses, Rachael held on to her mother as the minister sprinkled dirt on Willie's coffin, sending him into a black hole for the very last time. Minutes later the scene was repeated a few feet away at Jed's grave. Among the wailing and soulful cries, Rachael saw Sammy Joe walking away from his father's grave. She sidled through the small crowd and caught up with him. "I'm sorry about yer pa, Sammy Joe," she said softly.

"Thanks, I'm sorry about Willie, too," he replied.

Rachael wiped a tear from her face. "I can't believe he's gone. His life ain't even started and now it's over. I hear you and yer ma are leaving Bent Creek. Is that true?" she asked.

Sammy Joe nodded. "Yep, we're goin' to Ohio to live with my aunt and uncle. Can't stay here. We ain't got no money now and I'll be damn if I'm gonna go to work in the mine. I never said it, but I'm like you, Rachael, I've always wanted to leave this place. But not like this, losing my pa and all. I'm almost nineteen, the same age as Willie and now he's outta here for good." Rachael could hear the sobs catching in his throat. She turned to leave. "You take care of yourself, monkey ears."

"You too, Rachael roach," he answered.

Inconsolable, Ida Mae had to face the reality that she had given one of her children to the mine. The sadness that engulfed the Riley house lasted for weeks. Roy took to his bed and said he was ailing and wouldn't come out of the bedroom. Ida Mae, who once bragged that she was probably the only woman in the hollow to raise six children to adulthood and not lose a one of them from sickness or accident, joined the other women who mourned their dead children. The rest of the Riley kids moped around the house and every once in a while one of them would break into tears. They huddled together on the porch giving comfort to each other. The boys especially harbored a fear that they could be the next one to die in the mine.

Afraid and angry the mineworkers decided to ban together and talk to the managers about the unsafe conditions and the constant threats of a cave-in, but they were listened to with deaf ears. The foremen said either go to work or quit, but the miners picked a third option, they went on strike. In the spring of 1928 the men refused to enter the mine and laid down their picks. They stood fast. Over the next few weeks there were meetings, but nothing was accomplished and Fridays came and went without paychecks in their pockets.

Soon the realization hit home that the strike was changing the lives of everyone in Bent Creek drastically. The only income in the Riley family was the money that Rachael was making. With the mine's company store now closed, the other businesses in town began to follow suit. The lack of money was evident everywhere. She started working as many hours as she could get in the dry goods store. And so her life had taken on a rhythm to a tune she did not like. And it never seemed to get better. They were once again living in extreme poverty.

Chapter Four

Summer had come to the holler bringing the sizzling heat and constant torment of insects biting deep into your skin. Even though the river was just down the road they stayed clear of it. The river's bank was covered with debris the high water had deposited during the spring floods. Tangled masses of tree branches hugged the muddy shoreline. The undertow was swift and treacherous, along with a good number of water moccasins occupying the river. The only release the Riley kids found to relieve themselves of the heat was to trek partway up Black Mountain, to an old abandoned quarry that was filled with ice-cold water. After their chores were finished, the four oldest would escape before their mother found something else for them to do. Emma Jane was left behind. She was much too young to go with them and afraid of the quarry from the stories Paul had told her about the monsters that lived in the water. Ida Mae would watch as her children disappeared into the woods, wishing she could go with them.

By the time they reached the quarry to join the other kids already swimming, their clothes were soaked with sweat. The boys peeled off their overalls and jumped into the water in their underwear. Rachael was forced to swim in her clothes like most of the other girls. Diving off the edge of the quarry into the dark blue pool of water was instant relief. Rachael had learned to be a good swimmer after being tormented by her brothers who would drag her out into the deep water and let her go. She screamed and paddled and somehow made it to the bank, while they laughed at her. In time they gave up the game since she could easily make it to shore.

No one was sure how deep the quarry was. Some said as deep as seventy-five or eighty feet. Whatever it's depth the Riley kids made sure that they stayed within reach of the bank and always on the left side of the quarry. That was the rule their father had given them on the first day he brought them up to the deep pool.

"If'n I ever ketch you a swimmin' over thar," he said, pointing to the other bank," I'll cut me a big switch and beat yer ass all the way home. And I kin sneak up thar whenever I get a hankerin' to and check on you." They believed him.

The right side was a ledge of quarry rock that shot straight up into the sky. Over the years sturdy vines and small trees had grown into the crevasses. The branches would sway in the wind like long arms reaching out with a warning for them to stay on their own side of the quarry.

On a hot July day, the Riley kids trudged up the mountain and jumped into the cold water, feeling the gratifying release from the summer's torment. After a few hours of splashing and playing in the quarry they lay on the huge, gray rock, the warm sun dried their clothes; Rachael rolled over and sat up. "I reckon we should be going home, soon. Momma don't like us stayin' up here too long."

"What fer?" Paul asked. "What we gonna do at home. Taint no food in the house ceptin' them damn turnips and taters. I'm sick of them."

Jesse let out a grunt. "My belly is so hollow I could play a tune on it. How bout we look around fer some berries or nuts?"

"Damn, nuts or berries. I want food, real food. I want big hunks of meat and bread. Real good bread like Momma used to make," Paul added.

"We'll be gettin' some of that pretty soon. When we get to boot camp. They feed you good in the army," Ben said.

Rachael bolted upright. "Army, what are you talkin' about, Army?"

"Well, we was gonna wait to tell ya'll together, but me and Paul is goin' up to Lynch tomarra to join up. Thangs ain't gettin' no better round here, Rachael," Ben said.

"Oh Lordy, Ma is gonna have a fit when she finds out. She still ain't over losin' Willie and now with you two leaving, oh Lordy," Rachael said shaking her head. "But, I don't blame you. Leastwise you'll get away from here." They walked home in silence. Each one thinking about their own future and the changes coming in their lives.

At the supper table Ben cleared his throat." Well, I've got somethin' to tell ya'll. Me and Paul are goin' up to Lynch tomarra to join the army. They got a man up there that kin sign us up." Paul continued to stare at his empty plate waiting for his parent's to say something.

He was surprised at his father's reaction. "Don't says that I blame you one darn bit. You ain't got nothin'to hold you here. Leastwise the army will pay you and maybe you kin see yer way clear to send yer ma and me a few dollars."

"Why you want to go away and get yerself kilt in the army?" Ida Mae mumbled.

Paul slammed his fork down on the table. "How we gonna die in the army? Ain't no war right now. We're dyin' a slow death here, Ma. What if the mine doesn't open? What then? We jest gonna' sit here and starve to death. This old cabin won't stand another winter and it's already July and we don't have no money. Ain't no work round here for any of us. Sides they got all kinds of programs in the army to teach you things. Maybe I kin larn a trade that will help me make a livin'."

Ida Mae never had an answer for those kinds of questions. She knew there was none.

"Don't ya worry about that, boys. That mine will be up and runnin' in a couply months."

"Yeah and some more kin can get kilt thar," Paul said. "Jest like Willie."

That was the wrong thing to say to Roy Riley. He slammed his hand down on the table causing the dishes to rattle and spoons to fall on the floor. "Workin' in the mine is damn hard work and yeah, we all know it's dangerous. Willie knew that. Nobody twisted you boys arms to work thar. Ain't no call for you to remind me that I lost my son. You jest go on off and join the army." He left the room, slamming the door behind him.

The day after Ben's announcement the two Riley boys packed up their meager belongings and left on foot to meet up with the others that were going to enlist in the army. Rachael kissed them both and hugged them goodbye. Her mother cried, saying she would probably never see her boys again. Rachael's father shook their hands and wished them well. He turned and hurried into the house. It was a sad time even though it meant two less mouths to feed and Jesse would have a bed to sleep in. Roy was counting on the money they would be sending him. They were just boys, but they seemed so grown-up today as they walked down the road and away from Bent Creek.

Chapter Five

Rachael opened the door of the truck and slid in next to Jesse. "Thanks fer pickin' me up," she said, "You know how I hate walkin' home when it is almost dark and rainin' to boot."

Jesse nodded and struggled to keep the truck in gear as it chugged down the street. " It's a real toad strangler out there, Rachael. You best enjoy this ride, little sis, cause Pa is sellin' the truck. He's got someone comin' to look at it tonight. He says usin' the wagon and the mule is as good as the truck and costs a lot less."

"That is too bad, but I got bad news, too. This was my last day at the store cause it's closin'. I only had one customer today and she spent twenty cents. So now, I'm out of a job." She stared out the window at the gray and white scenery as they passed by the stripped land just above the mine.

"Maybe you could marry Billy Tate. I hear he has a crush on you," Jesse said, grinning.

"Billy Tate! I hate Billy Tate," she spewed out. "He's a slimy little weasel and he gives me the creeps. Anyway I am not gonna git hitched to Billy or anybody else livin' in this holler and have a mess of kids and be stuck here. I'm gonna leave soon. I'm gonna go to Florida."

"Well, Emma Jane is lookin' round fer a fella. She's afeared that pa is gonna find somebody fer you and her to marry."

"Well he can just forget that idée . I ain't ever had much to say about what goes on in my life, but I know'd for sure marryin' Billy Tate will never happen. Beside Emma Jane is only thirteen," Rachael replied. She's too young to be even thinkin' about gettin' hitched."

The last turn off the gravel road and into the rutted mud path leading to the house always made Rachael want to close her eyes. How could anyone actually live in this hovel? Half of the front porch was missing since the last storm hit and the yard was strewn with chickens and rusty tools her daddy picked up off the road. Ragged clothes hung on a line strung between two trees. An old Billy goat stood beneath the line chewing one of the pant legs. Rachael jumped out of the truck and shooed him away. It didn't really seem to matter much; the other pant leg was already ragged.

Since the men went on strike her father was always on the porch when Rachael came home from work with her meager pay. He had laid a board over a barrel and sat playing solitaire with a soiled deck of cards that had the three of clubs missing. He would sit for hours just watching the road, waiting for someone to come and tell him that the mine was open again. Today was no different. "See what I mean, Rachael," Jesse said. "Pa is sitting there pretendin' that every thang is gonna be all right and it ain't. "He should be out startin' to cut wood for the winter. We're gonna need a lot of it to keep that drafty, old house warm. I'm plumb tired of doin' all the outside chores round here."

Rachael saved her bad news until after supper. The family sat in silence and ate the boiled potatoes and turnips seasoned with a little deer meat. As her father pushed his chair away from the table, Rachael blurted out, "I don't have a job anymore. The store closed today."

Her father rubbed his head. "Bad news just keeps pilin' up in a heap. Truck is bein' sold tonight. Should give us a little money til the mine opens."

Around six o'clock two men came to the house and after talking with her father, Roy handed them the keys to the truck and they gave him an envelope. He stood in the yard and watched until the truck was out of his sight. He was despondent that he had to sell it, but nothing hurt the family more than when the radio was sold and soon after that all the electricity was cut off.

Chapter Six

"These people livin' around here are just plain stupid," Rachael said, throwing her pad of paper on the kitchen table. "I'm tryin' to do some good and they look at me like I got two heads. Alls I wanted was for them to come to a meetin' and hear what I have to say. They tell me they don't have time— they don't have time! That's a joke. They're jest sittin' round waitin' fer I don't know what. That's what I want to know, what are they waitin' fer? Are they waitin' fer one of their kids to starve to death or freeze when winter comes. I reckon that must be it." She plopped down in the chair, folding her arms over her chest. "Grandpa Abe's the only one that got any sense. He's been cuttin' wood for the last two weeks. He's got a real big stack goin' for him, but he's jest as bull-headed as the rest them. He won't come to my meetin' either."

"What did you spect them to do, Girl? They ain't never had no youngin' goin' round tryin' to set up meetins'. Hell, they probably think yer plumb loco."

"That's the point, Daddy. If they'd jest listen to me I could have told them what it was all about. We could help each other this winter. Instead of jest sittin' on their front porches drinkin' swill and spittin' in cans. Some need wood; others need food or a new roof like us. Maybe by puttin' all our resources together we could come up with a good plan."

"What's a resource?" Roy asked. "I ain't got no resource and I don't tend on buyin' one.

"Oh forget it," She stomped off. Talking to herself and kicking clods of dirt from the road, she didn't even see the figure coming toward her until he said hello.

"Oh, my gosh, Paul, what are you doing home? She threw her arms around his neck and kissed his cheek. "It's only been six weeks, I thought that boot camp lasted eight weeks."

"Does, for most. I didn't make it, Rachael. They said I twern't what they was lookin' fer. They done sent me home. They said I wasn't army material, so they gave me five dollars and a bus ticket home."

"Well, that's okay, Paul I'm sure not everyone is cut out to be a soldier."

"Ben's still there, Rachael. I seed him right before I left. I'm bigger than him and a lot stronger, too, but the sergeant jest kept a gittin' on me. Jest cause I couldn't make it through them trainin' sessions. I tried reel hard, but they were jest too hard fer me. It's my legs, Rachael. I'm plumb bowlegged. I done fell over my own feet." He wiped his nose with the back of his hand. "I'm jest a damn failure."

Rachael put her arms around her brother. "No, yer not, Paul. You'll be fine. I'm glad to have you back."

It didn't take long for Paul to sense that he was a big disappointment to his father. The words were never spoken out loud, but given out in small doses, like telling Jesse to help Paul with the chores since he might not be able to do them. Also, there would only be Ben's allotment sent home to help the family.

Ida Mae was happy to have at least one of her boys home safe. She even went so far as to blame herself for Paul's failure to make it in the army. "I shoulda bound yer legs when you were a youngin'. That's what that old midwife tole me, but I didn't do it. It's all my fault, Paul."

Nothing anyone said seemed to help Paul. He took the little money the army had given him and bought tobacco and moonshine. He slept late and spent the rest of the day sitting on the porch drinking from a jug. By evening he usually was too drunk to even make it in the house and spent many a night sleeping in the yard. Other times he would go off with Billy Tate and some of the other boys from the hollow to drink and raise a ruckus. Ida Mae worried constantly about him, but Roy told her to leave him be. He would come around in his own time.

By the end of the summer everyone in the house was totally fed up with Paul. He picked fights with Jesse, told his mother to mind her own business and called Roy a sorry excuse for a father. Even Rachael felt his wrath. When she tried to help him up when he had fallen he pushed her to the ground and cursed her. He became just one more aggravation to compound the already dire situation in the Riley house.

Paul had also taken up with a girl named Nancy who lived in Lynch. She was plump and short and six years older than him. He began spending all of his time with her.

Laying on the front porch, his hat pulled down over his eyes, Paul didn't hear Grandpa Abe coming, until he was knocked completely over by his grandfather's swift kick. "What'd the hell you do that fer? Damm you scart the beeJesus otta me."

"You don't cuss at me, Boy. Git off yer lazy ass and come help me pull some stumps."

"I ain't pullin' no stumps today, it's too damn hot. Now leave me be."

Grandpa Abe stepped over him and went into the house.

"I heard you out there givin' it to Paul," Rachael said dropping another biscuit into the hot grease. "I wish someone could get him movin'. He's done ate three biscuits already and has been yellin' for more."

"I'll take one of them biscuits, Darlin'. Yer ole grandpa is hungry." He kissed Rachael on the cheek. He had a gruff nature about himself, but always showed his soft side to her. Whenever he needed something read or written, he would come to her. Grandpa Abe considered himself a real mountain man until he took a job at the mine. He and his wife had nine children and kept food on the table for them. He was a trapper in his younger years, selling pelts to the livery stable in Bent Creek. He made a decent living at it until the mine came along and no one wanted to buy and sell pelts. He had always cursed the day he went to work at the Five Star wishing he would have never stepped foot in the tunnels.

In the past twenty years, Grandpa Abe had buried his wife and eight of his children; leaving only him and Roy as the last of a generation of Riley's. In his whole life he had never been more than twenty-two miles from his home. He said he would have gone further but that's the spot where the mule died and it was a real long walk home. He lived alone and liked it. He made homemade corn liquor that he drank from a wooden jug he had whittled himself. He liked to play his fiddle and kick up his heels, but time was taking it's toll on his old body and it killed his soul to have to ask anyone for help, especially someone like Paul.

When Paul first came home from the army, he constantly complained about being sent home. Grandpa Abe's only words to him were, "Git over it, Boy. Taint the end of the world." It didn't make Paul feel any better.

"What's yer daddy up to these days, Rachael," Grandpa Abe asked, shoving another biscuit in his mouth.

"Same as every day. Jest sittin' around doin' nothin'."

"Well, he better git off his sorry ass and git this place in order fer winter comes. Roof's got a big hole in it and I don't see no woodpile."

Paul called through the open window. "I'm gonna go swimmin' up at the quarry with some of boys. You want to come, Rachael?"

Rachael ran her hand over the back of her neck, feeling the raw skin from the heat rash. "Maybe I kin come and jest soak my feet. You finish off them biscuits, Grandpa. We'll be back in an hour or so."

"I'm goin' too," Jesse said. "May be the last time fer awhile. I got me a tempry job over at the sawmill. They need extry help fer a few weeks."

"Well good fer you little brother. Let's go," Paul said sarcastically. He reached under the porch and pulled out a small, brown bottle. He put it to his mouth and took a long drink and shoved it into his overall pocket.

"You kids be careful in that thar quarry," Grandpa Abe yelled after them.

The quarry was full of the sound of laughter and water splashing as boys jumped off of the flat rock into the water. "Where'd all these people come from?" Rachael asked.

"Friends of Billy's. They come down from Lynch with him. He done vited them up here to swim. See that girl over thar in that black suit," Paul said, "That's my gal, Nancy. She and me have been doin' it over thar in the woods fer about two weeks now. I got a good case of poison ivy on my ass to prove it." He let out a loud whoop and jumped into the water.

Rachael watched as Paul swam over to the girl and splashed water on her. She let out a squeal and sat up, her breasts bulging out of her suit. She slid off the rock and joined him in the water, her arms wrapped around his neck. Rachael turned her head; this was too much for her. Climbing down to a lower ledge, Rachael stuck her legs into the water. She was worried about Paul. He had taken several drinks from the bottle before he threw it into the weeds. It was Billy Tate who interrupted her thoughts. "Why ain't you swimmin' today, Rachael? The water feels right nice. You got yer monthly?"

"Fer gosh sakes, Billy, you don't ask girls that! I jest don't feel like gettin' my dress all wet."

"Yer brother sure has been actin' crazy like since he come home. I let him drive my truck last week and he done almost wrecked it. Almost seems like he don't care whether he lives or dies. Bein' in no damn army wouldn't mean that much ta me."

Billy no sooner had the words out of his mouth than Rachael heard Nancy screaming. She looked up to see Paul on the other side of the quarry climbing up the vine covered rocks. "Oh, my gosh, what is he doin'?' She cupped her hands around her mouth and called to him, but she knew he couldn't hear her since all of the boys were clapping and laughing as Paul climbed higher and higher. Finally reaching a sturdy branch, he put his arms around it, and then swung his legs over the top. Sitting on the branch he let out a whoop. "So the army says I ain't strong. Did ya'll see that? I'm stronger than most them assholes they got runnin' around in uniforms. Skinny ass little soldiers with big guns. Watch this." Paul put one foot on the branch and then the other. Holding on to the ledge, he teetered for a moment and then stood up. Everyone was silent.

Nancy had climbed up the bank and was now standing next to Rachael. She called out to Paul." You ain't provin' anythin' up thar, Paul. Now you git down fer you kill yerself."

Without warning, Paul leaned forward and jumped feet first into the water. Several boys still swimming below him yelled out as his body plummeted passed them and disappeared under the surface. Rachael let out a gasp and covered her mouth to keep from screaming. *How long would it take him to surface, fifteen seconds, half a minute…surely not any longer than that. How deep did he go? The seconds were ticking by. Where was he? Why wasn't his head popping up out of the water?* And then the scream escaped from her throat. "Paul, Paul, where are you?" She was in the water, swimming out to the middle, diving under the surface along with Jesse and a few other boys. Holding her breath as long as she could, she saw nothing but dark, dark water. Diving below the surface over and over until her lungs were burning like fire and her arms were too weak to hold her on the surface she felt her body sinking deeper into the quarry. Someone's arms went around her waist and she struggled to free herself. "He's done gone, Rachael. I ain't lettin' you be next." Jesse pulled her to shore. She was too tired to resist.

The bank was lined with a row of somber boys and sobbing girls and they stood looking into the now calm water as if Paul was going to miraculously appear from beneath the deep. As darkness set upon the quarry, the crowd disbursed leaving Rachael and Jesse to go home and tell their parents that Paul, their oldest son, would not be coming home. Billie Tate put his arm around Nancy and said he would notify the sheriff as soon as he got back to town.

The sheriff called the State Offices and a team of divers was sent to look for Paul's body. Two days later Rachael waited with her parents on the bank of the quarry as each diver descended into the depths only to return empty handed. Pulling himself out of the water, one of the divers approached the Riley's.

"There's a large outcropping of rocks on the far side that forms almost cavern-like crevasses. When Paul dove into the water he must have landed in one of those cracks in the rocks or he may have gotten tangled in the tree roots. I'm sorry we couldn't find your son, but the water is too deep and too dark."

Ida Mae collapsed into Roy's arms and wailed. He could hardly hold her up as she flailed about screaming Paul's name.

To honor Paul, a white cross was put in the cemetery next to Willie's grave. Rachael sat down next to the cross. She wondered what his last few minutes of life were like. She wondered if he knew he was going to die as he struggled to free himself from his watery grave or is that what he had planned to do when he climbed onto the rocks. She wondered if that was what he really wanted.

A 'No trespassing' sign was put up on the road leading to the quarry. No one really wanted to go there to swim anyway.

Chapter Seven

As the years passed, the leaves on the trees were beginning to wear their fall colors. The sound of the cicadas filled the air during the day and the evenings were becoming a slight bit cooler. It was September and the mine had still not opened. The town of Bent Creek had become desolate except for an occasional truck or wagon that came through to pick up the boards that were falling off the abandoned buildings. They would be used for repair or firewood for the people who still tried to eke out a living until the mine reopened.

It wasn't long until Mabry's general store and the livery stable were the only stores left on the dusty street. One small section of Mabry's was turned into the post office. Each week when Joe Mabry, who was now the postal clerk, went to Lynch to pick up the mail, he would bring home a wagonload of supplies. He brought flour and sugar and salt and coffee and anything else he could afford that week. He'd mark everything up a few cents and hope that someone would come in that week with enough money to buy a few staples and didn't ask for credit. Most days he just sat around the pot bellied stove with a few other men who wandered into town to break the silence and loneliness in their own lives. Puffing on their corncob pipes they would still lament over the closing of the mine and contemplate their miserable future. On the days Joe Mabry made his trip to Lynch, Rachael would watch the store in case someone came in to pickup mail or buy something. Joe paid her twenty-five cents and a half-pound of coffee.

At home, Rachael and Emma Jane spent their days foraging through the woods looking for anything edible. They gathered nuts and berries and wild garlic. Along with Jesse they harvested the rest of the vegetables from the garden and the fruit from the few remaining trees. Except for a few laying hens and the old rooster, all of the chickens had been eaten. Ida Mae refused to butcher the cow saying milk was more important than meat. Jesse spent his days hunting, bringing home a few rabbits or squirrels each day. And Roy still sat on the porch playing solitaire, letting the rest of the family do all the work. He watched as Jesse and Ida Mae chopped wood and stacked it next to the house. His life seemed to be frozen in time. He was no longer a part of the family, just a bystander with hopes that the mine was still going to open so once again he could provide for his family.

Laying in bed at night along side Emma Jane, Rachael prayed that things would get better for the family. Sometimes they would hug each other and cry and Emma Jane would ask over and over what they were going to do. It was a miserable existence for two teenage girls. Other times they would talk about what they would do if they had money to spend. Emma Jane always had the same wish. "I would buy a car and go into Lynch. I would walk into one of them stores and buy me a whole box of Butterfingers and eat them all and then I'd buy me another box to take home." The remembrance of a candy bar she had over three years ago still stuck her mine. She had nothing else to think about. Rachael's dreams were more complicated and Emma Jane usually fell asleep while Rachael was talking.

When Rachael heard about an organization in Lynch that would help out people in need, she mentioned it to her father. She never saw him get so mad. He knocked over a chair and pointed his finger at her. "Don't you ever, and I mean ever, go tellin' anybody our business. We ain't starvin' and I ain't gonna accept no handouts. I ain't gonna be beholden to anybody. You mind yer business little girl and stay outta' mine." Why did he call her little girl? She was almost eighteen years old, two years older than her mother when she married.

Two weeks before Christmas as the icicles formed on the inside walls of the bedrooms and the snow collected on the roof, Jesse returned from Bent Creek with a letter in his hand. It was scribbled in pencil on a smeared envelope. Roy could hardly make out the writing. The letter was postmarked almost two months previous. He handed it to Rachael and she carefully opened it. It was from Ben. In his barely legible script he wrote that he was still in California. When he was given a physical, the doctors found that his eyesight was not good enough to send him overseas. Ben was kept on the base and was going to school to learn how to repair jeeps and tanks.

Ben talked about the electric lights in his barracks that were on all the time and the warm water in the showers. He said that he was fed three times a day. He hoped that everyone was well. The best part was he enclosed a ten-dollar bill, folded in another piece of paper. When Rachael handed it to her father, she could see the tears in his eyes and a smile on his face. She had no idea if he was happy because he got the letter from Ben or that he could go now have a chaw of tobacco that he missed so much.

Because of Ben's generosity, Ida Mae made sure that each of the children was given something small for Christmas. Rachael received a box of three handkerchiefs trimmed in blue. Emma Jane got a crocheted hat that Ida Mae had made out of new yarn and Jesse was given a pocketknife. Ida Mae made chicken and dumplings and a rhubarb pie. Even Roy seemed happy on Christmas day as he sat by the stove with his pack of tobacco and the six dollars left over from the trip to the store in his pocket. He only wished that his two eldest sons were there to celebrate with them. Grandpa Abe came to the house and brought his jug of corn liquor. Roy got out his banjo and was joined by Jesse playing the fiddle. It was a good Christmas. As it turned out it would be the last one Grandpa Abe ever have.

On New Year's Eve, Grandpa Abe started celebrating early. By nine o'clock he had already finished one jug of moonshine and by ten he was all-lickered up. By eleven o'clock he had his rifle out and was shooting branches off the trees all around his cabin. He was staggering down the road in his red long johns, waving his gun in the air when two of his friends saw him and took him back home. He was cussing and screaming that the owners of the mine didn't give a damn that his family needed work. The men put him to bed and left. Sometime after midnight he must have gone outside to go to the privy. He fell head first into the rain barrel. A neighbor from down the road found him two days later. His head was still in the frozen water and the jug of corn liquor lay on the ground next to him. When they pulled him out he had a wreath of ice around his blue face.

Now that Grandpa Abe was gone, Roy decided to move his family into his father's house. It had one more room than their own, a watertight roof and the porch was still attached to the house. So the day after his funeral, the Riley family packed their belongings in the wagon and drove the mile and a half to their new home—a run-down shanty just a tad bit better than their own.

Most of Grandpa Abe's things had to be thrown out. They smelled of mildew and were almost too dirty to get clean. Ida Mae and Rachael packed up all the old blankets and bed sheets and took them outside. They swept all the floors and turned the mattresses. They hadn't brought much with them but within a few days Ida Mae had the cabin looking as decent as she could with her old furniture and newspaper covering the walls.

When Ida Mae found eleven dollars in a Mason jar under the sink she breathed a sigh of relief. It wasn't much, but along with Grandpa Abe's guns that they could sell maybe they could make it to spring.

Moving into Grandpa Abe's cabin also came with the awareness that for the first time in their lives they had neighbors living just a few hundred feet away from them. The house next to Grandpa Abe had been vacant for sometime before the Haines family moved in. It was little more than a frame with boards nailed on in every direction. In the first few days in their new home, Rachael counted over ten people living in the house next door and there was probably more that she hadn't seen. They were a rowdy bunch that had covered all the windows with bright colored rugs to keep the cold out. She and Emma Jane were fascinated with the idea that when they were outside in the yard they could hear people singing and sometimes shouting at each other. No one from the Haines family made any move to come over and talk to them and Ida Mae said to leave well enough alone. She didn't need any company and they were nothing but a band of gypsies. But Emma Jane's curiosity finally paid off, when after lingering in the yard for over two hours she met Jimmy Dell Haines. He was seventeen and Emma Jane thought he was the cutest boy she had ever seen.

"Rachael you go outside and holler fer Emma Jane. It's suppertime. I reckon she's over at the Haines agin," Ida Mae said.

Rachael stepped outside the door and yelled for her sister. She waited a few minutes and then called again. Rachael had never been in the Haines' house, but Emma Jane spent most of her free time with them. Emma Jane came running from the run-down barn in the back of the property. Jimmy Dell was right behind her.

"I swear, Emma Jane, straighten your dress and get the hay out of yer hair. What have you and Jimmy Dell been doing?"

"Nothin', jest sittin' out back talkin'. Don't tell mama." She ran ahead of Rachael and bounded up the porch steps.

Rachael positioned her hands on her hips. "You best stay away from my sister, Jimmy Dell. My pap finds you sniffin' around her he's likely to knock your head clean off."

Jimmy Dell threw his head back and laughed. "I'd like ta git mah hands on you, Girl. Whadda ya say me and you go out ta the barn?"

"You best better keep yer distance, Jimmy Dell or I'll tell my pa fer sure." He spit on the ground and walked away.

Roy shoved half a biscuit in his mouth and licked the gravy off of his fingers. "Yer mama tells me you been goin' over to them gypsies house and she can't never find ya, Emma Jane. That true?" he asked.

"To begin with, I don't know why you call them gypsies. They ain't gypsies, thar migrant workers. Thar jest waitin' fer the tobaccy plantin' ta begin and then they'll all be workin'. Sides, I like havin' friends," Emma Jane said.

"Migrants, gypsies, same thang. Ain't no tobaccy plantin' round here til spring. They ain't got no right squattin' in that house. Alls they do is drink and raise hell. You stay away from them, ya heer. I don't want no daughter of mine gettin' a bad name or somethin' worse from them people. I ketch you over thar agin I'm gonna whop yer ass." Roy was done talking and there was no arguing with him. All the kids knew that.

After supper while the girls cleaned up the kitchen, Emma Jane hummed to herself as she put the dishes in the wash pan.

"What are you so happy about? You best be careful messin' with that Jimmy Dell. He ain't no kid. He's been around, if you know what I mean," Rachael said.

"Them people are fun to be around. They laugh and play music and have a good time. They don't sit around moanin' all the time like everybody in this house. They make the best of a bad time. And besides I really like Jimmy Dell. Why is everybody always bad mouthin' the Haines?"

"Most everybody around these parts agrees with Pa. They say people like the Haines just roam around and squat where ever they find an empty house. They make thar livin' by stealin' and cheatin' people outta their money," Rachael said.

"That's stupid. Who around here has anythin to steal? I'm tellin' you their migrants," Emma Jane replied in an angry tone. "Sides, Jimmy Dell thinks I'm cute and I like him."

"If they ain't gypsies how come those men go away in their trucks for a couply days and come back with food. I bet they steal it. They steal from poor folks like us. None of them got jobs," Rachael said in a commanding tone. "And how come so many of them live in one house? I bet thars neigh on to fifteen of them squattin' in that house."

Emma Jane stomped her foot. "Well, none of us got jobs, so what does that make us? I ain't gonna argy about this any more. I get real tired of stayin' in this house every night listenin' to mama read the bible. I know it by heart and it sure ain't done us much good. Daddy sits around waitin' on the mine to open and Jesse is off huntin' all the time or hidin' from daddy ta keep from doin' any chores. Least wise the Haines have good food once in a while." Emma Jane threw down the towel. "Besides it ain't any of yer call how they make their money. Quit asking me so many questions." She grabbed her coat off the hook on the wall and went outside slamming the door behind her. Rachael knew where she was going.

Two months later, on a snowy, Sunday the Riley's returned from church to find the house the Haines had occupied empty. Emma Jane jumped down from the wagon. A look of surprise crossed her face. The door to the shanty was open and the few remaining panes of glass had been removed from the windows. She ran to the door and peered inside. Only a few pieces of broken furniture remained. Tears welled up in her eyes and she leapt from the porch and hurried to her own house. "Now, what's gotten into her all of a sudden?" Roy said. "I'm damn glad thar gone. I kin sleep better at night now. I knew'd they wuz gypsies. Thar off and runnin' agin."

Emma Jane was lying across her bed when Rachael walked in. Rachael kicked off her shoes and pulled her Sunday dress over her head. Sitting down on the bed, she tugged on her denim pants. "I'm sorry, Emma Jane, I know you liked Jimmy Dell, but that boy was jest plain bad news. You'll get over him. You kin do much better than him."

Emma Jane's head was buried in her pillow. "You don't understand," she said in a muffled voice. "Jimmy Dell knew his family was thinkin' bout leavin', but he said when his family left he would stay behind and be with me. He lied to me. God, what am I gonna do? I'm expectin', Rachael. I done missed my second monthly and my titties are gettin' real sore. Pa is gonna kill me when he finds out. I will be yer dead sister, Emma Jane."

Rachael's mouth dropped open. "Pregnant. You had done let yerself get pregnant! Damn. Emma Jane, yer so right, Pa is gonna kill you. I didn't know you and Billy Dell were doin' it. I thought you was just messin' around."

Emma Jane sat up and rubbed her nose. "We only did it twice out back in the barn. The first time it hurt real bad and so he talked me into doin' it agin to show me it wouldn't hurt the second time. But it did. He said he loved me a whole lot and that I was his woman. What am I gonna do?"

"You ain't got a choice, Emma Jane, you have to tell ma and pa and the sooner the better, if you ask me."

It took Emma Jane another month before she got the courage to tell her parents. Her stomach was starting to protrude and she got tired of wearing her coat in the house to hide the bump. Her mother cried and her father slapped her across the face. "Now see what you gone and done. Yer gonna bring a bastard child into this family and worst yet a bastard child of a damn gypsy. I'm gonna go after the little son of a bitch and make him come back and marry you proper like. Thang is I ain't got no idée what direction the Haines went when they left. Maybe I'll jest call the sheriff and let him deal with them people."

Emma Jane cried until her eyes were almost swollen shut. She begged her father not to call the law. She said she didn't want to have a baby. After a few days her father stopped his ranting and resigned himself to the fact that he was going to be a grandpa to his sixteen-year-old daughter's bastard child.

Chapter Eight

Rachael sat by the stove drying a pair of socks she had washed in the sink. It was cold and damp in the house with the rain dripping into four buckets placed on the kitchen floor. Spring was in full force and soon the daffodils and hyacinth that grew along the road would be popping up their sleepy heads. The creek in back of the house would once again be full of crawdads and turtles. It was good not to shiver all the time.

She heard her father and Jesse outside talking loudly. They had just returned from fishing. Her father burst into the room. "Rachael, whars yer ma. I need her right quick! I got news." He laid a string of six catfish on the table. "Whar is she?"

"She's outback with Emma Jane. They're cleanin' out the cow's stall. What's the news, Daddy?"

"Thars some men at the mine. Company men all dressed up in suits and there is a whole line of trucks comin' into town. By cracky, that mine is gonna be fixed and up and runnin' real soon. Hot damn, I know'd if'n we waited long enough them sumbitches would come round to our way of thinkin'. Tell you ma that I'll be back a fore dark. I got to see fer myself what's goin' on."

It was the first time Rachael had seen her father smile in a long time. Rachael breathed a sigh of relief. If her father went back to work she could leave. There would be enough money coming in to take care of the rest of the family and she could finally tell her parents that she was leaving Bent Creek.

She had no idea where she was going, or where she would get the money to get there, but she was leaving. She watched her father go down the road in his rickety, old wagon. She prayed he was right and the mine was going to reopen, even though she knew the dangers.

Roy pulled up in front of the Mabry's. The road was crammed with trucks and wagons. He shook off his hat and entered the room already crowded with other men from the mine. He nodded to a few he knew and pushed his way closer to the stove. Holding his hands out to warm them, he grinned. "Good news, ain't it?" he said out loud. A burly man standing next to him spat a wad of tobacco into the spittoon, nearly missing Roy's foot. "What's yer beef, Riley? I thought you waz lookin' forward ta goin' back ta' work? Why you so happy that the mine is closin' for good?"

"Whoa, hold on," Roy said. "I thought them men were here to tell us that the mine was gonna open. Why'd they bring all them trucks? Ain't all that equipment to fix the shafts?"

"Naw," the man replied. "Them trucks are takin' away everythin' that wuz left behind. The others are here to come up and give us all our walkin' papers. The mine is closed for good. Those bastards don't care one bit that we kin sit up here and starve to death. I hate them bastards." There was a loud grumble that filled the room.

When the men from the mining company finally came up to the main street, it was already getting dark and rain was still pelting down. Protected by four of the truck drivers the two men who entered the store tried to explain to the angry crowd that after a thorough inspection they found that the mine was just too dangerous to reopen. It was going to be condemned and dynamited shut the following week. Every man who worked there would get a check for twenty dollars just to show the goodwill of the company. The company men turned and left quickly as a roar of discontent rumbled through the throng.

By nine o'clock that night, Ida Mae was wringing her hands with worry. She paced back and forth across the room, looking out the window and then the door. She was sure that some harm had come to Roy. He would never stay away this long, especially if he had good news. "I know'd somethin's done gone wrong. Maybe he's somewhars on the road hurt. Maybe that old mule stepped in a hole in all this rain. I'm gonna go look for him."

Before anyone could object there were sounds of footsteps on the porch. Ida Mae opened the door and Roy fell in. He reeked of corn liquor and could barely keep his balance. He staggered across the kitchen and plopped down in a chair, muddy water dripping from his boots.

"Roy Riley, whar you been? I swear I been half sick with worry and you come home all lickered up. I wuz jest gettin' ready to send the boys out to look fer you."

Roy held up his hand. "Don't you go lecturin' me woman. I had enough lecturin' for one day. Ain't no good news. The mine is closed for good. Strike or no strike, them bastards closed it down. So…what do you think of that?" He let out a loud belch. "I guess we better think up somethin' to make some money this year. If'n I had enuf money I'd open a sawmill. Yes sir, that's what'd I'd do. Can't do that with the skinny money they be given us for all them years of bustin" our asses for them. Twenty measly dollars."

"I'm sure sorry, Roy. Sure sorry," Ida Mae said.

"I got a little bit of news. Ain't the best, but anyway, while I wuz in town, Nevers Bains came into the store. He said he wuz lookin' fer a couply people to come live over at his house for a while. He wants someone to stay behind with his wife and help her out with the chores and keep the varmints away from his livestock. He says he got a whole heap of trouble runnin' his place and trying to trap at the same time. Says he's a lookin fer somebody to help him run traps. Me and him made a deal." He pointed an unsteady finger at Rachael. "I'm gonna send Rachael and Jesse over there to help him out. Nevers said he would send me five dollars a week for thar help. That's a heap of money right now."

Rachael jumped up from her chair. "Oh, no. No way am I gonna go live with Nevers Bains. He's a mean old man and I ain't a goin'." Rachael folded her arms across her chest in an act of defiance.

Roy fell against the table as he stood up. He grabbed Rachael and pulled her close to him. "You lissen to me, Gal. Yer gonna do what ah say. We ain't got no money and yer sister is layin' in the other room with a big belly and no husband. Ya'll do what I say. Ya hear me? I plan on settin' up a sawmill when Ben comes home. Thar's big money in lumber."

His hand squeezed her arm tightly and she could smell his foul breath. For the first time in her life she was afraid of her father. Undoing his fingers, she stepped back. "I'll do it for momma and Emma Jane but I won't do it for you! And it won't be fer long, so you better find work. You been settin' around here for over a yar jest waitin' fer that mine to open, you could have been doin' somethin'. Why put all yer troubles off on me and Jesse? Besides, what makes you think Ben wants to come back to this hovel after he seen what is really going on in the world. I sure wouldn't come back." Rachael could see the stunned look on his face as she finally said out loud what everyone in the house was thinking. She bolted from the room before he could snatch her back. If he had been sober she would have gotten the whipping of her life.

Rachael knew all about Nevers Bains. He had been the source of gossip for as long as she could remember. He lived way back in the hollow, his house invisible from the road and he liked it that way. He kept his shotgun by the door and would fire shots at anyone who came to his house unannounced. He was a cussed man who had been married twice and both of his wives had died. The first supposedly drowned in the swollen creek after a flash flood and the second died from eating a piece of bad meat. Nevers didn't have a funeral service for either of his wives. After he got a release from the coroner, he buried them in a small plot he called the family cemetery in the back of his house and stuck wooden crosses over their graves. When the mine's company store closed, Nevers tried to buy up all of the sugar in town. The storeowners refused to sell it to him, saying everyone was low on sugar and he had no right to all of it. The next night bullet holes riddled the windows and siding of the town stores. Everyone knew that Nevers did it, but they were afraid to accuse them. Once when he overheard a stranger in Lynch calling him a hillbilly, he picked them up and threw them against the side of a building. When the sheriff was called, Nevers refused to back down. The sheriff finally let him go knowing that if he didn't he would be the next one on Never's list. He had threatened so many people in the past that everyone steered clear of him. Nevers was a trapper by trade. He would come through Bent Creek with a load of smelly skins on his truck and take them to Lynch to sell. Every town had a bully and Nevers filled the bill quite well.

When Nevers married a mute girl named Lily everyone was surprised. Rachael wondered how her family could let a young girl like Lily marry an ornery old coot like Nevers. She had gone to school with Lily for a few years. Lily dropped out in third grade when she had to go to work in the fields to help her family survive. How could her parents marry her off to someone three times her age?

Chapter Nine

Emma Jane leaned on the bedpost and watched as Rachael put her few pieces of clothing in to a canvas sack. "I'm gonna be so lonely without you, Rachael. You always took a care of me. What am I gonna do if that old rooster comes after me and what am I gonna do when this baby comes and yer not here to help me?"

"Don't you worry none, Emma Jane, I don't plan on being gone too long. If daddy don't find work soon, I'll come and get you and we'll leave this place."

Emma Jane threw her arms around her sister and sobbed. "Daddy hates me now and momma won't even talk to me. They think I'm jest a common whore. I love you Rachael and I'll be waitin' for you. I'm so afeared to be here without you." She repeated herself, "What if the baby comes and I ain't got nobody to help me?"

"You got a few months ta go, Emma Jane. We'll worry about that when the time comes. You jest take care of yerself and try to eat some greens now and then. I love you baby sister."

After everything was loaded into the wagon, Rachael said goodbye to her mother. "Now, Momma I'm gonna be just eleven miles down the road. If you need me, you send somebody to get me. I want you ta be nicer to Emma Jane. She's jest a little girl herself and she made a bad mistake, but she's still yer daughter and she needs you."

"I'll try, Rachael. But this is all wrong. Ain't no call fer the two you ta be going to Nevers."

Ida Mae was upset, but it was Roy's decision and she wouldn't go against it. "You be careful, ya heer? You stay close with yer brother." She hugged Rachael and whispered into her ear, "I know it ain't right sendin' you two off to Nevers' house, but we aint't got no choice. You watch him, Rachael. Don't let that old man git around you." She stood with Emma Jane as Roy turned the wagon around in the yard.

About a mile from Nevers' house, Roy reached under the seat and pulled out a small sack. He handed it to Rachael. "This here is one of Grandpa Abe's handguns that I kept. It's only got four bullets left in it, so if'n you have to use it, you better aim good." He set it on her lap. "I don't reckon you will have any trouble with Nevers. He knows if he doesn't do right by you and Jesse, I'll come a lookin' fer him."

Rachael turned her head. Nevers wouldn't be afraid of her skinny, old daddy. He would laugh in his face.

When they arrived at the front of the property Rachael and Jesse jumped down from the wagon and retrieved their bags. Rachael stood with her hands crossed over her chest while her father drove away. She still refused to talk to him.

Walking up the winding road, Rachael stopped for a moment and tied her shoes. "I don't hate Pa, but he sure is a lazy ass. He 's always on me about being a dreamer, but I ain't ever seen anyone that can't see more than a foot in front of his face like our pa. I sure hope he knows what he's doing by sending us to live with Nevers Bains.

When they got to the gate, Rachael pulled on the cord that set off the clanging of a large, barn bell. She wanted to make sure that Nevers didn't shoot them before they got to his house. She swung the gate open and closed it behind her. It felt like the prison gate had just closed on her.

"Damn! Would you look at that? That's a right nice place. I wouldn't have thought that Nevers had a house like this," Rachael said aloud when she first caught sight of the house sitting in a grove of pine trees.

The foundation of the house was made of creek stones that extended up into a fireplace chimney. Layered with round logs, the front of the building was covered with a porch made of sturdy uprights and the roof was bright red tin. In front of the porch there were wooden containers filled with flowers, wild vines covered with red roses climbed up the side of a trellis.

Rachael walked slowly up the path and stepped on to the porch. A swing hanging in one corner rocked gently in the breeze. The door opened and Nevers stood in front of them. He wore a clean plaid shirt and coveralls. "Well, don't jest don't stand there gawkin'. Yer lettin the flies in. Come on in, but wipe yer feet first."

How could this be possible? This is not at all what Rachael had expected. She imagined a filthy cabin reeking of dead animals instead of a kitchen with the table draped in green oilcloth. There were curtains on every window and the floor was covered with red and white linoleum. Neat rows of dishes and pans filled the shelves lining the wall over the four-burner cook stove. A small refrigerator had a place of honor next to the sink.

"This is reel nice, Nevers. I mean it, real nice. Damn, you got lectricity and a radio," she said, pointing across the room.

"Not what you expected, eh? Guess you thought I lived in cave somewheres? This is why I don't like people comin' round. They don't need to know what I got up here. This is real nice, ain't it? I done it all myself. Ain't nothin' like that shack yer family lives in. I like a clean house. I got me a Kalvinator refrigerator," he said, leaning against the white metal box.

"Sent fer it from the Sears-Roebuck catalog. My lectric line runs clear across the county line. Ain't too many of us in these parts got lectricity," he boasted.

Rachael put her hands on her hips. "Don't you worry, Nevers Bains, when I get my own house it will have rugs on the floors and maybe two or three radios."

"Yeah, I bet," Nevers said grinning.

"Where's yer wife?" Rachael asked.

"She's back yonder gettin' yer rooms ready. I want them rooms kept clean, you heer? Now, let's talk about what I expect outta you and yer brother for my five dollars a week. I got at least twenty traps to set in the next couply days. Me and Jesse might be gone fer two or three days at a stretch. So that leaves you and Lily to keep the wood cut when I'm not here. You gotta help Lily with this house and the livestock. She ain't keepin' up reel good lately. I got me a couply cows, some chickens and rabbits. Don't keep no pigs, can't stand the smell. You know how to cook, girl?"

Rachael rolled her eyes. "Of course I kin cook. I been helpin' my momma since I was knee high to a grasshopper."

"What I want ta know is kin you make a decent biscuit?" he asked.

"I sure kin," she answered.

"That'll be good. That woman of mine sure ain't no cook. She kin do most everything else if she has a mind to, but she sure can't cook worth a damn." Nevers got up and poured a cup of coffee out of the enamelware pot on the stove.

Lily came into the room carrying an armload of blankets. She dropped them on the floor and began folding them. She smiled at Rachael. Rachael had only seen her at a distance in the last couple of years. Sometimes she would come into town with Nevers, but she stayed in the wagon. She was fair-skinned with light hair and a thin, straight body. She was much too nice looking to be married to Nevers Bains. "Hi, I'm

Rachael." She extended her hand. Lily just continued to smile at her.

"Ain't no sense tryin' ta make talk with her. She kin hear you, but she's mute. Been like that fer some yars now. Sometimes she mouths words, but hell, I don't read lips. I can't figure out what she's sayin'. I got the best. Ain't nothin' like havin' a woman that can't talk." Nevers stretched his hands over his head. "Daylight is awastin'. Might as well get some wood cut so you women kin make up some supper. Come on boy, you kin help," he said to Jesse, who had been standing in the corner since he came into the house. Rachael had never been called a woman before.

After Nevers and Jesse left the house Lily once again smiled at Rachael. She took a pad of paper from her pocket and with a stub of a pencil wrote the words, 'hapy yer heer.'

"Well thank you, Lily, I'm glad someone is happy that I'm here." Lily took her by the hand and led her down the narrow hall leading to the bedrooms. She stopped and pushed open a door.

Rachael covered her mouth with her hand, "Oh, my God! You got inside plumbin'. Oh, my God! Ain't that sumthin'." Lily nodded and pulled her into another room. The iron bed was covered with a pink and white quilt and there was a proper dresser with a mirror. Lily pointed to Rachael and then patted the bed. "Are you tellin' me this is my room? Yer kiddin'." Rachael giggled and sat down. There was a pillow on the bed. She actually had a pillow. Without thinking she stood up and hugged Lily. Lily's arms went down to her sides and she backed away with a startled look on her face.

"Oh, Lily, I am sorry. I didn't mean to scare you, but you have no idea how much all of this means to me. Maybe livin' here won't be so bad." Lily dropped her head and stared at the floor. Rachael could be so jealous of Lily if it weren't for the fact that she was married to Nevers. That…she could not imagine.

That evening Rachael made biscuits to go along with the pot of ham and green beans that Lily had simmering on the stove. They set the table and Lily went outside and pulled the cord on the heavy dinner bell. Nevers came out of the barn. He stopped at the pump and washed his hands before coming into the house.

"Well, I'll be damn, biscuits!" After eating two plates of food and three biscuits, Nevers pushed himself away from the table and wiped his mouth on his sleeve. He let out a loud belch. "That was a right nice meal. Right nice." He got up and went outside. "Now if'n' you git a hankerin' you teach Lily how ta make them biscuits," he said pointing his finger at Rachael.

After living at Nevers' house for a week, Rachael knew that Lily was deathly afraid of him. Lily cringed whenever he raised his voice. And over the course of the week his demeanor began to change toward Rachael. He barked orders at her constantly. He told Rachael to help Lily clean the fireplace, all the cupboards in the kitchen and wash all the blankets and quilts. Although the house looked clean to her, Nevers told Rachael to scrub every floor. She cooked almost all the meals and helped feed the livestock. At night she would fall into bed exhausted. Even having a nice house to live in didn't make up for being Nevers' slave. She had to do something about it, but what?

Jesse complained about Nevers nonstop. He said he hated him and wanted to go home. He had thought about running off, but if he went home his father would probably whip him good and send him right back.

Chapter Ten

On a balmy Saturday night with the glow of an almost full moon shining on the porch, Rachael and Lily sat in the swing. Jesse rested on the railing strumming on his guitar. It was a nice evening until the door burst open and Nevers came out carrying a mop and bucket. "That kitchen floor needs a moppin' Rachael. Thar's somethin' sticky all over it. Git to it!" He pushed the mop toward her.

Rachael jumped out of the swing and threw the mop on the porch. "You lissen to me, Nevers Bains, I ain't been hired on as no slave. Me and Jesse are workin' for five dollars a week, which we don't even get to keep. When the kitchen is cleaned after dinner I am done for the night. I ain't workin' on Sunday, except fer cookin' and every other weekend I want you ta drive us home so that I kin see my family. You been bossin' us around like you owned us. Well, you don't and if'n you don't like what I jest said, me and mah brother will leave right now. I don't know whar we're goin', but it will sure nuf be better than stayin' here."

Nevers glared at her, clenching his fist. Lily sat in the swing with a horrified look on her face. She expected at any moment for Nevers to lash out and slap Rachael. Jesse sunk down as low as he could against the wall of the house.

"You got a mouth on you, Girl. I should tech you a lessen."

Rachael steeled herself for Nevers' wrath, but instead of hitting her, he dropped his hands to his sides. "But, I'm supposin' that's fair," He pointed his finger at her. "You better make sure yer work is done before you start lollygagging out here on the porch. Lily, you come in now, it's time for bed." Lily slowly followed him into the house. Nevers stood holding on to the door, "You two stay out here for a piece. I got some business with my wife."

The next morning when Lily came into the kitchen she had a bruise on her left cheek. Rachael noticed it right away. "Did Nevers hit you last night?"

Lily shook her head no.

"I know yer a lyin'. I'm so sorry, Lily, I didn't mean to get you in trouble. He took his mad out on you. Does it hurt real bad?"

Once again Lily shook her head and busied herself cutting up bacon. She jumped when Nevers came into the room. "Git the vittles on now! I'm going up the mountain and put out some traps, I'm takin' Jesse with me. Might be gone all night. Ya'll make sure them animals are fed and put up fer the night. You hear them varmints out there, jest go outside and make noise and they'll run off. Do you understand, Rachael?" Rachael did not answer him.

"You two stay in the house. Don't go wonderin' off nowheres. You stay in the house and that's an order." He took his jacket off the hook on the wall and motioned to Jesse.

Rachael waited until the truck was out of sight before she threw her arms in the air and danced around the room. "Yahoo, the old bastard is gone for awhile." She turned on the radio and began to sing. Lily watched her. A smile crossed her face.

"I swear, Lily, you are like a little whipped puppy. Come here." Rachael took her hands and pulled her out in the middle of the kitchen floor. "We're gonna dance." Shy at first,

Lily began to move her foot in time with the music and in a few minutes they were both jumping up and down.

Rachael fell onto the floor, holding her side. "I am out of breath, but that was fun, wasn't it?"

A small voice answered, "Yes."

Rachael bolted straight up, staring at Lily. "Oh, my God, Lily, you talked. You kin talk. Wait a minute, what's goin' on? How long have you been able to talk?" Rachael looked over at Lily. She still lay on the floor, tears rolling down her cheeks.

"I shoulda never done that and if'n you tell Nevers, I will say yer a lyin'. He won't believe you, Rachael. I ain't talked a loud in over four years. I swear he won't believe you. You made me do it. I forgot myself."

"You kin trust me, Lily. I promise you kin trust me. Jest talk to me. I am so glad you kin talk. How in the hell have you kept from speakin' all these yars? It had to be really hard."

"Hard ain't the word fer it. When Nevers was gone I used to go out in the woods and just stand there and scream until I really lost my voice. But if he know'd I could talk...I have no idea what he would do to me. I sure hope I kin trust you, Rachael." Lily grabbed both of Rachael's hands and held them tight. "You promise, on yer mother's life, you promise you won't tell a soul."

"I promise," Rachael replied. She helped Lily up from the floor and they went outside to sit in the swing.

Lily began to talk. "I was only fourteen when Nevers started comin' round our house and talkin' to my step-pa, Earl bout takin' me fer his wife. Nevers' second wife had just died and he said he'd takin' a fancy to me when he seed me in town. Nevers was done thirty-five years old. When I told Earl that ah didn't want ta marry that old man, Nevers said he would give Earl an old truck he had, plus some chickens and a kerosene stove. Hell, we wuz liven hand to mouth. Those things were better than gold to Earl. None of Earl's kin liked to work so didn't have anythin' to speak of. Since Earl and I didn't get along anyway it didn't matter none to Earl what happened to me. He was always tryin' to git at me and when I fought him off it made me reel mad. Earl was a nasty man. Sides gettin' all that stuff Nevers said he would give him, Earl know'd it was a good time to git even with me. Nevers promised Earl that he wouldn't touch me until I was older, but I knew that was a lie and Earl sure didn't care none cause I wouldn't let him git in my britches." Lily stopped and wiped her nose with the hem of her dress.

"I was scart to death that Nevers would kill me like I heard he done to them other women, plus I didn't want him touchin' me at all. Well, anyway, one afternoon I was outside our house and I seed Nevers comin' up the road. I took off runnin' and climbed up an old, hickory tree behind the house. I thought if I stayed away long nuf he would go away. When I tried to git down, I grabbed for a branch. I heard it crack and the next thing I know'd I was on the ground. I landed right on a big, old rock. It hurt really bad awful. The blood was runnin' out of my head and I jest laid there too scart to move. I musta swooned and the next thing I know'd is when I opened my eyes I was lookin' right up at Nevers. Lordy, that was a scary sight. My brothers carried me to the house and laid me on the bed. My momma sat by me and put cold rags on my head and prayed for me. And then it comes to me. I just wouldn't talk no more. No matter what they asked me, I wouldn't say a word. My plan worked real good. It scart them reel bad so the next mornin' Earl took me into Lynch and the doctor put a couply stitches in my head. He told Earl that the bump from the fall musta caused me some brain damage and that was why I couldn't talk, even though he hadn't ever seen that happen afore. The doctor wanted to take me into Campbellsburg to the hospital, but Earl said no. Since I was on my feet and didn't seem to be in any pain he would jest wait and see if my voice came back. It was really hard not speakin', but when Nevers found out, he stopped comin' around."

Rachael interrupted. "Yer really brave, Lily. I could never stop talkin'."

"That's cause you never had to think about marryin'someone like Nevers. Anyway, I hated not talkin', but I figured he would find someone else and then I could talk again. But, my plan didn't work fer too long. A few months later, Nevers started comin' round agin. Then one Saturday in the spring, my momma laid out my church dress on the bed and took me to the creek to warsh. I seen Nevers drivin' up the road and I know'd what was gonna happen. We went to the courthouse in Lynch and I was married to him." Lily stopped talking for a moment and looked around as if she expected Nevers to jump out at her from some hidden corner.

"I cried all the way to his house. A silent cry and I made up mah mind that I would never talk agin, specially not to him. Them first months were jest plumb awful. He wouldn't leave me alone. My bottom parts were so sore I thought they would jest fall out. Then he let up some and went back to trappin'. I larned some ways ta keep from bein' put upon every night. I made sure I didn't take a bath when he was around. Cause I didn't want him ta ketch me naked. I stayed up reel late at night and waited fer him ta fall a sleep first. Course when I had ta do it, I larned how ta move a certain way and then it would only last a couply minutes. He wouldn't come near me when I wuz havin my monthly, so I always made it last at least a week. I had thought about takin' my own life and then I thought about jest killin' him while he wuz sleepin, but ah don't want ta go to hell." Lily stopped for a moment. "I sure am talkin' a lot ain't I. I been here three years and it twernt hard when it was jest me and Nevers. I got nothin' to say to him. But since you been here it's been plumb awful. So now you know my secret and the sound of my own voice is makin' me happy for once. But, remember, you promised you won't tell him or anyone, okay? Sometimes Nevers gets reel mad at me cause I don't talk and he says maybe he should divorce me and send me home. I'm hopin' real hard that it will happen. But then sometimes I'm real scart he might jest kill me off."

"Nevers, hits on you, don't he?" Rachael asked.

"Yeah, he hits me all the time."

"If you told your family that he hits on you wouldn't they do somethin' bad to him?"

Lily let out a big sigh. "No. Earl hits on my momma and me so he won't care. He says a little beatin' keeps a woman in her place. I wished it was jest the hittin' that he did to me. There are other things I hate even more..." She put her head down. "I don't want to talk about it anymore. I done went and said too much already, so don't ask me, but I want to tell you to be real careful. Never has a bad temper. He's got a mean streak wider than the stripe on a skunk. When he drinks, I run and hide. You be real careful round him. All this nice crap he is doen is jest an act."

"What about other people? Doesn't anyone ever come around here and why didn't you just run off when he was gone away trappin'?

"Most times he was gone it was cold outside. I couldn't run off, Rachael. Every time he left he took my shoes with him and sides, where would I go? Yeah, sometimes there would be some men comin' up here, but Nevers always met them outside. He made me stay in the house. Sometimes he would take me into Lynch, but that was not very often. And lessen' he was buyin' me somethin' to wear, I had to wait in the truck."

"I wonder why you ain't never got pregnant? Come to think of it, Nevers ain't had no children at all by none of his wives," Rachael said.

Lily shook her head. "No he ain't got no kids. Nevers tole me one time that he had the mumps when he was jest a little kid and them mumps went down in his weenie sack and he thinks it made him so he can't make babies. I'm sure nuf glad fer that. I want youngin' someday, but not by him. God, them kids would be butt ugly." Saying it aloud sent Lily into a fit of laughter.

They talked for a couple more hours about everything they could think of. Lily wanted to know all about Rachael's family. She wanted to know about school since she only went for a few years. She said at first she missed her family; all except Earl and wished she could see them. Nevers wouldn't let her visit them and refused to let them come see her. He said they would come around asking for a handout and he wasn't about to help them. She was his prisoner.

Rachael yawned. "I'm tired, Lily. I need to go to bed."

Lily took Rachael's hand, "Yer my friend now ain't you, Rachael. Yer my best friend and you promised to keep my secret."

Rachael hugged her. "Yes, Lily, I am your friend and no one will ever know yer secret lessen you want to tell them."

Rachael lay in bed for over an hour trying to make sense of everything that had happened tonight. Maybe she should tell someone…but she promised. Then again, who would even care what happened to Lily. Everyone in the holler had their own set of woes.

Chapter Eleven

"He's home, dang it. He's back already." Lily said, pulling back the curtain as Nevers truck turned into the yard. "Guess my talkin' time is over. Back to being a mute."

Rachael laughed, "Leastwise I know yer a talkin' mute." Rachael peered out the window. "Jest look at him, Lily. With them big bushy eyebrows and hairy knuckles he looks like one of them gorillas I saw in my schoolbook. See the way he walks, all hunkered over and swingin' them arms. Yep, he looks like a big, ole gorilla."

Lily covered her mouth. "You quit, yer gonna make me laugh when he comes in. Jest hush," she giggled.

Nevers pushed open the door and dropped his canvas bag and boots on the floor. His eyes traveled around the room looking for anything out of place. "You two do okay?" he asked. "Anybody come by? How bout them coyotes, any of them been around?"

"We did fine," Rachael replied. "No one come by and not even a sign of a coyote. All yer livestock is safe, except one chicken. It had blood feathers and the other hens were pickin' on it. So I put her out of her misery. She's a cookin' in the pot right now."

Nevers sat on a chair and took off his dirty socks. He picked them up and padded across the floor to the bedroom. "Jesse's outside warshen up, he done fell in a muddy hole."

With Nevers once again at home, Lily became the meek, young woman, afraid to even move when Nevers was in the same room. At first it was difficult for her. There were times when she wanted to talk to Rachael but she couldn't be sure that Nevers wasn't lurking around some corner. She knew he was always spying on them. It was only when he was out of the house that Rachael and Lily had snatches of conversation. After awhile it became a game and the girls began to enjoy their secret. Rachael and Lily made up signs for certain words. Holding up two fingers meant that Nevers was being an ass again and they tried hard not to laugh aloud. Wiggling one's nose meant that they could meet outside in ten minutes. Within two weeks they had developed a language of their own. They had to be careful. Nevers had a keen eye and when he saw Rachael wiggling her nose he said, "What's the matter with you, Girl. You got a tic or somethin'?"

Even though Rachael was happy with her newfound friend, it was Jesse who was miserable. When he wasn't doing chores, he spent most of his time in his room to stay out of Nevers way. After returning from the mountain he pulled Rachael aside. "Come on, walk down to the river with me. Grab that bucket in case Nevers is watchin' us."

"What's wrong?" Rachael asked as she tried to catch up with him.

"I'll tell you what's wrong. Nevers ain't jest a mean bastard, he's teched in the head, too. I don't want to go back that mountain with him and I know he is gonna make me. When we got almost to the top of the ridge, he pulled the wagon over in front of an old lean-to bout ten feet from the edge. It was a smelly place with two old cots and a buck stove. He told me that was where we was gonna stay at night. Then we walked part way up the path. He stops me and makes me sit down on a big ole rock. I'm supposed to stay there and if anyone comes up I'm supposed to whistle for him. He says the animals are used to his smell and if'n I go with him they won't come round his traps."

"I never heard that one," Rachael said. "Is that true?"

"I'm thinkin' its bullcrap, but I got no choice but to do what he says. Bout six damn hours I waited with the woods crackin' all round me. I'm sittin' thar with no gun, not even a slingshot. I'm jest waitin' for some cougar or bear to come make me thar dinner. I was really scart. I didn't even git up ta take a pee. When he finally comes down, I tell him I was scart and he jest laughs."

"That sounds like the old coot," Rachael interjected.

"Yeah well, when we was in that lean-to he opens two cans of beans and hands me one. Cold beans and water. That was dinner. Then he lays down and goes to sleep. I tell you Rachael between his snorin' and fartin' I never got a lick of sleep. The next day I fall asleep sittin' on that rock and I didn't heer him a comin'. He hits me in the back of the head and knocks me clean off that rock. I ain't goin' up thar no more, Rachael. I'm gonna go home at the end of the month. The following day, Nevers announced that they were going up the mountain again. Jesse gave Rachael a pitiful look, knowing that he had no choice but to go with Nevers.

It had seemed like forever before Nevers and Jesse were ready to leave again and only seconds for Lily and Rachael to begin talking nonstop. Sitting on the porch shucking a bushel of corn, Lily hummed softly to herself. "I like it when Jesse plays his guitar. Sometimes I jest wish I could sing along. I have to warn myself not to do that. Tell me about Jesse, Rachael."

"What do you want me to tell you? Him and me are twins. I'm the smart one. Sometimes I think that Jesse is just plain dumb, other times I think he jest puts on a good act ta git out of doin' things he don't like. He's always getting' himself into the damdest messes' cause he never stops to think about what he's doing. My momma always says he ain't got the sense he was born with. Why you want to know about him? You see him all the time."

"I think he's kind of cute. You know, when he smiles. Yep, he's real cute," Lily said. "He ain't never tried to talk to me, but sometimes I catch him lookin' at me. I'm guessin' he's real afeared of Nevers."

"You better believe he is. You jest watch yerself, Lily. You go hangin' round my brother yer likely to get both of yerself kilt. Nevers would do you both in without thinkin' twice."

"I know that. But, a girl kin think, can't she? She can think about somebody with smooth skin rather than a wrinkly old body and a shriveled up weenie." Both of the girls howled with laughter. This time Nevers and Jesse were gone for just one night.

The next afternoon Jesse knelt on the ground, cleaning fish on a flat rock. Lily leaned against a tree watching him. Knowing she could no longer keep her secret from him she blurted out. "I kin talk, Jesse."

"Well, damn, when did you git yer voice back?"

"I ain't ever lost it. I jest been pretendin' fer a long time. It's a long story and I can't tell you it now, but you got ta make sure you don't tell Nevers. Me and you and Rachael is all that know. You promise?"

"Yeah, sure, I promise."

"Do you think I'm purty, Jesse?" she asked.

He glanced up at her. "Well, I'm not sayin' yer ugly."

"If we was livin' back home, would you give me a second look?"

"Maybe," once again Jesse glanced toward her, this time staring at her breasts. "Why you askin' me all these questions?"

"I never had a chance to have a real boyfriend. Alls I had was Nevers." Lily ran her finger down the bark of the tree. "You ever kissed a girl? I ain't never been kissed,"

"You mean you and Nevers don't kiss?" he asked.

"No! He's got them green teeth and nasty breath. I ain't gonna let him kiss me, besides he ain't interested in kissin'." Lily walked over and kneeled down in front of Jesse. "Do you want to kiss me, Jesse?"

"What's the matter with you, Lily, you gone nuts?" Jesse scrambled to his feet. "You get away from me. You gonna get us both kilt." He reached for the bucket of fish and took off running up the hill.

"Dammit," Lily cursed and stomped up the hill toward home.

Nevers was standing in the shadow of the house. When Lily passed by he grabbed her by the arm. "What you been doin' down at the river with that boy. You lettin' that boy tech you?" Lily shook her head and tried to release his grip. "I'm tellin' you right now. You stay clear of that boy. Yer mah woman." Lily pulled harder on his fingers. His free hand reached up and slapped her across the face. She staggered backward and fell to the ground.

"You leave her alone," Jesse shouted. "She ain't done nothin' wrong."

Nevers glared at Jesse. "Oh yeah, well when I'm through with her yer next. I catch you lookin' at her agin, I'm gonna knock yer eyes right outta yer head. You understand me boy?" Nevers held his fist up and Jesse took off out of sight.

"That's right. You go on and run boy. I bet you wouldn't save yer momma if the pigs were after her. Yer a chicken-shit, yellow coward." Nevers howled at his own joke.

Lily ran into the house and into the bedroom. Nevers came in after her. Jesse steeled himself for what was going to happen next. Instead of coming after him, Nevers went to the sink and began to wash his hands. "If'n I didn't have somethin' to tell ya, I'd knock yer teeth out right now. I got news this mornin' when I was up at the store. One of yer neighbors come by and said that you two need to come home. Seems like yer folks got a visit from some men in uniforms from the government. I'll bet it ain't good news, but I'll let them tell you. You get yer sister and git. You kin take that brown mare."

When Jesse told Rachael the news she ran to the barn. "Hurry on, Jesse, we got to get home. That damn ole Nevers, I wonder when he was plannin' on tellin' us?"

After a bumpy ride on the old horse, Rachael hopped down and ran up the front stairs. She opened the busted screen door. Her mother and Emma Jane were sitting at the table crying.

"Momma, what happened? Who is it?"

"It's Ben, her mother said. "He's had an accident. He's in the hospital. They ain't sure he's gonna make it. They was doin' some trainin' with ammunition and he got blowed up.

"Let me talk to daddy first. Where is he?" Rachael asked. Her mother nodded toward the bedroom.

Rachael walked into the darkened room. "Daddy. Is it all right if I come in?"

Roy sat up in bed and looked at Rachael with red-rimmed eyes. "It's my fault. I told them boys it was okay for them to go and now lookee. My last good son is fixin' to die. We was gonna open a sawmill when he come home. Now he ain't never comin' home. He's in somethin' called a coma. "

Rachael knelt next to the bed. "It ain't your fault, Daddy. Ben wanted to go. He could have just as soon could have been killed in the mine. I'm sorry, too, Daddy. But, he ain't dead yet. Ben is strong. We'll all get down on our knees and pray he makes it."

Some of the neighbors came by when they heard the news and there was a lot of bible reading and wailing. The women sang mournful hymns as they rocked back and forth. The strains of Amazing Grace went on for hours.

Later that day, Roy and some of the other men shared a jug of corn liquor. They cursed the war and the government and poverty and their lot in life. Rachael sat by her mother and tried to comfort her. "Momma, if you want me and Jesse to stay here, we will. We can help out a lot. Ida Mae put her hand on Rachael's head. "I know that, Rachael. I need fer you and Jesse to keep workin' at Nevers. Who knows what's gonna happen. That money will help to keep us from starvin'. Specially now with the baby comin' we need the money. What if'n Emma Jane's milks no good? We need to buy a cow."

"What happen to our cow, Momma?"

"Oh, Rachael girl we done butchered her bout a week ago. We had nothin' to eat. Neither Emma Jane or me have got shoes to wear when the weather turns. And right now other than the food the people brought when they come to visit, we ain't got a lick of nothin' in this house. I surely hope yer daddy gets work soon."

"Maybe Jesse could stay here. He is so miserable over at Nevers' place. I can go back. But maybe he could stay here and help out. This house is falling apart, Mama. It ain't gonna hold together much longer."

"You know yer daddy wouldn't allow you ta go back to Nevers' place without yer brother. It ain't proper and we don't trust Nevers Bains. You both got to go."

Rachael laid her head on her mother's lap. She felt sorry that it was so hard for her mother. "Okay, Momma, me and Jesse will go back for a while."

Two days later Nevers showed up to collect Rachael and Jesse. He said he had been patient but he had work to do and needed them right away. Rachael said goodbye to her family knowing that it might be a long time before she would be home again. Jesse once again begged his father to let him stay home, but his pleadings were in vain. "I'm settin' here wonderin' if'n Ben is gonna live or die and you want to give me trouble. You know yer ma and me need that money. It's done a heap of good and with winter coming soon, we'll be needin' it even more. Now you go on and git back over to Nevers and stop complainin'," Roy said in an angry voice. "You got it damn good over thar. You got inside plumbin' and two meals a day. More than you git here. So go on git in that truck." Roy slapped Jesse across the back of his head and the conversation was over.

Rachael held on to her mother's hand for the last few minutes. "Now, Momma, when the baby comes you send someone to fetch me. You promise? And most important, if'n you hear anythin' about Ben you let me know right away." Her mother nodded and walked away.

Chapter Twelve

No one knew all the reasons why Jesse was so unhappy at Nevers. There were the obvious ones like being scared of Nevers, hating all the work he had to do and spending time up on the mountain. There was another reason why he was miserable. At night he would lay in his bed in the small room off the kitchen. It was just a few feet from Never's bedroom. The walls were thin. Jesse would listen to the noises coming from that room. He knew what was going on. He could hear Nevers plain and clear, but never even a moan from Lily. Jesse was almost nineteen and had never been with a woman. It was weighing heavy on his mind and his body. Sometimes he felt as if he was going to burst wide open. Since his daddy told him that if he didn't leave his weenie alone he would go blind, he suffered even more. And now he had to go back once again and be tortured by something he wanted so desperately. The other reason that nagged at him constantly was his fear of being alone on the mountain while Nevers was off trapping. He hated it more and more each time.

The day after they arrived back at Nevers, Jesse barely had time to catch his breath and the truck was already packed and ready to go up the mountain early the next morning. Nevers said they would be gone for two nights. To comfort Jesse, Rachael made some extra biscuits and a big piece of fat back, which she wrapped in a napkin and stuck in his sack. If he had to suffer through another trip at least he wanted to have something to eat and something to keep him warm. He just had to make sure that Nevers had no idea that he had brought food along.

"Git yer ass in the truck, boy. We ain't got all day," Nevers yelled from the yard. Jesse slowly trudged outside and gave Rachael a limp wave goodbye.

Settling into the front seat, Jesse slumped down and closed his eyes.

"What's that smell?" Nevers said sniffing the air. "I smell bacon. You got bacon on you, Boy?"

"Naw, I jest et a piece fore I came out the door."

"Well you jest better make sure you don't bring food. I told you them varmints would be after you like flies on horse crap."

As soon as the truck was out of sight, Lily threw her arms around Rachael's neck. "Oh, please, don't ever leave me alone agin. Not even for one day. You don't know how many times I almost talked. I hate him. I hate him so much I want him dead. He had me doin' the deed twice a day since we had the house to ourselves. I hate him, Rachael. I've been tryin' to stay out of his way while you were gone. I done cleaned this house which way and over agin."

Rachael pried Lily's arms loose. "Okay, I'm back so you can rest for a spell. What would you like to do today?" Knowing that what Lily was going through was too much for anyone to handle.

"I want to go to Lynch and go to the picture show. That's what I want to do. Nevers said he was gonna be gone at least two nights."

"I swear, Lily, you must be teched. We can't leave. Besides we don't have no money and no way to get to Lynch. That's a long way away. Besides, if Nevers found out he would beat both of us silly."

"I got money, Rachael. I got fifty cents. Them two quarters fell out of Nevers pants one night when he was getting undressed and when he was asleep I took em. The show only cost about a dime and I ain't never been to a movie, have you, Rachael?"

"No! And we ain't going today."

"Then I'll go by myself. I'll walk down the road and wait til somebody comes by and then I'll hitch a ride to Lynch. I'll go to the show and be home afore dark. You comin' or not?"

Rachael looked at Lily and suddenly she knew that the life Lily was leading was closing in around her. Living with Nevers was taking its toll on Lily. If she ever faced him down he may really hurt her. "Okay, I'll go, but if we get caught we are gonna be real sorry."

Lily began to jump up and down and squeal. "Oh, I'm going to the show, a real movie show. Oh, I can't wait." Then suddenly she stopped and her mood changed. "What am I thinkin' about? I can't go. I ain't got no shoes to wear. Nevers done took them agin. You can't git into the picture show without shoes."

"But, he didn't take mine," Rachael said. "I got these I got on and another old pair that are jest bout ready to be pitched. They got holes in the bottom but that don't matter none. We'll stuff some paper in them." She ran to the bedroom and pulled the ragged shoes from under the bed.

Lily squeezed her feet into them just like one of Cinderella's sisters trying on the glass slipper. "They hurt, but I don't care. Let's go."

Lily took the shoes off and carried them until they reached the road. "Somebody's bound to come by soon. Let's make up our story right now, okay?"

Rachael thought a moment and then spoke. "I'll say that yer ailin' and you need to see a doctor in Lynch. So you got to act sick, Lily. Maybe cough once in a while."

"I kin sure do that," she replied.

The two girls walked about half a mile when they heard the sound of a grinding motor coming down the road. Rachael stood close to the edge of the road and began to wave her hand up and down.

The truck came to bumpy stop just a few feet from them. The driver ducked his head and peered at the two girls.

"Oh, my God, it's Billy Tate," Rachael said in a whisper. "Jest our luck. Pretend like yer stomach is hurtin'. Double over or gag or somethin'."

"Well, I'll be damn, Rachael Riley. What you doin' walkin' down this here road? Yer a far piece from home ain't you?" Billy said.

"I'm livin' at the Bains place now. I'm helpin' out round the house. Look, I got Never's wife, Lily, with me. She ain't well. I really need to get her to the doctor in Lynch. Nevers is out trappin' right now. Can you take us as far as yer goin'? She really needs ta see the doctor."

Billy smiled. "Sure, I kin. Matter a fact I'm on my way to Lynch myself. You git in and I'll have you thar real soon.'

Billy leaned over the seat and opened the door. "You better sit next to me, Rachael. It ain't proper for me to sit next to a married woman." Rachael slid in next to Billy trying to keep a space between them, but with three in the front seat, she was crammed up next to him. He reached over and patted her leg. "Now, you jest relax."

That a fact that that girl can't speak a word?" he said looking over at Lily.

"It's a fact," Rachael replied. She shoved his hand off of her leg. She wanted to slap his face, but she also wanted to get to Lynch. She cringed and squeezed up next to Lily who was pushed against the door.

"Why ain't you nice to me, Rachael? What I ever done to make you not like me so much?"

Rachael rolled her eyes. "Well, fer one thang yer pushy and yer just one rung up from where I am now. I want to get to the top of ladder. I want to make somethin' of myself."

"Aw, go on. You ain't never leavin' the hollow. Yer stuck here jest like the rest of us. Besides I ain't got no idée why yer livin' at Nevers' house. He's a mean, old bastard."

"That's my business,' she replied. He's as mean as a skunk, but every once in awhile he shows a little good side. It's like whoever made him so ornery and nasty never really finished the job. Now you jest be quiet and drive."

Thirty minutes later the truck stopped on Main Street in Lynch. "You girls need a ride home. I got some business, but I reckon I should be done in a couply hours. You want me to wait fer you?"

"No, that's okay. We'll be jest fine," Rachael said as she bounded out of the truck and on to the sidewalk. "Thanks for the ride, Billy."

Lily and Rachael crossed the street and walked slowly until they were sure that Billy was gone. When they turned the corner the marquee of the Lynch Theater was right in front of them.

Lily walked up to the window and bought two tickets. Handing one to Rachael they walked into the theater and found a seat right in front. When the movie started they both sat there grinning from ear to ear. It was like a miracle. There they were, the giant faces of Norma Shearer and Chester Morris starring in The Divorcee.

When the movie was over, Lily just could not stop smiling. It had been the most wonderful experience she had ever had. Rachael took her hand and they walked outside the theater. "Can you believe it, Lily? We done saw a real movie."

"This is the best day of my whole life and I ain't never goin' ta ferget it." They walked in silence for a few minutes. "That's what I want ta be, Rachael. I want ta be a divorcee like the lady in the movie. Alls she did was ask the judge and he gave her a paper and she was free ta do what she wanted. Do you think I could do that, Rachael?"

"I ain't real sure about that, Lily. I think that's somethin' only rich people kin do. Still lost in the movie it took a loud honk to bring them back to reality. It was Billy Tate again. He was sitting in his truck right in front of them. He stepped out onto the sidewalk, blocking their way. "Well, I guess Mrs. Bains must have had a good recovery since you went to the movies."

"Yeah, she's much better now. Dr. Glass gave her a shot and it really helped her. We didn't go ta the movies. Whar'd you git that idée?"

"Yer lyin' through yer teeth, Rachael Riley, you never went to the doctor. You went right to the picture show. I done followed you. How'd it be if I told Lily's old man what you done?"

"What do want, Billy Tate?" Rachael asked in a demanding voice.

"I want you ta let me come courtin' once in a while and when I come around you stop treatin' me so mean." He reached out and ran his hand down her arm.

Rachael pulled backed. Letting Billy Tate court her— that was never going to happen!

"What if I was to tell Nevers that we came to town ta see the doctor and you were makin' advances at his wife. You know, talkin' sweet to her and touchin' her. How would you like that? Nevers has a real bad temper. Some say he even killed two or three people. Who you think he would believe?

When I tell him Lily was real sick and you was pawen all over her. Isn't that right, Lily? Billy was flirtin' with you wasn't he?" Lily slowly nodded her head.

"Billy's eyes widen. "Okay, I don't cotton to dealin' with Nevers Bains. You win this time, Rachael. I won't tell. But you and me are gonna talk agin real soon." He climbed into his truck and pulled away from the curb.

"How we gonna git home, Rachael?" Lily asked.

"You see, that's what I mean, Lily. You jest wanted to see a movie picture. You never made any plans on how we were going to get home. You always leave it up to me." Rachael began to walk faster, with Lily running behind her.

Just on the outskirts of town, Rachael and Lily waved down a produce truck. They climbed in the back among the boxes of potatoes and turnips. Rachael leaned against the rail and closed her eyes. After a few minutes Lily pushed her on the shoulder. "You asleep?"

"Well, if I was, I'm awake now. I was jest thinkin' about the people in the movie. Did you hear how they talked and the way they dressed. That's what I want. I always knew I wasn't meant to live in Bent Creek all my life. I think I was born to the wrong parents. Somebody messed up really bad."

"Thar's that silly talk agin," Lily said. "How'd you ever be born to the wrong folks? That's plumb crazy."

"No crazier than bein' miserable all the time. Look at you. Spendin' your life with that old coot, Nevers. Always bein' afraid. Pretendin' you can't talk. Isn't that all crazy? And me...jest as bad havin' to work for him. We need to make a plan, Lily. We have to figure out how to change all of this. Yep, I'm gonna have to work on that." She closed her eyes again and was back inside the movie.

Chapter Thirteen

While Rachael and Lily were in Lynch staring at the movie screen, Nevers and Jesse were going up the mountain. Usually Jesse never spoke, but today with the food Rachael had given tucked safely in his blanket he seemed to have more courage than usual. "Nevers I was wonderin' if we could get some better food to eat when we come up here. Those beans are tearin' up my stomach and I'm tired of them."

"You jest don't understand, boy. Didn't I jest finish tellin' you that you can't take a bunch of food to the shack. There are hungry critters that would come callin' and tear the hell out of the place and maybe us, too. Them beans is safe in the cans. This is my business. Ya got to put up with somethins ya don't like to git the things ya do like. That's why I got a nice house and I'm thinkin' about gettin' me a telephone in a couply weeks. How bout that? A telephone. That's somethin'. I'll tell you what, Jesse. you quit yer bellyachin' and bitchin' and ah may be willin' ta pay you an extra dollar a week. That would be jest for you. How does that sound?"

"Good, real good. I ain't ever had any money of my own. Okay, you jest tell me what you want me ta to and I'll do it. Even eat them beans." Jesse let out a laugh.

"That's right, boy. You mind yer business. I'll give you a bit of advice, Jesse. You watch yer back. Make sure you know what yer doin" and watch yer back. You make sure whats yers is yers and don't let no one take it way from you. Money

81

will buy you what you want, Boy. Jest be smart. You got that, boy?"

Jesse nodded his head. He had no idea what Nevers was talking about.

Positioning Jesse at his usual spot, Nevers handed him the rifle. "I'm gonna give you this ta make you feel better about waitin' here. Now remember, you don't fire that rifle lessen someone is comin'. I'll be back in about four hours."

Making sure Nevers was out of sight, Jesse quickly opened the package and ate one of the biscuits and half the fatback. Licking his fingers he wrapped up the rest of the food and stuck it under a rock a few feet away from him. With a full stomach, he lay down on the grassy patch under a towering pine tree and closed his eyes. The sun was warm and it didn't take him long before he drifted off to sleep.

Half an hour later, Jesse awoke to the smell of bacon fat coming from a hot breath. He opened his eyes and stared into the face of a huge, brown bear. Stinking drool fell from the bear's mouth and landed on Jesse's shirt as the bear shook his head back and forth. Jesse wanted to scream, but he knew better. He had to lay still and pretend he was dead, his heart thumping in his chest. He had been taught that since he was young. He had to pee and he wanted to cry, but he lay still. He should have known better than to let the rest of the food so close to him. Nevers had warned him and now he looked into the eyes of death. The bear nudged him with his nose and pawed at his side, tearing his shirt to shreds. Jesse could feel the warm blood begin to trickle down his side. The rifle lay only a few feet away. If he could get to it he may have a chance. The bear moved a few steps and sniffed at the ground where the food was hidden. He scratched at the ground and pushed the rock over. While the bear devoured the remaining food, Jesse rolled over as quickly as he could and reached for the rifle. The bear reacted quickly. Standing up on two feet, he let out an ominous roar.

Leaving the gun, Jesse rolled over two more times, scrambling to his he feet he ran for his life. He shimmied up the trunk of the first pine tree he came to. He knew he wouldn't be safe for long. The bear would probably follow after him, but Jesse prayed the beast's heavy weight would break the slender branches and keep him from reaching the upper branches. Half way up the tree, Jesse stopped for a moment and looked down. The bear seemed to have lost interest in him. He was licking at the barrel of the gun. He must have smelled the grease from Jesse's hand that was left on the rifle. Picking the gun up in his teeth, he splintered the heavy wooden stock as if it were a toothpick. It was a big mistake. One of his canines hit the trigger and with an ear-splitting blast, the bear fell backward, blood spewing from his chest. Jesse let out a scream. He didn't know, why but it just came out at the same time the stream of yellow pee trickled down his leg. Holding on tight to the tree branch, his hands and knees bleeding from the climb, he waited to see what would happen next. He was shaking so hard that the branches of the tree were moving. The bear's body jerked three or four times and then lay still. Deciding to wait a few more minutes before he came down from the tree, he didn't see Nevers running down the hill. Nevers suddenly stopped. Taking aim at the bear, the crackle of the tree branches made him spin around, his gun still in firing position. "Don't shoot, Nevers, it's me! Don't shoot!" Jesse slid down the tree, catching more splinters and cuts on his hands.

"What in the Sam hell is goin' on? I heard the shot. Did you shoot that bar?" Nevers asked in a stunned voice.

"Yeah...I sure did. I shot him once, but he charged at me and grabbed the gun. He just went crazy, bittin' and chewin' on it and I run for the tree, but when I got up thar he just keeled over dead."

"Well, I'll be damn. You done got you a bar. It's a big-gin, too. That pelt will fetch a pretty penny."

Beginning to settle down, Jesse asked, "Kin I keep the money from the skin?"

"Hell no, boy, you done owe me a new rifle. We may jest break even. Now let's git him down the hill before the coyotes come round.

As the day turned into evening, Lily and Rachael begin to get more and more nervous over what they had done. They should have never accepted a ride from Billy Tate. Why didn't they just tell Billy that they were out for a walk. If Billy told Nevers about them going to the picture show they had no idea what would happen to them. When they heard the sound of the truck coming down the road they both ran to the window. "Oh, Lordy, he said he'd be gone for two nights and here he is back already," Rachael groaned.

. "Hurry, Lily, git in the bed. Now try to act sick," Rachael said. "You stay in that bed and don't move. We jest got here by the skin of our teeth. I wonder what thar doin' home so soon?"

"I ain't sorry, Rachael. I'll take whatever Nevers does to me. I got to see a movie and he can't take that away from me. I jest hate the idea that he may hurt you, too."

"Don't you worry any about me. There ain't no way that Nevers is gonna touch me."

Rachael went outside as soon as the truck stopped. Before she could say anything, Nevers opened the door and jumped down. "Yer brother done shot himself a bar. Come see, it's in the back of the truck. We had to come home before the varmints came sniffin' round and tried to take it away from us. I got to go in the shed and take care of it. You ever eat bear meat, little girl?"

Rachael shook her head. He hadn't even asked about Lily. Jesse followed Rachael into the house after Nevers went into the shed. "I can't believe you shot a bar," she said.

Jesse's face turned pale and he began to shake all over. "Oh, God, Rachael, I ain't never been so scart in my whole life. I had a bar lookin'me straight in the eye. He was standin' right over me and I thought I was gonna die." He began to sob and Rachael let him fall into her arms before he hit the floor. "It was plumb awful. I ain't never goin' up that mountain again. I ain't cut out for this kind of work." He wiped his nose with his sleeve and continued to cry. "I'm still scart. That bar meant business." He pointed to his torn shirt and the scratches on his side.

"You'll be all right, Jesse. Wait till daddy hears about this. He's gonna to be real proud of you. In a fortnight everybody in the holler will know you done kilt a bar. Ain't many who live to tell the tale when they get that close to a bar. Now why don't you go lay down for a while and I'll fix you somethin' to eat."

"Where's Lily," Nevers said as he came into the kitchen.

"She's in the bed. She's feelin' real poorly. I had to take her into the doctor today in Lynch. She was in real bad pain," Rachael said, trying to sound convincing.

"What do you mean?" How'd you get to Lynch? Didn't I tell ya not ta leave this house?"

She could see the anger in his face. Rachael began to talk fast. She didn't want him to interrupt her lie. "We had ta go, Nevers. I thought Lily was gonna die. She was wailin'and doubled over in pain. I had ta almost carry her. A real nice man and lady took us there and they waited till the doctor saw her and brought us home. She's gonna be okay. The doctor said it was the bug got into her belly. He done gave her a shot and told her to stay in bed the rest of the day."

"I ain't cotton to you takin' her out of this house without me knowin' about it. Was she really that sick?" he asked in an irritated voice. "What'd you think yer doin' ridin' with strangers?"

"I didn't have no choice, Nevers, she was real sick. She was doubled over in pain and her face was green and she was throwing up everywhars. We barely made it to the road and she jest keeled over."

Nevers opened his bedroom door and looked in on Lily. She lay in the bed with a cloth on her head and the covers pulled up around her neck. "Well, she must be ailin'. She ain't one to stay in the bed. I still ain't likin' the idée of you all goin' to Lynch but I guess you done what you had to. I'm gonna go gut that bar."

Rachael waited until he was out of sight before she went in to see Lily. "Now you heard my story. You better stick to it or we're gonna be in big trouble. Lucky for us he didn't ask how we got down to the road with you being so sick and he didn't ask who the people were. We got to make sure he stays away from this subject. If'n it twernt fer that bar he'd be really riled and probably ask a lot more questions. "

Lily stayed in bed for three days afraid to get up. When she realized what she and Rachael had done, she knew that if Nevers found out he would probably beat her to death. What was she thinking? She got to see a movie, but was all this worry worth it. She just hoped Billy Tate kept his mouth shut. Especially since Nevers said he was making a trip to Lynch. Oh lardy, she could be in such big trouble.

Nevers came into the bedroom. "Lissen, girl, I'm going off ta Lynch to pick up some supplies. Do ya want me ta stop in at that doctor's office and see if'n he can give you some medicine ta git you out of that bed?"

Lily rolled over and slowly sat up. She pretended to yawn. She stood up and smiled. Pointing to herself she mouthed the words, "I feel better," very slowly.

"Yer sayin' yer better?" he asked.

She shook her head up and down as fast as she could.

"Well, alrighty then. You git back in that bed, I kin git supplies tomarra." Nevers pulled his suspenders off his shoulders and left his pants fall to the floor. He climbed in next to her. Lily closed her eyes and cringed.

In the morning Nevers pulled Jesse out of bed and they headed into Lynch. The streets of the town were busy with Saturday shoppers. Nevers pulled the truck up in front of the livery stable. "You see that man standin' over thar, Jesse. That's Rooster. He's a mean sum bitch. Him and me don't cotton to each other. He ever comes anywhars near you, you jest walk away. Don't talk to him. He won't mess with me. He knows better. You stay here and I'll be right back."

Jesse watched the man leaning against the building for a few minutes and then slipped down in the seat and closed his eyes. He opened them with a start when something hit the truck with a loud thud. Rooster was standing at the window with a stick in his hand. "Wake up boy. What are you and Nevers up to?"

"We ain't up to nothin'. You better stop beatin' on this truck fore Nevers catches you."

Rooster threw his head back and let out a loud cackle. "You think I'm afeared of Nevers. That's a real good one. I reckon you ain't gonna tell me nothin' cause I kin see he's done got you scart ta death of him. Well, he ain't so tough." He turned and sauntered away.

Nevers put the bags in the back of the truck and got in. "
I seed Rooster talkin' ta ya. What'd he want? You tell him anythang?"

"Nope, didn't tell him a thang."

"That's the best answer you gave me all day. Now let's
git on home."

Chapter Fourteen

Billy Tate sat on the wooden bench outside of the Lynch Drugstore. He was waiting for his mother to get her medicine. He watched as Nevers Bains pulled his truck into the alleyway between the livery stable and Orby's General Store. His truck was loaded with skins. Fifteen minutes later, Nevers pulled out on to the street and got out. He began loading cardboard boxes that Clyde Orby had set on the sidewalk. Billy sauntered across the street and stopped next to the truck. "Ya need any halp?" Billy asked.

"Got damn, you scart me. Why'd you sneak up on me?" Nevers said.

"Sorry, Mr. Bains. I thought you seed me comin'. Do you want me to halp you? Them look like heavy boxes."

"No! I don't need no halp. Now step back." He pushed in front of Billy and heaved another box into the truck.

"I like ta ask you a question. I was just wonderin' if'n you need any help out at yer place, Mr. Bains? I got some free time before the next tobaccy crop comes in. I'm a hard worker and I kin work cheap. What'd ya think about that?"

"Seems ta me you already asked me two questions. I don't need no help," he growled. "Now step aside." He climbed into the truck and chugged down the street.

Billy stood looking after the truck. He best not ever tangle with Nevers Bains but he sure would like to see what was going on out at his place. It would be nice to have a chance to be around Rachael.

Nevers truck bumped down the rutted road leaving Lynch behind. He hated coming into town every week. He always ran into some ass that wanted to talk to him. He never bothered them townspeople, why wouldn't they just leave him alone. Maybe he should hire Billy Tate and tell Jesse to hit the road. He was tired of Jesse's whining all the time. But he may as well leave things as they were. He liked Rachael's cooking. He was in a bad mood today.

When he turned off the road into his yard, Nevers was surprised to see Lily in the yard hanging clothes on the line. She was finally out of the bed for good. It had been a week and she was still acting puny. He slid across the seat and yelled to her. "Git me a cup of coffee, I'll be right in." He stopped by the side of the steps and took off his boots and smelly socks. Lily was still hanging clothes. "Well, I'll be damn," Nevers said as he hobbled across the yard. "Didn't you hear what I said? You deef as well as mute?" He grabbed her by the arm and pulled her up the stairs and into the kitchen. Tossing her across the floor, she landed against the wall like a rag doll. He was over her, his calloused hand already in the air ready to swoop down and hit her across the face. Without warning a wooden spoon came sailing across the room and hit him in the head. Nevers grabbed his head. "Got damn," he said, turning around.

"Don't you hit her again, Nevers Bains. What's wrong with you? People don't treat their cur dogs as bad as you treat her." Rachael reached down and helped Lily up. "Look at her, Nevers! She don't weigh a hundred pounds drippin' wet. Yer three times her size. Yer nothin' but a mean, old bully." Rachael stomped her foot with conviction.

"Oh yeah, well let me tell you somethin'. Lily is mah wife and I kin ..."

Rachael took the boning knife that she was using to cut up the chicken and jammed it down into the wooden sink drain. "Don't you even say it. I'm tellin' you right now if'n you don't stop hittin' her you may go to bed some night and it could be yer last night on this earth." She clenched her fingers around the knife.

"You tellin' me you're gonna do me in." He threw his head back and laughed.

"That's what I'm sayin'. So maybe you better start sleepin' with one eye open."

"Well, I jest outta send your skinny ass on down the road, better yet I outta show ya ta mind yer manners."

"Go ahead and when I leave I'm takin' Lily with me and then I'm goin' to call the sheriff and make up a whole bunch of lies about you."

Nevers squinted his eyes. "Aw go on. Yer as nutty as yer old man." He rose from his chair and went outside. Rachael had gotten the best of him for once.

Lily moved behind Rachael and whispered, "Thank you," in her ear.

Quietly Rachael answered. "That's okay. Oh, you should feel my heart. It's about ready to jump out of my chest. I was so scart. Whew, I hope that settles him for a little while."

Rachael opened the screen door and yelled to Nevers. "You best get washed up, Nevers. Supper will be ready in about ten minutes."

"You come on out here, Girl. I got a horse with a bad shoe. I need some help. I can't find yer dumb-ass brother."

Rachael walked slowly to the barn, wondering if she was making a mistake. She hoped she had given Nevers enough time to cool down and he wasn't luring her outside to beat on her. She stood at the door of the barn until Nevers led one of the horses to the anvil iron.

"Hold onto this rope while I git his shoe off," Nevers said to Rachael as he tried to steady the mare.

Rachael grabbed the rope just as the horse reared up knocking Nevers to the ground. "Got damn. What you tryin' to do, git me kilt? I told you ta hold on to it. Yer just as crazy as yer old man."

Rachael grabbed the rope again and held on tight. "That's the second time you called my daddy crazy. Why do you keep sayin' that, Nevers. My daddy ain't crazy. He's goin' through a hard time but that don't make him crazy. He don't have work and Ben is still not doin' so good."

"Hard time, you betcha. I guess you don't know about what he's done? He went up to Lynch to cash that check that he got from the Army. It was some money Ben had comin' ta him fer gettin' hurt. I reckon it was a couply hundred dollars. It was supposed to be kept safe fer Ben, but yer pap didn't care. He tuk it fer his own. While yer daddy was in town he met some stranger in the bank. He started tellin' the man about his plan to open a sawmill and that he had money to do it. That man told yer pappy he had a whole bunch of sawmill equipment for sale real cheap. He took yer pappy over to an old buildin' and showed him the machinery. Yer daddy liked it so he went to the bank with the man and cashed the check. He give that man all of it. When he went to collect the equipment, he almost got kilt. The fella who sold it to him didn't even own it. The man who owned it almost shot yer pappy when he saw him in his building messin' with his stuff."

"Oh no! Did he find the man? Did he get his money back?"

"Hell no. That shyster was long gone. He knew yer old man was an easy mark. That's why I call him crazy. By the way, yer pappy got another one of them letters from the government. Thar sendin' Ben home. He done come outta that deep sleep. He ain't no good to the army anymore."

Another shock for Rachael. She stomped her foot. "Why don't you ever tell me about this stuff? It's important. What's wrong with him? What happened?"

"Hell if I know. Taint my business ta take care of yer family's business. All's I know is that he is comin' in on the train to Lynch on Thursday and yer daddy don't have no way to go up and git hem. Nobody at Mabry's had a truck that could make it that far. I reckon Ben will jest have to set up thar until someone comes and fetches him."

Rachael began to cry. Why, why was all this happenin' agin? "Nevers can Jesse and I use…"

Nevers interrupted her. "Don't be askin' me ta use my truck."

"I'm beggin', Nevers, please."

"What'd you gonna give me if I let you use it." He grinned and licked his lips."

"Forget it. I'll walk and carry Ben home on my back if I have to."

"Aw, go on, use it, but I'm takin' a dollar outta yer pay for gas and wear on my truck."

Early the next morning, Jesse and Rachael pulled the truck into their parent's yard and laid on the horn. It didn't take long to rouse everyone out of the house. "

With her mother and Emma Jane in the truck cab with Jesse, Rachael and her father climbed into the back.

After a few minutes Rachael spoke. "Do you know what's wrong with Ben? Did the letter tell you what happened to him?"

Roy shook his head. "Nope. It jest said that he had per-manent injuries. I ain't sure what that means. But it don't sound good."

Rachael wanted to talk to her father about the money. She wanted to tell him she was sorry, but she knew that anything she said would only bring back the shame he felt already for falling for a scam. She knew that the old men at Mabry's had probably already given him a real hard time and calling him an old fool. It was better to leave that subject alone.

Standing on the wooden platform in front of the train station, Rachael said a silent prayer that Ben would come bounding off the train and tell them that he was all right. Maybe he had just a little dent in his head or a missing toe. As the train rattled to a stop and the whistle sounded for the last time, she waited patiently as the passengers filed down the steps. When it seemed like everyone was already off the train, a nurse in a crisp, white uniform pushed a wheel chair down a side ramp. A young soldier followed behind her carrying Ben in his arms.

Ida Mae put her hand to her mouth and let out a small cry as the soldier sat Ben in the chair. A blanket was placed across him to cover up the place where his legs should have been He never looked up. Everyone seemed to be frozen in place until Rachael went to his side. She put her arms around his neck and kissed his cheek. "Ben, it's so good to see you."

Ben did not answer. He just continued to look down. The nurse stepped forward and extended her hand to Roy. "You must be Mr. Riley. Is that correct?" Roy, still staring at his son, slowly nodded his head.

"Ben had injuries to his head and also severe injuries to his legs. Once out of the comma his head trauma was healed, but he developed infections in both of his legs. We were not really sure that he would recover, but he has made good progress. Unfortunately for Ben, both of his legs had to be amputated. We wanted to tell you, but he refused our request to let you know. I'm afraid at the time he was hoping he would just die. I'm so sorry, Mr. Riley, but with therapy and care your son can live a full and productive life. Your son is a wonderful young man."

"How would you know?" Roy spate out. "You don't know my son. You sent him home without his legs. You jest go on and leave us alone."

She seemed uncomfortable. "I need to give you some instructions for his care. Can any of you read?"

Before anyone could answer, Rachael stepped forward. "Tell me, I kin read. I'll take care of him." As the nurse talked with Rachael the rest of the family gathered around Ben. Ida Mae gently hugged him and Roy patted him on the shoulder. It was Jesse who hung back too afraid to open mouth and say the wrong thing.

Jesse loaded the wheelchair into the back of the truck and lifted Ben into the front seat. Everyone else climbed into the back. They needed some time to digest what they had just seen and what they were going to say to Ben.

Rachael pulled Jesse aside before they went into this house. "I want you to tell Nevers that I will be back in a week. I'm gonna stay here with Ben until he gets used to the house. Momma and daddy don't know how to handle him and I'm afraid he is just gonna lay in bed all day. That's not good for him. The nurse said he had to get up and move around. If Nevers gets mad, that's jest too bad, I can't leave now."

Rachael would not leave Ben alone. She sat by his bed and talked nonstop. She told him all about Emma Jane and about the baby that would be coming soon and living at Nevers' house. She told him about how sad they were that Paul had died and she asked him what it was like living in California."

"Will you stop talkin', Rachael. I need to rest," Ben said in an irritated voice. "Alls you do is talk. You talk about everythin' except my missin' legs. Is that what you want to know? Well go on and ask me. Get it over with."

"Tell me what happened, Ben. Tell me all about it."

His voice choked and his chest heaved as he began to sob. "They cut them off, Rachael. They cut them off without even askin' me. They took my legs. They said they were too mangled and if'n they didn't take them off the infection would kill me. I wished I woulda died." His arm went up over eyes. "I was under the jeep, workin' on the axle, my legs was stickin' out. I smelled the gasoline and saw the fire from the explosion comin' toward the jeep. I tried to get out, but the fire was all around me, so I had to scoot way under the jeep. And then I heer'd another loud blast. That's the last I remember. I woke up bout four days later with half a body and burns all over me. Then I went into that comma. I jest want to die. Jest go get a gun and shoot me and put me out of my misery."

Rachael put her arms around him. "Please, Ben. Give it some time. You'll get better."

"I ain't never gonna be better. I can't grow no new legs."

Rachael refused to let Ben feel sorry for himself. When he said he wanted to wash and shave she would not let her mother do it for him. Rachael brought him a basin of water and a razor and set it on the stand next to his bed. She laid a clean nightshirt next to him. "Now you sit up and wash yerself and shave. Change yer clothes, yer startin' to smell."

"I can't," he said.

"Oh, yes you kin. Yer arms ain't broken." She turned around and left the room, pulling the curtain closed behind her.

Rachael knew that she had to get back to Nevers soon. Ben came home with about twenty dollars in his duffel bag, but it may be months before he would begin getting a monthly disability check from the government. He didn't know about the money the government had sent home and Rachael didn't want to tell him what her father had done. It would probably only be enough to take care of his own needs and not much left over. She was beginning to feel a sense of panic coming over her. What would they do when winter came? How would they be able to take care of Ben and Emma Jane and the new baby with no income and no prospects?

After a week, Rachael made her announcement. "I hate to leave you, Momma, but I got to go back." Actually other than filling her time with Ben, she was having a hard time living in the hovel that her parent's called home. Going to the privy outside and fighting the bugs that came in through the open windows was not something that she enjoyed. It was time to go and help Lily and Jesse.

"You gotta get Ben to take care of himself. He kin do a lot more than you think he kin. Maybe daddy could fix some sort of ramp so that Ben could at least git outside to the privy."

"I jest don't know, Rachael. I don't think I kin take care of him. I kin hardly git him out of bed and Roy won't even go near Ben. He acts like he scart of him. We don't have much food round here. I'm guessin' we have no choice but to take care of him. Emma Jane is getting' so heavy in the belly she can't help."

Rachael had no idea that Ben was awake and heard everything that was said.

"I sure wish you could stay here with me, Rachael," Emma Jane said. I'm so lonely I can hardly stand it. I can't wait fer this baby ta git here so I kin see my toes agin." She gave Rachael a hug. "But I know'd without the money you give daddy things would even be worse."

Bent Creek

Mr. Mabry agreed to take Rachael back to Nevers' place when she was ready to go. On the day she was to leave, Ben asked her if she would wheel him down to the pond for a few minutes. He wanted to get outside for a little while and do a little fishing. Struggling with his chair, she shoved and pulled him down the mud path leading to the water. Pushing with all her strength the chair finally bumped across the makeshift dock. Out of breath she lay down on the warm boards, she let out a sigh. "Damn, we have to get you a lighter chair." She rolled over on her stomach and watched the light dance on the water. This used to be one of her favorite places, before the algae took over most of the surface, yet it was still good for fishing. "Remember when we were kids and we used to come down here and swim and catch crawdads? That was fun. That was before this pond got all scummy."

"I hate to ask you, Rachael, but do ya think you could go up to the pump and get me some water? I'm parched," Ben asked. "I plumb forget ta bring some with me."

"Why didn't you say somethin' afore we come down here. Now I gotta walk all the way back?" She stood up with a groan, "I'll be right back." She brushed off the back of her jeans and started slowly up the path. Climbing the last few feet to the top of the hill, Rachael suddenly heard a loud splash. She let out a scream. Running as fast as her legs would carry her, she passed the empty wheelchair sitting on the dock. Rachael jumped in just as Ben's body began to sink beneath the water. Holding her breath she dove under the murky, green surface and grabbed the back of his shirt. Struggling to hold on, she gasped as her head broke the surface of the water. Ben pushed at her, thrashing back and forth, he screamed, "Let me go, Rachael, let me go."

Rachael continued to pull him as she paddled with one arm to the shore. Her feet sinking into the mud, she heaved his body into the shallow water. Dragging him on to the grassy

98

bank she began to pummel him with both fists. "Damn you, Ben Riley, damn you."

Ben tried to cover his head with his arms. "If yer gonna beat me ta death, why don't you jest let me drown?" he sputtered. "I heard what momma said. She don't want me here. I ain't good fer nothin'. Jest let me die."

"I want you to live! You're not gonna do this to me, Ben Riley. You still have your eyes and ears and mouth. Yer brains must have been in yer feet when they cut them off. You ain't gonna kill yerself and make me mourn fer you. I done lost two brothers and I ain't gonna lose you. I'm gonna take you to Nevers house with me. There's only one step to the house and he's got an indoor toilet. Now sit right thar while I git yer chair. Don't you dare move." Pulling his wet body into his chair, she knelt down and put her arms around him. "I love you, Ben. Please don't give up. It's gonna be okay. I promise you." They clung to each other, crying muddy tears.

Sobs wracked his body. "Why'd they take my legs, Rachael? They didn't even ask me, they jest cut them off."

Chapter Fifteen

Her decision to take Ben to Nevers' house with her was met with a sigh of relief from both her parents. She bundled him into Mr. Mabry's truck and kissed her parents goodbye. No amount of talking seemed to lift his spirits and he settled into his shroud of depression. "Yah see what I mean, Rachael. Did you see the look on their faces? Thar damn glad ta git rid of me."

"Don't blame them, Ben. Thar jest backwoods folks. They ain't got no smart bout this kinda thing and they ain't got no idée what yer goin' through. And I got ta warn you. Nevers ain't gonna be a bit happy when he sees you, but pay him no mind. I can handle him."

When they arrived at Nevers, Rachael had to deal with the tirade that she was expecting when she wheeled Ben into the house. "Ya gotta be kiddin' me. What the hell do you think I'm a runnin' here, a boardin' house fer Riley kids. And now here's one that can't even git round. If'n I wasn't leavin' this minute, I'd kick the lot of you outta my house. He ain't gonna be of no help ta me and I sure as hell ain't gonna pay fer his keep. Anythin he eats comes outta yer pocket, ya heer?"

Nevers already had the truck packed and ready to go into Lynch. He needed Jesse with him and he knew that Rachael was in no mood to messed with. If he raised too much of a ruckus they would all leave. He could see that look in

Rachael's eyes. He grumbled out loud as he tromped out to the truck. "Got damn mistake hirin' them Riley kids. Got to lissen to Jesse's bellyachen, Rachael's smart mouth and now Ben sittin' in a chair with no legs. Damn, what did I do to deserve this? We're gonna have a talk about this situation when I get back." He turned around and yelled, "Ya'll get some work done around here. I want dinner ready when I git home, Girl. And don't forget to make a mess of them biscuits, " He shook his head, "Damn, I sure don't know what I did to deserve this."

"You're a mean, old bastard, that's why," Rachael yelled out the door. "Don't you worry none, I'll take care of my brother." She ran back into the kitchen and started laughing.

Ben raised his head and a smile came across his lips. Yes, that was his sister, Rachael. If anyone could tame Nevers Bains it was her.

Lily was busting to talk to Rachael and now she had been to contend with another person in the house. She huffed off into the bedroom while Rachael began pulling things out of the pantry. "Lily, I need some eggs, go out to the hen house and get me some," she yelled.

Lily slowly walked into the kitchen, picked up the egg basket and headed outside.

"Ben, I have something to tell you. Up til now it's been me and Jesse's secret, but this arrangement ain't gonna work unless I tell you. Now you got to promise me that you'll keep it a secret. If Nevers finds out, we all might be in for a big hurting. She told Ben all about Lily.

When Lily returned to the kitchen, Rachael spoke up. "You kin talk to me, Lily. I told Ben. He ain't gonna tell Nevers. How you been since I been gone.?"

Lily's face lit up. "I've been pretty bad. Nevers been drinkin' a lot and been pretty mean and when some men came round last week he chased them off with his gun. I don't know who they were." She turned to Ben. "Oh, Ben, I'm so sorry about what happened to you. It's jest plain awful. Does it hurt much?"

Ben shook his head. It would take him a while to get used to the two women who would be around him most of the time.

"Where am I gonna sleep?" Ben asked. "I think I'll go lay down."

"You're gonna share a room with Jesse, but right now you kin help us." She put a bag of potatoes and carrots on the table and handed him a knife. "Here, peel these. I'm makin' stew. When yer finished you can cut some small kindlin' fer the stove."

Ben just stared at her.

"Well, go on. Your hands ain't broken are they?" she said. "We all got to earn our keep."

He slowly picked up the knife and began peeling the potatoes.

On the second day after Ben's arrival, Nevers and Jesse left for the mountains, Lily and Rachael finished their chores and then spent the afternoon smoothing out the path leading to the river. They wanted to make it easier for Ben to get his chair down the path. They cleared out the rocks and poured buckets of dirt into the ruts and then ran a board tied to a rope down the middle. Ben watched from the kitchen not really sure what they were doing.

"Thar, that should be good," Rachael said. She brushed her hands on her pants knocking the loose dirt off of them.

"Ain't you scared he might try to kill himself agin?" Lily asked.

"I can't sit around and worry about that every day. If he really wants to do it, he will, but not when I'm around. The idee is to keep him busy and make him feel like he has some worth. That's all everyone wants, Lily. To feel like thar needed. If he kin catch us some fish a couply times of week it would be good for him and us, too."

"Yer a good sister, Rachael. I wish you were my sister. You wouldn't have let Nevers take me away from home."

"I surly would have tried to keep you safe, Lily. Now let's go fix Ben a fishin' pole and let him catch us some catfish for dinner."

Ben protested, but Rachael turned a deaf ear and maneuvered his chair out the door, down the plank she had laid across the steps. She put the can of worms on his lap, slung the pole over her shoulder and pushed him down the path. "Now, catch us some damn fish. I don't feel like eatin' stew again." She sat down next to him on the bank. "How much longer are you gonna protest livin' in this world? Tell me if I'm wastin' my time on you."

"You jest don't understand, Rachael. It ain't easy. Sometimes I jest want to scream. I want my legs back."

"I know it ain't easy for you, Ben and I don't have a clue what I would do in yer place, but one thing I know for sure is that I wouldn't want to die. Being dead is forever and it will happen to all of us soon enough. Gosh, Ben, I still got so much livin' to do, I'm just bustin' at the seams to get started. When you get yer pension we can take you up to one of them army hospitals and they can make you some wooden legs. Oh, I know, it ain't the same, but at least you could stand tall."

Ben sighed. "I'll stay around fer you. At least for a while anyway."

"Does that mean I kin go back up to the house and you ain't gonna jump in this water? I ain't really in the mood fer a swim."

"You go on, Rachael. I'll stay put."

Chapter Sixteen

Jesse sat on his usual rock, his new gun resting across his lap. He had learned his lesson after the incident with the bear. He would never lay it down again. Picking up a round branch he pulled out his pocketknife and began to whittle. It was something to do to pass the long hours while he waited for Nevers. Jesse had already carved several small animals, which he intended to give to Lily. He wanted to do something to show Lily that he liked her. Ever since that day at the lake, he seldom talked to her. Surely, she had to understand how afraid of Nevers he was. If he had caught them together Nevers would have beat Jesse to a pulp or maybe even shot him. No one would blame a man for making sure his wife stayed true to him, even if it meant killing her lover.

Lost in his daydreams and carving, the two blasts from a shotgun almost made him fall off the rock. He bolted upright, wood shavings and his gun falling to the ground. Knowing that was a signal from Nevers, Jesse grabbed his rifle and began running up the steep slope. Another barrage of gunfire rang out, causing Jesse to fall flat to the ground. After a few minutes he got up and ran the rest of the way up the incline. Out of breath, he was relieved when he saw Nevers truck. When he came upon it he found Nevers lying on the ground next to it holding his leg. Blood was dripping out of a tear in his pants.

"Damn, what's wrong? You been shot?" Jesse asked.

"No! I cut myself. Get me a rag ta tie off my cut."

"What was all that shootin'? I heard lots of shots fired?" Jesse asked as he stripped off his shirt and tore the bottom part off the sleeve. Nevers let out a loud moan as he let go of the wound and wrapped the blue cloth around it. "It was jest me, twernt sure you heard the first shot. Get me in the truck! Take me down to the lean-to. Now, dammit! Jest don't stand thar and let me bleed to death."

Leaning on Jesse's shoulder, Nevers staggered to the truck. He lay with his head on the seat while the truck bumped its way down the path with blood dripping onto the floorboards.

"Now lissen to me, boy and lissen good," Nevers said. "You gotta take this truck into Lynch and deliver this load to Clyde Orby at the general store. Pull round back and knock on the door. Tell him I sent you. Help him unload and then he'll give ya a bag. Don't open it! Then come back and git me."

"I can't do that," Jesse said. "You got a bad cut. I ain't leavin' you up here all alone, you need ta git to a doctor."

Nevers pointed his shotgun at Jesse. "You better do what I say, Jesse or I'm gonna take this gun and shoot you in the head right now. Now git."

Jesse pulled the door shut on the lean-to and jumped into the truck. At the bottom of the mountain, he turned left instead of going right. A few minutes later he pulled the truck into the yard. Opening the door, he yelled for Rachael.

"What are you doing back so soon? Where's Nevers? What happen to yer shirt?" she questioned.

"He's hurt, Rachael. He's hurt reel bad. He's up at the shack. He said he cut his leg, but I think he done got shot cause he's got a hole in his leg that goes clean through ta the other side. Didn't look like no cut to me. He was gonna shoot me if'n I didn't take this load of pelts into Lynch before I went back and fetched him. But I can't jest let him lay thar and bleed to death. I need yer help. Git Lily. I need you both." Jesse was almost choking on his words.

"Settle down. Tell me what happen?" she asked.

"Thar's no time. We gotta go git him right now."

Rachael yelled for Lily. "Come on, we got to go, Nevers been hurt. We'll be back soon, Ben. You jest stay here in the kitchen. Boil some water, get some clean rags out of the closet." They were gone before he could answer.

On the way up the mountain, Jesse told them what happened. "He's gonna be real mad at me when he sees me back with you two. We might have to tie him up and make him come with us."

At the top of the ridge Jesse pulled the truck under a tree and got out. He ducked his head as he entered the shack. He stood there for a moment looking at Nevers and then called to Rachael and Lily. "He ain't movin'. I think he's dead. Thar's blood everywhere." Jesse poked him with his boot. "Yep, he's dead as a doornail."

"Dang blame it, Jesse, you don't need to be pokin' him with your foot. Tech his chest and see if'n he's breathin'."

"I ain't touchin' him. You do it," Jesse said, backing away.

Rachael slowly moved toward the cot. Nevers face was a pale gray. His mouth hung open reveling a purple tongue. Putting her hand on his shirt she could feel that his body was already beginning to become rigid. "Yep, he's dead, all right." Pushing back the leg of his pants, Rachael saw the gapping wound from a shotgun. "Yer right, he didn't cut himself, he's been shot fer sure. I reckon we better put him in the truck and take him down to the house." She turned to Lily. "Are you okay?" Lily shook her head and bolted toward the door. Standing off in the weeds she heaved up her breakfast and lunch.

"Go clear some of those skins out of the truck. We'll wrap him in these blankets and put him in the back," Rachael said, knowing that neither Jesse nor Lily knew what to do. "Oh

Marlene Mitchell

forget it! I'll do it myself. You just stand there like two dummies." She stomped off and climbed into the bed of the truck. Rachael began throwing the pelts over the side of the truck. A few minutes later she let out a yell so loud that Lily and Jesse came running to her. "Would you look at this? I'll be switched. Moonshine! Jars and jars of it. That Nevers wasn't a trapper at tall. She held up a mason jar filled with a clear liquid. That old sum bitch wuz runnin' moonshine. That's why he wanted you to take it into Lynch right away. Damn, this changes everything."

"He ain't no moon shiner. I been up here ten times with him. He always comes down with a load of pelts," Jesse said.

"Yeah, the same old pelts every time. Hell, these skins are so old that half of them are goin' bare. Now help me get him into the truck. We got to get to the house real fast."

With Nevers' body tucked between two blankets Jesse headed down the steep road. "What are we gonna do, Rachael? What are we gonna do with the hooch? Should we go straight to the sheriff's office?"

Rachael put her hands over her ears. "Be still, Jesse. I have to think. Just let me think on this for a minute. We have to make a plan." Rachael knew the sheriff would ask a lot of questions. He would want to see the location where Nevers injured himself. If they took the sheriff up to the shack he might get a notion to follow the trail of blood leading further up the path. Then what? If he found the still the revenuers would take everything—the truck, the house and everything in it. Then what would Lily do?

"What should we do with the body?" Jesse asked as they drove into the yard.

"I guess we could put it in the barn. At least for tonight."

107

Once inside the house, Lily blurted out the story to Ben, telling him every detail. "And then we took him off the truck and we put him in the barn."

"Sounds like somebody else know'd what Nevers was doing up on that ridge. I reckon when they come up on him they shot him. Jesse did you see anybody else up thar when you went up to fetch Nevers?" Ben asked.

"Naw, it was jest him, layin' by his truck. I didn't see nobody," Jesse replied. "I ain't got no idée who was doin' all the shootin' but fer sure he had company up thar."

"I want everybody to sit down and be quiet. I have a plan." Rachael unscrewed the lid on the jar of alcohol she had brought into the house. She gathered up four mismatched glasses and poured the liquid into each glass. "Lets take a drink of this stuff. Maybe it will calm our nerves."

Rachael coughed, Lily gagged and both Ben and Jesse asked for seconds. They said it was good stuff.

"Okay, here's what I think we should do. First off, me and Jesse have to take this load into Lynch and deliver it like Nevers said to. If we don't, Clyde may come lookin' for him. We can't let that happen. While we're gone, Lily, I want you and Ben to tear this place apart and see if you kin find any money or recipes that Nevers may have stashed somewhere. When we get back, we have to go up to the mountain and follow that trail of blood and hope to gosh we can find that still. Then we need to burn down the lean-to and come back here and bury Nevers."

"Damn, Rachael, when did you figure all this out?" Ben asked.

"On the way here. Now lets go, Jesse, we got to get this stuff to town."

Lily began to cry. "When my family finds out that Nevers is dead they're gonna come over here to live. It's gonna be jest awful."

"Look, Lily, they aren't gonna know he's dead. Least wise not for a while. He didn't like yer family. Didn't you tell me he always chased them off when they came here?"

"Yeah, but what if'n they show up agin?" Lily asked.

"We'll just have to pretend that he is still alive. You know, set up a decoy. Don't worry about it right now. Jesse and I have to go. Just remember, don't let anybody in this house while we're gone. If anybody comes round you just tell them Nevers ain't home."

Jesse was nervous. "But what if Clyde asks where Nevers is and what if'n he asks us some questions? I'm real afeared, Rachael and what if'n whoever wuz up thar with Nevers comes round lookin' fer him."

"You hush, we ain't got no time for what ifs. Come on, Jesse get in the truck, I'm gonna drive. I'll figure that out on the way." Rachael took off down the road, the old truck running wide open. Jesse hung onto the window frame for dear life.

Chapter Seventeen

Clyde Orby looked at his watch and let out a string of profanity. *Where in the hell was Nevers? He had to have the shipment ready to be picked up by six and it was already almost four. Damn that Nevers. What would he tell his customer if Nevers didn't show up? They wouldn't be too happy.* He walked outside and looked down the street. He let out a sigh of relief when he saw the old, black truck rounding the corner. He quickly went in to the store and to the back door.

Rachael pulled around to the back of the building just like Nevers had always done when they came to Orby's Store. "What the hell...where's Nevers? Yer late," Clyde growled.

"Nevers is sick. Reel sick. He had me and Rachael bring in yer order," Jesse said, trying to sound as if they knew all about the still. Sorry we're late, but I had to tend to him before we could leave."

Clyde bent his head and looked into the driver's side of the truck. Spying Rachael who he had never seen with Jesse when the delivery made before him a little ill at ease. "Ain't like Nevers to let no girl drive his truck. You best be tellin' me the truth. I ain't got time to worry about Nevers right now. Come on, help me unload this stuff."

When the last box was put into the back room of the store, Clyde disappeared. He returned a few minutes later and handed Jesse an envelope. "Okay, here's what I want. I need ten cases by next Thursday. We're gonna get top price cause the revenuers are sniffin' around couply miles over and all them stills are shuttin' down. So I got to make sure I kin supply what everyone needs. Reacon you know, this stuff ends up in Chicago." Clyde seemed real proud of that fact. "What the hell is wrong with Nevers? I ain't know'd him ta be sick."

"Don't rightly know, but he's feelin' real poorly. We'll have yer stuff here next week," Rachael replied. "I reckon we better git goin'." Opening the door of the truck, she froze when Clyde yelled at her.

"Wait! Ain't you gonna take yer supplies. How you gonna cook me a batch without yer supplies?"

Rachael smiled. "Oh, sure, I was jest gettin' to that." She followed Clyde into the store as he began handing her heavy, white bags and three gallons of some kind of liquid. She smiled to cover up her quivering lips. With everything loaded into the truck, Rachael opened the door to get in. Clyde put his hand on the door. "Now, next Thursday I spect you to be on time. My customers don't like to be kept waitin'. I'll spect you here no later than noon. Do I make myself clear? I been dealin' with Nevers for over ten yars and we ain't had a problem. I don't spect the two of ya to cause me none either. If'n you do, Nevers will hear about it." He opened his jacket and laid his hand on a forty-five tucked in his belt.

Rachael gulped. "Yes, uh, sure. We'll be here on time." She ducked under his arm and climbed into the seat nodding to Jesse to get the heck out of there as fast as he could.

Still shaking from the experience, Rachael forgot all about the envelope until they were almost home.

"Geez, look at this, Jesse. We got almost a hundred dollars from Clyde. Can you believe that? Damn that Nevers. Here we were workin' fer him fer five bucks a week and he was pullin' in all this money. Have you ever in yer life seen so much money, Jesse?"

"I'm scart, Rachael," Jesse said. "I ain't never done nothin' like this and you done made Clyde a promise we can't keep. You know what's gonna happen if we don't show up next week. Why'd you go and do that?"

She patted his knee. "We're gonna be jest fine, Jesse. You wait and see. Everythang is gonna be okay. We got a whole week to ponder on it."

It was almost dusk by the time they got back to the house. It was too late to go up to the mountain to look around again, but not too late to bury Nevers in the backfield. Placing his body, still wrapped in the blankets into the newly dug grave, Lily made a feeble attempt at saying a prayer and they quickly covered him with black soil. "Should we put a cross or somethin' on his grave?" Lily asked.

"No, we don't want anyone to know he's here. Jest draw a cross in the dirt. If God wants his soul he'll find him, but I doubt if he'll come lookin' fer him. He'll have ta spend a lot of time repentin' afore he can go to heaven," Rachael said. Putting her arm around Lily they walked back toward the house. "Are you sad that he's dead, Lily?"

"I don't think I am, but I ain't sure. There were very few times when he was nice to me, and mostly I felt like a prisoner. Now I don't have ta do the deed anymore and I won't git hit every time I move and I kin talk alls I want. Nope, I ain't sad he's dead. I'm a widow now, Rachael. I ain't even twenty and I'm a widow. And all these yars I was so dumb I didn't even know what he was a doin' up on that mountain."

Rachael washed her hands and splashed water on her face. She was hungry and tired. She sat down at the kitchen table and took a drink of strong, black coffee. "So, old Nevers was bootlegging for a long time and when Clyde handed me that hundred dollars I was both mad and happy at the same time. What about you and Lily? Did you find anythin' while we was gone?"

"We sure did," Ben replied. We found this box under the floorboards in the bedroom. We can't git it open. Jesse needs ta take it outside and put and ax to the lock."

After hacking away at the box for a few minutes, Jesse put it on the kitchen table and four heads peered into it. There were soiled notebooks filled with writing and almost three hundred in twenty dollar bills.

Rachael took the money and fanned it out in her hand. "I ain't never seen this much money in my life and I probably never will agin." She reached for one of the notebooks and flipped through the pages. "This is mostly scribble I jest can't read. I'm just too tired. My eyes are going crossed. We'll ponder on all of this tomorrow. Alls I know is that right now we got four hundred dollars."

Chapter Eighteen

Morning came too soon. Rachael opened her eyes as the sun rose high enough to shine through her window and the crowing of the roosters started just seconds later. The goats began to bleat and the cows gave out low bellows, signaling that they needed to be milked. As Rachael sat up, she groaned. Moving the heavy bags and Nevers' body had given her a backache. A reminder of what had transpired in the last twenty-four hours. What would this day bring?

Rachael stumbled out into the dimly lit kitchen and lit the burner under the kettle and put three scoops of coffee in the pot.

"Good morning," Ben said.

Rachael jumped, spilling coffee grounds on the floor. "Damn, Ben, you jest about scared the tar outta me. What are you doin' up so early and why are you sittin' in the dark?"

"I couldn't sleep. I've been sittin' here tryin' ta make some sense out of our situation. I suppose Jesse should go into town and get the sheriff."

"No!" Rachael blurted out. She knelt down in front of Ben's chair. Putting her hand in front of her face she said, "You see this, Ben I've been doin' some thinkin' too. Before today this was our future. It was just as far as the hand in front of my face. You been through enough hell. Do you want to go back to our old house and sit there the rest of yer life? Ya'll freeze in the winter and eat whatever scraps they give you. Is that what you want? I jest want enough money to get us all to Florida. You know a lot about fixin' engines in vehicles. You kin open a shop, maybe teach Jesse enough to help you. I want to see momma and daddy and Emma Jane on the beach. I want to see them playin' in the sand and getting' some color on their faces. They'll be happy there, I jest know it."

"We got four-hundred dollars, Rachael."

"And when that's gone. What will happen then, Ben?"

"What if'n we get caught, Rachael? You ready to face jail time?"

"Couldn't be any worse than livin' in the holler. Least wise we'll get two meals a day and inside plumbing. I promise I'll take all the blame if we git caught. Heck Nevers was doin' if fer over ten yars and he never got caught. We kin do this. I know we kin and then we kin git the hell outta here."

A meek voice came from the back of the room. "What about me?" Lily stood leaning against the door. Do I have to stay here all alone?"

"Of course not. You and me are going to Florida and open some kind of business, too. Maybe we'll sell oranges, or I don't know, we'll figure out somethin'." A smile covered Lily's face.

The next morning they all piled into the truck and headed up the mountain pass. Jesse found the spot where he last saw Nevers hobbling down the hill. "I figure he come from that direction over thar," Jesse said, pointing to a spot overgrown with vines and bushes. Leaving Ben in the truck, the three began to carefully scan the bushes and tree branches looking for any clues that would help them find out what really happened to Nevers.

Lily was the first to see specks of blood on the leaves. Following further into the thicket the route became even clearer as a trail of blood led them down a small slope and below a ledge covered with large fir tree branches. "What's that smell?" Lily said putting her fingers on her nose. Thar is somethin' dead up here fer sure." Pulling down one of the branches, Jesse ducked under the overhang. "Jesus, Joseph and Mary, thar are two dead bodies up here." The smell was so acrid that he began to gag as he backed away. The men lay face down in the dirt with thousands of insects attacking their bodies. The carnivores in the area had been working on stripping their bones of flesh."

Rachael stepped back not anxious to see the carnage. "That's what them shots were. Nevers must have killed them after they shot him." Tying his handkerchief over his face, Jesse slowly walked past the remains and began looking around. "Hey, I think this one over here is the man that Nevers and I saw in town. His name was Rooster. I member that red, plaid shirt he was wearin' and them boots with the chains on em". Turning away from the body, Jesse went further up the hill. The grass was worn down and matted in an opening leading to a rocky overhang. He crawled under the ledge covered by a tangle of vines. "Here it is. I found the still and it's a beauty. It's all copper and thars lots of boxes of hooch too."

"Let's get out of here," Rachael said. "Let's go back to the truck. Some of them wolves and bars may still be around here. They won't be too happy if we interrupted their dinner." Rachael filled Ben in on what they had found. "Jesse said they twernt revenuers. He said Nevers knew one of the men. I think they're jest moonies lookin' to take over Never's still and so he kilt them. What should we do now, Ben?"

"I say right now we go home and let nature take over them bodies. We'll come back in a few days. We can't move that pile of mess."

"Do you think anyone will find them a fore we get back here, Ben?" Rachael asked.

"We jest got to keep our fingers crossed and hope that no one comes up this way. All that time we thought Nevers was delivein' skins, he was runnin' moonshine to Clyde. Man, ain't that sumthin'."

Two days later they returned to the mountain and nothing was left of the two men except a pile of ragged clothes and a few bones. The scavengers had done their job well. Rachael began to take a good look around. Under the outcrop were boxes of empty jars and more copper pots. "Look how he had this rigged up," Jesse said. "The smoke from the still goes right under this ledge and disappears before it reaches the clearin'. No wonder I ain't never seen nothin' comin' from up here. So all this time I been a lookout for Nevers. I could have got kilt jest like him. Damn."

"It's gettin' dark. We got to hurry before them coyotes we heard yowlin' pick up our trail and end right here at our feet. Looks like some of them have been here already," Rachael said, pointing to the paw prints in the soft earth. "Then we gotta take these remains and bury them."

"Are you nuts?" Jesse said loudly. "Why we gotta bury them bones?

"Look even bad people have a right to be buried and besides if we don't take these bones someone else might find them. Then they'll call the sheriff and before you know it there will be lawmen crawlin' over this place. We can't let that happen. Now here," she said, throwing a blanket at him, "Wrap them in this."

After covering the entrance to the still, Rachael and Jesse grabbed handfuls of branches and swept them back and forth across the ground. They pulled the bloody leaves off the bushes and stuffed them in a gunnysack. All of the boxes of whiskey were loaded into the truck. After making sure all of the debris was cleared away, they headed for home. "Now what we need is a real gully washer to take care of the rest of the stuff we might have missed," Rachael said. Rachael got her wish. Just after they finished putting the remains of the two men in a shallow grave next to where Nevers was buried it rained for the next two days. They were all now involved in a scheme that could send them to jail. There was no turning back. They had enough whiskey to make one more delivery to Clyde.

Ben decided it would be best if they just laid low for a while in case the two men Nevers killed had friends in the area. They would stay away from the still until they calmed down and could figure out what they wanted to do next. "Hell, it ain't that hard ta make moonshine. If Nevers been doin' it all this time and makin' money, I don't see why we can't." He seemed animated when he talked about running the still. It seemed that at last he had a purpose, even if it was an illegal one. "We'll jest build us a still. We'll set it up behind the house and brew some bootleg. It'll be good stuff." Their moods became one of almost giddiness. Lily was free of the abuse from Nevers, there was money in the house and the radio stayed on most of the day.

As usual, it was Jesse who was worried. "I know that Clyde Orby doesn't care who delivers his moonshine to him as long as he thinks that Nevers is still makin' it, but we don't know how ta make the stuff. Daddy makes moonshine but it's jest old squint not really fit for drinkin'. The stuff Nevers was makin' was a lot better than that. Clyde will know the difference. Then soon as them revenuers come sniffin' round and if'n they do, I'm gonna make a run for it. I'm scart enough jest talkin' about all this. If I'd a knew'd that Nevers was makin' moonshine when I was sittin' on that rock I'd a been gone by now. And now we done covered up three murders. Oh lardy, the four of us is in a deep hole. I think yer jest about plumb crazy, Rachael, but I'll stick around fer a while." He gave a furtive glance at Lily.

It took three days for the still to be assembled in the rear of Nevers house. After gathering enough wood to get the fire started, Ben and Jesse added the sugar and mash. The first batch tasted too sweet and the second was so strong it burned their tongues. Spitting out a mouthful of the third batch, Jesse threw the tin cup on the ground. "I knew'd it. Thar ain't no way we're gonna pass this stuff off on Clyde. It tastes plumb arful. I'm sure glad we got enuf to make one more delivery to Clyde."

"There's only one person I know who knows more about white lightnin' than anybody in this county. His name is Joe Seminole, but he ain't been around these parts fer a long time," Ben said.

Rachael beamed. "Good, how do we get hold of this Joe?"

"I ain't never met him, but Pap used to talk about him once in a while. He lived up on Black Mountain. I ain't even sure he's still kickin'. Beside I don't think anyone kin coax him down from thar. He's been up there about twenty years."

"Well I reckon we better find a way to sweet talk him off that mountain. We got some shine ta make."

Chapter Nineteen

Lily spent a few days of remorse over Nevers and then let it go. She decided that it had never happened and she wanted to keep it that way. She told Rachael that she was a born-again virgin and from now on she would live her own life. Lily decided she didn't want to cook or clean the house anymore and she was going to go to the picture show at least once a month. She played cards with Ben and picked wildflowers for the kitchen table. Her face seemed to soften and she now wore her hair loose, cascading down her back instead of pulled back in a knot. And Jesse took note of everything she did.

While Rachael cooked, Ben spent most of his time sitting at the kitchen table making some kind of drawings on paper bags. No one was sure what he was doing. Rachael and Jesse took the cow, two goats and about ten chickens to her parents. There was just too much livestock for them to take care of.

Thrilled with the prospect of fresh eggs and milk her mother hugged her for the first time in years. She handed her father the twenty dollars for the month. Her father grumbled, saying the animals were going be a lot to take care of.

"Look, Daddy, you can't have it both ways. You either tend to the livestock so you have somethin' to eat or jest let them run. You can't have it both ways." She decided that nothing she did would ever make him happy. It was all about the mine.

After Rachael and Jesse made the second delivery to Clyde's the box under the floorboards was growing. Still fretting about the deteriorating situation at her parent's house, she knew if she gave her mother more money questions would begin to surface. She couldn't take that chance. Her mother had questioned her at length as to why Nevers gave them all those animals. She told her mother that Nevers was tired of feeding all the livestock and was just going to let them run loose. He had enough meat with all of the trapping he did. The varmints lurking around the farm would probably kill most of the chickens anyway. Rachael said she bought them from him for five dollars, which she had to pay back to him in the coming weeks. She hated lying to her parents and when the time came she would make it all up to them.

On her visit to her parents, Emma Jane told Rachael that she was very lonesome and with the impending birth of her baby she was too cumbersome to do much around the house even though there was always work to do—laundry, tending to the small garden, searching for berries. She was lonely and had no one to talk to. Her parents were still upset about her pregnancy and had little to say to her. She couldn't wait for Ben's allotment checks to start so that Jesse and Rachael could come home. Rachael hugged her and said that it wouldn't be too long before things would be much better for all of them.

Stopping by Mabry's store, the old men sitting on the outside bench were surprised to see Rachael driving Nevers' truck. Nodding to them, Jesse and Rachael went inside. Mr. Mabry looked behind Rachael as she came toward the counter. "Where's Nevers? We ain't seen hair of him fer over three weeks. He sick or sumpthin'?"

"Yeah he's been reel sick. He's got an infection. He's got a bad foot steppin' on a rusty nail. It swolled up and made him real sick." Rachael pulled up her sleeve revealing a purple bruise on her arm that she got when she fell against the truck door. "See this, he is still as mean as ever. I got this from him yesterday because I didn't move fast enough. You know Nevers. He doesn't like talkin' to people. He said since he is payin' Jesse and me he might as well make us do his errands. We need to get a few things," she said, changing the subject.

While Rachael put her purchases on the counter, Jesse wandered around the store. Calling to Rachael he pointed to a gold locket on a thin chain displayed in a glass case. "I'm gonna git that fer Lily," he whispered.

"No! That's three dollars! We can't be buyin' anythin' that expensive. That thing has been in that case a fore the mine closed. If'n you buy it, Mabry will start asking questions. Here get a few of them butterscotch candies."

After totaling their bill, Mr. Mabry packed the coffee and other staples into a box. "These for you?" he said holding up the candy. Rachael smiled and nodded. "Now you tell Nevers I said hey and I hope the old coot's foot gets better. Maybe I'll come out and see him someday."

"You do that, Mr. Mabry. Jest be sure to honk a fore you come in the yard. He don't cotton to people comin' on his property without him knowin' their comin'." As she turned to leave she hesitated for a moment. " I was jest wonderin', Mr. Mabry have you ever heard anythin' more about Old Joe Seminole? You know, if'n he's still alive."

"Lordy, Girl, why you askin' bout him. Ain't heard anyone mention his name in a coon's age," he replied.

"Oh we wuz jest makin' conversation with my parents and his name come up." She feigned a laugh. "I think my daddy was talkin' about moonshine."

"Far as I know, he's still livin' up on Pine Ridge. Some hunters come round here last fall and they said they seed smoke a comin' from an old cabin up thar. That must be Old Joe.

Ain't no one else crazy nuf ta live up thar in the winter. Now you best run on, it's gettin' neigh on ta dark."

Getting into the truck, Jesse asked, "Why'd you say that to Mabry? He jest may come out and then what? And give me those candies."

"You know he won't come to see Nevers. He doesn't like him one bit. If'n I told him not to come, he'd be thar a fore we got home."

Jesse sulked all the way home. Complaining that he wanted to spend some of the money. Nothing Rachael said would make him stop. It was only when they pulled into the yard and Jesse saw Lily sitting in the swing that his mood changed. She wore a white cotton dress and a blue ribbon in her hair.

"You sure do look purty," Jesse said. "I ain't seen you in that dress a fore."

"This is the dress I wore when I got married. After that, Nevers wouldn't let me wear it. He said I shouldn't show my legs. I got it out of the back of the closet today."

"You really do look nice," Rachael chimed in.

Jesse smiled at her and hurriedly helped Rachael carry in the supplies and then went outside to join Lily. Sitting down next to her he reached into his pocket and pulled out the two butterscotch candies. "Look what I got fer you, Lily," he said.

"Why isn't that nice of you. I love butterscotch." She unwrapped the shiny paper and popped one into her mouth. "Hmm, this is so good." She put the other one in her pocket.

"Lily, I got to tell you somethin'," Jesse said nervously. "I reckon you know that I'm sweet on you. I was wonderin' if maybe you liked me, too?"

"I think yer real nice, Jesse, but…" before she could answer Jesse put his arm around her shoulder his hand resting on her breast. "What in the hell you think yer doing, Jesse Riley?" Lily said jumping off the swing.

"Well, you said you liked me," he replied.

"I want to be courted, Jesse. I ain't ever been courted. Jest cause I'm sort of soiled don't mean I can't be treated decent like. And grabbin' my titties ain't how you court. I've been grabbed at enough by Nevers. Are you just tellin' me yer jest harney or do you really like me? Rachael told me there's a difference."

"Why do you always lissen to Rachael," Jesse asked. "She don't know everythang. She ain't ever been courted."

"Well, she knows a damn side more than I do. She read books."

"I'm supposin' I'm both, Lily. I like you and I'm also wantin' more than holdin' yer hand. Can't I jest kiss you one time? Then I'll be real nice till you say it's all right for me to touch yer titties agin."

Lily thought for a moment. Nevers didn't believe in kissin'. Maybe just one kiss would be all right. "Okay, jest once and then I'll ponder on it," she replied. Closing her eyes she waited for Jesse to kiss her. Putting his arms around her, his mouth pressed against hers, Jesse's lips parted and his tongue pushed into her mouth.

"Damn it! That ain't kissin'. You jest spit in my mouth. That's not the way they did it in the picture show. I don't want no more kissin' from you. The next time you or anybody else disrespects my body I'm gonna get a gun and shoot them. Do you understand me?" Lily shouted at him and tromped across the yard.

Jesse trotted after her. "What picture show? And what I was doin' is what yer supposed to do. It's called French kissin'. Give me another chance. Come on, Lily, let me kiss you agin."

"This time you keep yer mouth shut, you heer? Don't be doin' that French thing." Jesse kissed her again. His lips closed tightly as he pressed his mouth on hers for a few seconds. Without warning he pulled her tightly to his body and his erection pushing into her groin. Lily pushed him away. "Yer nasty! You jest stay away from me, Jesse Riley. I don't want you courtin' me. Not till I'm good and ready." Making a fist she landed a blow on the front of his pants. Jesse dropped to his knees and groaned.

Rachael and Ben looked out the window after hearing Lily shouting. "What's goin' on?" Rachael asked.

"I suppose it's jest a lover's quarrel. One minute thar kissin' the next minutes she popped him."

Rachael looked at her own reflection in the window glass. Her hair was a mess. She tried to push it behind her ear. Looking down at her clothes, Rachael realized that her jeans were ragged and she smelled of perspiration. There was grit under her fingernails and the tops of her feet were dirty. "I'm going to go take a bath," she announced.

"Now? It's the middle of the week?" Ben said as Rachael disappeared into the bathroom.

Chapter Twenty

Rachael put the last of the skins over the cases of whiskey and jumped into the driver's seat of the truck. "You git out of thar, Rachael. I'm drivin'," Jesse said.

"Not this time. I still need the practice. I gotta learn how ta drive real fast." She shifted the car in to gear and it began to roll with Jesse still hanging on to the door. "I swear, Rachael, you are jest gittin 'too big fer yer britches."

Clyde was waiting for them to arrive as usual. Pulling around back, Rachael went inside. "We only got eight cases this week. Do you want them?"

"Yeah, I reckon I'll have to settle fer them." Clyde replied. "Where's Nevers? This is the third week in a row you two have been makin' the delivery. How sick is he?"

"He ain't sick, Clyde, he's dead," Rachael blurted out. "He done died three weeks ago. He was up at the still and he dropped a box of glass jars on his arm and cut himself real bad. Damn fool bled to death." Jesse let out a loud gasp at Rachael's confession to Clyde.

Clyde stared at her. "You go on. He's dead. Is that a fact? Yer lyin'."

"No I ain't, Clyde. It's the truth. Me and my kin are gonna be runnin' the still as soon as we get a plan. So, you got a choice. Keep yer mouth closed and we kin go on and do business as usual or we can jest put an end to the business all together."

"You wait jest one minute, girl. You come in here tellin' me this story and I ain't even had time to ponder on it."

"We need the money, Clyde jest like you and this has got to be kept a secret. If anyone else finds out about Nevers, his wife, Lily will lose everythin' and I suppose the rest of us will go to jail. So what do you say, Clyde?"

Clyde grinned. "You sure have got some mocksey for such a youngin'. But I ain't settlin' fer no second grade swill. My customers are reel particular. They'd have my head if'n I tried to pass off some bad stuff on them."

"I ain't got time to be a youngin and don't you worry none we'll be bringin' you first class stuff, maybe even better than what you got from Nevers. Do we have a deal?" They agreed on the same terms that Clyde had with Nevers. Instead of bringing in the skins, the cases of moon would be covered with produce. No one would ever suspect a couple of young holler kids to be runnin'a still.

"Sometime I may bring in a load of chickens. I gotta make sure that no one gets suspicious." She tucked the roll of bills into her pocket and headed for the truck. She felt as though she was going to be sick to her stomach. It was a hard day and there would be another one to come. The jars at home were empty. Not a drop of moonshine in any of them.

Arriving at home, Rachael placed the money in the box and put it back under the floorboards.

"What smells good in here?" Rachael said entering the kitchen.

"Ben is teachin' me how ta make cowboy stew. I got every thin' in here you kin imagine." Lily stirred the pot and added another cup of fresh peas.

"With buttered biscuits and a bowl of stew in front of them everyone was quiet for a few minutes. "That was real good, Ben," Rachael said. "It sure hit the spot." Clearing her plate away from in front of her, Rachael pulled out a pad of paper and a pencil from her overall pocket. "I got somethin' I want to talk to all of you about. First off, I want to find Joe Seminole and see if he'll help us. Then I want to move Nevers' still down here to the house."

Jesse let out a whoop. "Are you nuts!"

"I surely may be, but I think Joe Seminole could make us some fine whiskey and by havin' the still here we could make a lot more. It sure is a plain sight better than that old rig we put together. I'm plannin' on us all building a smokehouse out back. A real big smokehouse. We kin divide it in two with a wall. We kin smoke all kinds of meat to sell and with all the smoke coming from it, I reckon no one would ever suspect that it's a cover for a still."

Ben slapped the table. "Damn, Rachael, I think that is a real smart idée. Real smart. We got plenty of lumber round here and lots of good rocks. I think we could do it. Now, findin' Old Joe may be a whole different matter. You act like you kin jest walk up ta him and say hey, Joe. That ain't gonna happen. Let me tell you about old Joe." Ben leaned back and began his story.

∾ ∾ ∾

The legend of Joe Seminole had been a topic of conversation at many a gathering of the clans in the hollow. Tipping the glass jars to their mouths, one of the old men would usually start talking about Joe. Usually wondering if he was still alive. Every winter when the snow was on the ground and animals were easy to track, someone would return from the ridge saying that they had seen smoke rising over the trees. So everyone figured he must still be up there."

The story everyone told was pretty much the same. Joe professed to be a direct descendant from a Seminole Indian chief. He claimed that his tribe was responsible for making the first moonshine in the state. A fine, clear liquid that went down smooth and kicked your insides into a battle of fire.

When Joe got tired of trapping, he set up his still near the top of Pine Ridge. Joe had a clear view of the valley and the trail leading up to his cabin, which meant he could draw a bead on a stranger without them even knowing they were about to be shot. His life was making and selling mountain whiskey and he was real good at it. Coming down from the mountain to drink and tell stories with the men in the hollow, he would laugh and slap his knees at his own tales. He said the recipe he used was handed down through the tribe and it finally came to him. When the fiddles were brought out, he could kick up his heels with the best of them and no one could out drink him. Long after the others lay stupefied on the ground or bent over the horse rail giving up their guts, he finished off the remains in the circle of brown jugs.

Then one day a group of men rode into town and tied their horses up at the general store. It didn't take them long to find out what they were about. They wanted his business. Heading up the mountain was a mistake because Joe saw them coming. When Joe called out to them, they just kept on approaching the cabin. Pulling out their rifles was their second mistake. By the time the air had cleared of smoke, six of the men were dead and one was running for his life down the trail.

That one man that was still alive went to the sheriff and told him what happened. He said they were just going up the mountain to do a little hunting. Everyone knew it wasn't a true story, but Joe was put on trial and was given twenty years in prison— five years for moonshining and fifteen for killing six men.

They took him away in handcuffs and nobody ever expected to see him again. The revenuers burnt down his cabin and destroyed his still.

Then to everyone's surprise, he rode back into town on an old mule. It was the Fourth of July, twenty years and six days since Old Seminole had been put behind bars. He didn't even nod to the men who greeted him, he just kept his eyes straight ahead and went right to the hardware store. He left a few hours later with his mule pulling a flatbed piled high with supplies. Everyone figured that before Joe was arrested he must have stashed a wad of money somewhere.

That was the last time he came down to town. He built a cabin on the side of Black Mountain. He fished and trapped animals for food and used skins to cover his feet in the winter. Every once in a while someone out hunting would leave him a few vittles in a bag tied up in an old oak tree about three hundred feet from his shack. That was as close as they would go.

Some people said that Old Joe was plumb crazy and would shoot you without even thinking twice. And others said he just wanted to be alone and they respected his wishes.

Ben had heard the story many times. And the last comment in the story was always the same. Old Joe Seminole had made the best white lightning in the county. Rachael hoped the stories were true. She was betting her life on it.

In the morning Rachael packed four biscuits and a pail of stew in her saddlebag. She took a canteen of water, a few apples and a blanket. Before she left the house she took the gun her father had given her and stuck it into her belt. She was scared to death, but bent on finding Joe Seminole.

"Now while I'm gone, I want you and Jesse to go visit momma and daddy. They need to know we are all right. Pick some of those peaches and take them with you and maybe give them this," She pulled a ten-dollar bill out of her pocket and handed it to Ben.

"I still think Jesse should be goin' with you," Ben said.

"No! If'n Old Joe isn't plumb loco, maybe he won't shoot a girl all by herself. We all go up thar after him and he ain't likely to ever come down."

Following the road to the end of Bent Creek, Rachael stopped for a moment and rested. She refilled her canteen from a cool spring and watered her horse. She veered off the road and headed into an unknown area. The remnants of a trail, overgrown with weeds and vines were barely visible. Halfway up the path, Rachael guided her horse into the thicket. She bent her head as her horse picked his way through the shadowed forest. This was the directions Ben had given her and she was hoping he was right.

After another ten minute walk the cabin came into view. She dismounted, took her saddlebag and began walking up toward the side of the house. Finding the big, oak tree, she stood behind it and called his name. There was no answer. She called again, this time even louder. The response was a rifle barrel sticking out of a window covered with burlap. Rachael could feel her heart pounding in her chest. Taking out a white piece of material she began waving it, hoping to get his attention. It did. A shot rang out scattering the bark of the tree onto her head.

"Damn you, stop shootin' at me. I jest want to talk to you. I ain't here to do you no harm," she yelled out.

The burlap slowly parted and a face appeared in the window. "Ya got a weapon?" came a graveling voice.

"No. I got some food, but I don't have a weapon." She pulled the gun out of her belt and laid it on the ground behind the tree.

"How many of you?" he asked.

Jest me, kin I come closer?" she asked. "I'll jest put the food on the stoop and leave."

"Why ya bringin' me food?"

"Just take it, okay. If you like it you kin open the door and maybe we kin talk," she answered.

"Put it by the door and step back," he growled.

Rachael slowly walked to the front of the cabin and placed the sack in front of the door She ran back behind the tree as fast as her legs would carry her, hoping he wouldn't take aim at her. She munched on an apple waiting for some response. Two hours later Rachael decided he was not going to come out. She stood up and brushed the leaves off her pants. Turning to go back down the way she had come, she heard the creak of the door. He waved to her to approach.

"You gonna shoot me?" she asked, her hands in the air.

"Ah don't kill woman folk. Ya kin come on up."

Steadying herself she ducked her head and went inside. It was just one room with a dirt floor. The walls were covered with animal skins and a pallet of straw lay on the floor. A small table and a buck stove took up most of the space. "Whadda ya doin' up heer? Ain't nobody posed to come up heer. Ain't no women posed to come up heer." He motioned for her to sit down on the rough-hewn bench next to the table.

"It's a long story," Rachael said trying to get comfortable.

"Ya got anymore of them biscuits? Ya got another and I'll lissen." He pointed his finger at her. "Ain't no way I woulda let you in heer ceptin' I ain't et nothin' fer two days."

Rachael dug in her backpack and pulled out the remaining biscuit she had saved for herself. He attacked it like a bear in a honeycomb, licking his finger to pick up the crumbs that had fallen on the table. "Well go on, tell me yer tale."

When she had finished telling him about her family and Nevers and the still, he threw his head back and laughed revealing a mouth void of teeth. "I know'd that Nevers when he was jest a youngin'. He was a bad ass. Jest like me. So you done put him in the ground." He laughed again.

"I reckon you know yer a legend down in the holler. People tell yer story all the time. Why didn't you come back to Bent Creek when you got out of prison?"

His face turned grim. "Ya git yer fill of people when yer in prison. Thangs happen ta ya that ya don't want ta talk about. I ain't that same person who left heer. Do ya reckon to know what I'm sayin'?"

"Yes, I think I do, but don't you ever jest get lonely?"

"Oh, I wasn't always alone. Yars back, some men that come up heer once in a while and bring me stuff. Ya know, coffee and salt and bullets. I always need bullets. Then I let em hunt back of the ridge. Damn fools think I own the mountain." He let out another cackle. "Ain't nobody been round in a whole lotta winters. People down below think I'm plumb loco, but I ain't. I'm smarter than the whole bunch tied together. But, now and agin, I'm startin' to get tired of talkin' ta myself. First twenty yars were okay, but now I'm getting" neigh on in age. You be the first in a long time ta talk ta me," he said, pointing his finger at her. What you want with me, girl?"

"I want your recipes for whiskey, the ones that all the people in the holler raved about. Could I buy them from you?"

"Ain't ever given that list of fixins'to anyone." He pointed to his head. "I got them all up heer. What the hell would I do with money, use it to start a farh."

"Well, thanks anyway. I'm glad I got to talk to you," Rachael said, standing up.

"Now you hold on a minute, Girl. I like ya. Ya ain't a feared ta speak yer mind. You come back tomarra with some more vittles and we might be able ta come to some terms."

Rachael stood up, her head almost hitting the low ceiling. "I ain't comin' back tomarra. If'n you want some real good eats, you kin come home with me right now. Times a wastin' and I got ta git that still up and runnin'."

"Now you jest sit down and maybe, jest maybe, you kin persuade me ta come down with ya. That is if'n nobody knows I'm with ya. It's got ta be a secret. Truth of the matter is I'm gettin' reel old, girl. I don't spect I'm gonna make another winter up heer. Bout froze ta death last year. I got a sore on my leg that won't mend and my sight ain't so good anymore. I'm havin' a hard time hittin' game with mah bow. Them wolves are caterwauling outside my door jest waitin' for me to lay still so they kin make a meal of me. I don't cotton ta be eatin' alive. Ain't ever thought I'd leave here, but a time comes for all of us. I could take a look see at that still and see what ya got going on. So you got lots of good vittles at yer house?"

Rachael smiled. "Why you old devil, yer jest tryin' ta outsmart me." She looked at this shriveled up old man and realized he would do almost anything for food at this point. "Do you have anythang you need to take with you?"

"Jest my gun, Girl, jest my gun."

"You kin call me Rachael," she said. "I was wonderin'; how old are you, Joe?"

"I reckon I'm goin' on ta ninety, best as I kin figure." He sat down and put on his rabbit skin shoes. "Who lives with you down yonder"

Well there's Lily—she's Nevers widow. Lately she has been actin' like a little princess, prancing around in her white dress and not doin' much around the house. My brother, Ben just got back from the army. He doesn't have any legs. They got blow'd off in an accident. And then there's Jesse. I swear I can't believe him and me are twins. But he's strong and most times he'll do what I ask him to. We got a real nice barn where you can bunk and we got lectricity and inside plumbin'.

With his crooked legs and bent back. It took Old Joe a few minutes to get on the back of the horse, Rachael slowly descended the trail wondering what she had gotten herself into now and knowing for sure that Joe Seminole was going to take a bath first thing.

Joe continued to talk as if he enjoyed hearing the sound of his voice. He reminisced about the early days when he was on top of the world. He told her about his time in prison. Some of the things she really didn't need to know. As they neared the bottom of the trail Rachael began to get anxious. She had no idea what her reception would be when she got home. She could just imagine.

"That right there is a nice place," Joe said as he climbed down from the horse. Rubbing his backside he hobbled up the steps. Rachael opened the door and yelled, "I'm home."

Lily came into the kitchen. She stopped short when she saw Joe standing behind Rachael. "Who is that?' she asked.

"This here is Old Joe Seminole. He's come to help us with the still."

It was Ben who chimed in next. "Well I'll be danged. How in the world did you do it, Rachael?" Ben looked at the stooped shouldered, old man with his hands in his pockets standing before him. "So yer the mighty Joe Seminole. I've heard a lot about you."

Ben's remark brought a wide grin to Joe's face. Rachael breathed a sigh of relief, hoping that Jesse would not be too against the idea. Pouring two cups of coffee she nodded to Joe to have a seat. He cupped both hands around the cup and drank it all in one long gulp, pushing the cup across the table. She refilled it twice more. Lily stood with her arms folded over her chest staring at Joe.

"What's that?" Rachael said. Hearing a wail, she turned her head toward the bedroom. "That's a baby! Damn, who brung a baby ta our house?"

Lily left the room and returned with a blanket swaddled in her arms. "It's Emma Jane's baby. I brung her here yesterday mornin'."

"Where is Emma Jane? Has somethin' happened to her?" Rachael began to panic.

"Oh don't get yer overalls in a wad. Ain't nothin' wrong with Emma Jane, not that I know of other than she's teched in the head," Lily said.

"Stop all this! What's going on?" Rachael demanded.

"We did like you said, Rachael, after you left, we went over to yer momma's house. That place is a sin, Rachael. Anyway, yer momma, she was in tears. Yer momma said that them gypsies had come round agin a fortnight ago and Jimmy Dell was with them. Yer daddy took his gun and was gonna shoot him, but Emma Jane grabbed the gun jest when it went off. Then her water come out and a few hours later she had the baby. She was a screamin and kickin', but yer momma got the baby out with no trouble ta either of them.

Last night Jimmie Dell snuck back to the house and talked Emma Jane into leavin' with him. Jest one day out of havin' a baby and she left with him. Them gypsies took all yer mammas' chickens and the two goats. Emma Jane is a real piece of trash. She claims she's still in love with Jimmy Dell and was missin' him reel bad. She left the baby behind without even giving her a name. She writ a note and said that the baby was better off with yer momma then travelin' from place to place. I jest couldn't leave her over thar, Rachael. It's dirty and wet and they ain't got no food for this youngin. I begged yer momma to let me bring her here and yer momma knew she would be better off with me. It was reel hard doin' all that without talkin'. Jest look at her, Rachael, ain't she the cutest thang you ever seed? She's my baby now. I named her Violet and I'm gonna keep her. I done been feedin' her goat's milk and she's a likin' it and it ain't givin' her the bloat. Yer momma, she don't like me none. She gave me some real evil looks, but she still gave me the baby. I reckon she figured you would be the one takin' care of her. I suppose I might have given her that idée."

"What happens if Emma Jane comes back for her?" Rachael asked.

"I'll tell her she died. I'll go up yonder and make a fake grave. She ain't gettin' her back."

"Yer young, Lily. You can have babies of yer own." Ben said.

"I don't care if'n I have a dozen babies, I'm still keepin' her. She's just like us, Ben. All damaged. You from the war, me from Nevers and now Violet was jest left behind like junk. I'm keepin' her forever."

"Them Damn gypsies. I hate them. And I hate Emma Jane, too. How could she go off and leave her baby?" Rachael stomped her foot and Violet began to cry. "Oh, I'm sorry, baby, I didn't mean to scare you." Rachael took her from Lily and cuddled her in her arms. She smelled of powder and her skin was as soft as velvet. Rachael had no fear that Lily would be a good mother to Violet.

Jesse opened the door in the middle of the chaos. Rachael pointed her finger at him, "And you, Jesse Riley, you don't say a damn thing." The look on her face was enough to keep him silent. He turned around and left the room.

After Rachael convinced Joe to take a bath, she gave him some of Nevers' clothes to put on. They hung on his body like rags on a scarecrow. Joe cinched up the waist of his pants with a length of rope. Lily and Rachael made dinner and everyone ate in silence except for the slurping noises Joe made as he sucked up the gravy off his plate. With blanket in hand he headed for the barn. Lily put Violet to bed in a dresser drawer padded with a quilt. She slowly rocked the drawer back and forth and hummed. Rachael leaned against the door and watched her for a few minutes.

She returned to the kitchen and sat down across from Ben. She put her head in her hands. It was Ben who finally broke the silence. "Well, Rachael it looks like our family is growin'. We got the old; we got the young, and everythang in between. I reckon we better make the best of it."

Chapter Twenty-One

Three weeks had passed since the bodies of the two men were found on the mountain. Ben and Jesse had almost completed the smokehouse. Ben crawled around on the ground, placing stones for the foundation and carried boards across his wheelchair to be nailed in place. Jesse grumbled and tried any excuse he could to get out of the work, but Rachael stood guard and threatened him if he didn't keep working. Her hands were raw from the rough boards and her fingers swollen from the many times she missed the nails. Old Joe tried to help, but he was always more in the way than working.

Rachael had a lot on her mind. She was worried about the condition her parents were living in, but she knew right now she couldn't tell them what was going on. She was worried that someone may come around looking for the two men that Nevers had killed or that Jimmy Dell and his gypsy clan may return for the baby. She was also concerned that the still would not be up and running in time to make the next delivery to Clyde.

Unlike Rachael, Lily had lost interest in the house and the cooking. With Nevers not there to make sure it was done, she left all of the work for Rachael. She was totally involved with baby Violet. She had delved into the role of motherhood and spent every waking hour with the baby. It was if for the first time in her life she had something to call her own and she was consumed by it.

Rachael tried to hold her tongue, but after working all day on the smoke house she was in no mood to find not even water boiling on the stove at suppertime. She had to deal with Joe following her around asking when they were going to eat and what they were going to eat. It had become his focus in life.

Tired and dirty, Rachael, Ben and Jesse came into the house and collapsed on the kitchen floor. "I'm starvin,'" Jesse said. "How come we ain't got no supper ready agin'?"

Rachael stood up and yelled for Lily. "Okay, here's what we have to do. We got less than one week to make our deadline. We have to get Nevers' still off the mountain and up and runnin'. The one we got ain't worth a crap. We'll bring it down if we have to carry it on our backs piece by piece. If Clyde don't git his order by Friday, that will be the end of us." She began to walk around the room. "You, Lily will probably have yer family livin' here with you. Old Joe, I guess you'll have to go back to your shack because me and the boys will be headin' home. Have I made myself clear."

There was silence in the room. "I'll go, I'll help, I promise," Lily said meekly. "I'll put Violet in a basket and take her with me."

"Me, too. I ain't gonna go back to that thar shed. I like it here," Old Joe said.

Of course, Rachael knew Ben was on board, but she worried about Jesse. "You with us, Jesse? You want to make a lot of money in a short time." Jesse lowered his head and nodded.

"Okay. Let's all get a good night sleep tonight. We got a lot of work to do tomarry. Grabbing cold biscuits and cups of day old coffee everyone went to their rooms.

Rachael lowered herself to the side of the bed and knelt down. She put her hands together. "Oh. Lord, I know I ain't got no right to ask you for favors, but if you just git me through till spring I promise I will never bother you agin. I know what we're doing here ain't exactly legal, but I promise we ain't goin' to hurt anyone and I'll make sure to give a big donation to the church before we leave here. Now, I'll let you get back to bigger things. I need help takin' care of these people, Lord. I'm countin' on you. Amen.

Taking the wagon, Jesse, Rachael and Old Joe went back to Black Mountain to take another look at Nevers still. Walking around it, tapping on it and running his hands down the tubes, Joe let out a low whistle. 'This here is one purty sum bitch. Nevers sure did do a fine job on this still. Ain't seen one this good in yars. It would do fine fer our brewin'. He likely started out with somethin' small afore he got into this one."

It took two trips to get the still to Nevers house. Jesse and Ben made a ramp out of old boards and the heavy boiler was pushed into the bed of the truck and carefully rested on a bed of leaves. Lily and Rachael held on to it as the truck made the bumpy trip down the trail. The tubes and coils came down pretty easy on the second trip. When the still was safely behind the false wall in the smokehouse, everyone gave a sigh of relief. Even though she was dead tired, Rachael fried chicken and made mounds of mashed potatoes. The look of appreciation on everyone's face was enough thanks for her. Tomorrow the still would be running. That would be her day of appreciation for all their hard work.

Joe Seminole pushed himself away from the table and wiped his mouth on his sleeve. "That thar was a right nice meal, Rachael. Right nice. You sure kin fry chicken good. I think I'll go out to the barn, take a chaw of backer and get some sleep. My bones is achin'."

"Wait just a minute, Joe, we got to talk," Rachael said. "I need to know if yer ready to start brewin' in the morning. I'd like to have one batch at least by Wednesday. She put a pad of paper and a pencil on the table and sat down next to him. I'm ready, now you jest tell me what ta do and I'll write it down."

"I gotta ponder on that, Rachael. I can't rightly recall everythin' goin' into the mix. I gotta ponder on it."

Rachael put her hands on her hips. "You jest better be funnin' with me, Joe. You better ponder real quick. You told me you made the best moonshine in these parts. I'm countin' on you."

"I wuz the best maker, but that wuz half a life a go. My mind ain't as good. You got book readin' maybe you kin help me out."

"I don't have a clue how to do it and where in the hell am I gonna get a book on how to make moonshine? Now what? Damn, I can't believe this!" Rachael stomped her foot and Joe took off out the door.

"I had everythang ridin' on him and now he tells me he can't remember. This is jest great."

"Now hold on jest a minute, Sister. We got them notes that Nevers writ. You and me are jest gonna have to cipher them out. Go get them, Lily," Ben said.

After looking through the papers, Rachael pushed them across the table to Ben." See if you kin figure them it. This scribblin' don't make one bit of sense to me. It's all smeared." She stomped out the door and plopped down on the stoop. Putting her head in her hands she began to cry. Ben wheeled himself out next to her, the notebooks on his lap. "Come on, Sis, don't cry. It'll be all right."

"How do you know that, Ben Riley? Nothin' ever turns out right for us. I was puttin' my faith in that old coot. I shoulda known better. Alls he wanted was a way to get down off that mountain and git a free meal. I'm so mad, I could spit."

"I'm tellin' you it's gonna be okay. Look yonder," he said.

Rachael looked up to where Ben was pointing. A thin trail of smoke escaped from the chimney of the smokehouse. "Either Joe is smokin' meat or that still is up and a runnin'. Let's go check it out."

Rachael hurriedly pushed Ben's chair across the yard. She opened the door to the smokehouse and pulled away the false wall.

"Well, hiddie, Rachael. I waz jest comin' to fetch you. I come in here and seed all them supplies and it all come to me. I got a batch a brewin'. Should be ready by mornin'. Least wise a few drops is startin' already."

Rachael watched as a crystal clear drop of liquid formed on the tip of the spigot. It teetered there for a few minutes, dancing about as if it were afraid to fall into the deep vat. Finally it let go and Rachael caught it on her finger. "Ben, taste this," she said, almost putting her finger in his mouth.

"Hold on, Rachael, I need a little more than that to taste. Rachael sat down on the floor next to Ben and they both sat hypnotized as each drop fell into the vat. After almost an hour Rachael dipped a metal cup into the vat and handed it to Ben. He slowly put it to his lips, letting the small amount of liquid play on his tongue before he swallowed it.

"Well, how is it, Ben? Is it good? Please say it's good," Rachael pleaded.

Ben smiled. "It's good, alright. Plenty good."

Rachael jumped up. She grabbed Joe Seminole and planted a kiss on his bald head. "Thank you, damn, this is great."

Joe gave a toothless grin. "Hot damn, I reckon we be in business. Now you two git and let me get to brewin'. I ain't had this much fun in yars. You jest keep the wood a comin' and maybe a few more pieces of that chicken and that vat will be full by sun up."

Chapter Twenty-Two

The Riley kids became a fine oiled machine. While Ben and Joe tended to the still, Jesse cut wood. Rachael washed the jars and filled them from the vat and packed them in the boxes. Lily was once again assigned to house duty, which she grumbled constantly about saying that it didn't give her enough time to spend with Violet. When there was no meat in the smokehouse to cure, Jesse would go into the forest and hunt for deer and rabbits. Just in case anyone came, they had to make sure there was meat hanging in the smokehouse. They would be eating smoked meat for a long time.

Joe fermented a barrel of peaches and produced a fine batch of peach liquor. When Rachael and Jesse took a sample to Clyde he ordered six cases on the spot. Rachael knew he was excited about the latest shipment, but refused to show it so that he could get it from them for a good price. They haggled for a while before coming up with the cost. Rachael told Clyde they were also going to make apple brandy. "Now are you gonna finally tell me who is helpin' you making this stuff? Sure is a cut above what Nevers was given me."

"I can't," Rachael answered. "I promised I wouldn't tell. If'n I do, the brewin' will stop. Do you want that to happen?"

"Aw, go on. Keep your secret." Clyde grumbled.

With an empty truck and money under the seat, Rachael and Jesse started home. "I've been ponderin', Jesse. Maybe we better let Nevers make an appearance so that the men up at Mabry's stop asking me questions about him. Every time I meet up with one of them they ask about him. I think thar beginnin' to wonder what's really goin' on at the house. "You know with us cartin' lumber and stuff back and forth all the time. I don't want them comin' round."

"How we gonna do that? We gonna dig him up?" Jesse asked.

"Don't be so dumb, Jesse. We still got some of his clothes. I'm gonna put them on Joe and drive past the store. Jest let them get a glimpse of him. Maybe I'll have Joe wave his hand out the winder."

Jesse shook his head. "I swear, Rachael, I jest wish you would stop thinkin'."

Old Joe wasn't happy about pretending to be Nevers, but a promise of a few chaws of tobacco convinced him. Rachael sat him up on two pillows in the truck and climbed in the drivers seat. Putting Nevers old hat on his head, she pulled his collar up close to his face. "Now lissen to me and lissen real good. I'm gonna drive by the store. If'n the men are outside, I'll jest honk and you wave. If'n they ain't, I'll have to go in. You don't talk to anyone or git out of the truck."

Joe pulled Never's hat down over his eyes. "I heer ya, Rachael. You done told me that three times."

Rachael drove slowly by the store and no one was sitting outside on the bench. "Damn, Wouldn't you know it, I have to go in." She pulled the truck over to the side of the building, in plain view of the window and went in. Three of the men from the hollow were gathered around the potbelly stove even though it wasn't lit. They turned when she entered.

"Well, hey there, Rachael," Mr. Mabry greeted her. "I ain't seen you in a coon's age. What you been up to? Is that

Nevers I see sittin' out thar in the truck?" All three of the men turned and looked out the window.

"It sure is. He can't come in. He ain't able to walk very good. He still ain't doin' good, that fection went clear into his belly. His toes all busted open. Ta beat that , he's got pleurisy and he coughs all the time. Never has me and Jesse workin' our fingers to the bone. Jesse's doin' all the trappin' and I'm takin' care of everything else. We got a smoke house now. We're gonna sell meat and hope ta make enuf money to help out my family this winter."

"Well, no wonder you ain't round much. I reckon you didn't hear that them gypsies are back in Bent Creek. They been campin' down by the river. Thars two truckloads of em this time. They come in here tuther day like a swarm of beetles on a corn crop. I had to watch them reel careful but I jest know'd they probably stole somethin' afore they left. We sent for the sheriff to go down and chase them off. I sure hope he did. I been stayin' in my store all night to keep em from robbin' me agin. They come around here agin thar gonna get a butt full of buckshot."

Rachael tried to hide her irritation. "No, I didn't know that they were back. I sure hope they move on soon. I better get Nevers' chaw and go a fore he starts honkin'. Maybe ya oughta throw in a couply boxes of them shotgun shells fer me jest in case them gypsies come out our way."

Rachael hurriedly paid for her purchase and quickly left as two of the men got up and started toward the door. She ran across the lot and jumped into the truck. Rachael backed up and took off before the men were off the porch. One of the old men scratched his head. "Whew, she done took off like greased lighten. Wonder what's her big hurry?"

"Dammit, dammit, dammit," she said, beating on the wheel. "I know'd it was too good to be true. Jest as soon as we get everythin' goin' good, here comes trouble again. Dammit."

"What you goin' off about, Gal?" Joe asked. "What kinda bee you got in yer bonnet now?"

"Them gypsies are back. That means that Jimmy and Emma Jane are probably with them. We got to get home and fast." She stepped on the gas and the old truck let out a loud backfire and took off down the road.

It was too late. When Rachael pulled up the road she noticed that the bolt had been cut and the gate stood wide open. Four men stood next to the two old trucks parked in the yard. There were several women inside of the trucks. Emma Jane and Jimmy were standing on the porch with Jesse and Ben blocking the door.

Rachael jumped out of the truck and ran up the steps. "What are you doin' here, Emma Jane? What do you want? You ain't got no call to come round here." She looked at her younger sister with pity in her eyes. Emma Jane's hair was tangled and dirty. She wore a faded blue dress that smelled of perspiration.

"I come fer my baby. I know that you got my baby and I want it. "

"It! Is that what you call a baby…it! You and Jimmy don't even care what you had, do you?"

"I ain't that dumb, Rachael. I know it's a girl. Ben and Jesse won't let us in. I done heard a baby in thar, so don't you be tellin' me it died. That's a lie."

"You left her, Emma Jane. Lily has been taken care of her and she's gonna keep her. So you and your kind jest go on and git the hell outta here," Rachael said, angrily. One of the men standing by the truck pulled a shotgun from the front seat and started toward the porch. It was Ben who stopped him, with a rifle of his own that had been hidden under the blanket laid across his lap. The man backed up and put the gun in the truck.

Emma Jane began to cry. "Look at ya'll. You livin' in a nice house, with lectricity and runnin' water and we ain't even got a pillow to lay our heads on. We come fer the baby."

"Where you gonna keep her? She can't sleep on the ground. You got any diapers and milk for her, Emma Jane? You know she's better off here. Jimmy Dell put you up to this, didn't he, Emma Jane?"

Jimmy stepped forward. "We come to fetch our youngin, so you jest git her right now."

"How much do you want fer her?" Ben blurted out. "Cause we ain't givin' her to you either way. So if'n yer smart you'll jest take some money and git."

Jimmy Dell walked back to where the others were standing. He returned a few minutes later. "Two hundred dollars. We want two hundred dollars fer the baby and then you kin keep her."

Ben clenched his fists. "You are a real hunk of crap, Jimmy. I'll give you one hundred dollars fer her. I jest got my army check money. That's all we got between us. You better take it if'n you know what's good fer you, lessen I might jest have to send Jesse to fetch the sheriff."

Jimmy Dell turned around and looked over at one of the older men. He held up one finger. The man nodded his head. "Okay. We'll take a hundred." Emma Jane began to cry.

"You git back in the truck, woman," Jimmy Dell yelled at her. "This is all yer doin'." He turned to Rachael. "It's all her idée to come back here and git the baby. I didn't want no part of this."

Rachael clenched her fists, wanting so badly to smack him in the face or better yet shoot him. " I don't believe you, Jimmy Dell, but it's no matter. You've done tainted my sister so bad that I don't even know who she is anymore. Before you leave you got to sign a paper sayin' that you sold her to us and if'n you ever try to get her back I'll have both you and Emma Jane put in jail. Do you understand?" Rachael said.

"Write the paper. We gotta git," Jimmy Dell said.

After Rachael wrote the paper, Jimmy Dell and Emma Jane both signed it and Ben handed Jimmy the money. "Now ya'll git. You come back here agin you ain't gonna git sech a good welcome. Next time it'll be the bullets that will be doin' the talkin'."

As they turned to leave, Emma Jane stopped for a minute. "What's her name, Rachael? Is she purty?'

"Her name is Violet and she looks jest like you." Rachael could see the tears welling up in her sister's eyes again and wondered how she had ever let herself get to this point. She wanted to jump off the porch and put her arms around Emma Jane, and tell her not to go, but she knew that she couldn't unless she wanted trouble. "How's momma and daddy? Are they okay?" Emma Jane asked.

Thar doin' okay. Momma still cries over you. You sure done her a bad one, Emma Jane. I feel sorry fer you."

Jimmy Dell yelled again and Emma Jane ran to the truck and got in. Rachael watched as they pulled out of the yard. She would never see her sister again. There were tales told of a band of migrants who showed up in Tennessee and were stealing crops from the farmers. They were caught and sent to jail and some had been shot in the raid. Rachael tried to believe that it wasn't her sister's clan and that maybe she was somewhere living a good life.

Inside the house, Lily sat in the corner of the bedroom with Violet wrapped in a blanket. She slowly rocked the baby back and forth, silently crying to herself. Rachael bent down next to her. "She's yer baby now, Lily. We got a signed paper. You kin keep her. Ben's done paid for her. She's yers to keep forever."

Lily laid the baby on the bed and put her arms around Rachael. Her shoulders shook as the sobs wracked through her body. "Thank you, Rachael. I kin never repay you fer what you and Ben have done fer me.. I love Violet, but I love ya'll, too. But what if'n they come back and want more money? What then?"

"They ain't comin' back, Lily. They know we mean business and if'n they come this way agin they'll be in really big trouble."

Lily picked up the baby and held her close to her cheek. "Yer my baby, Violet, and no one will ever take you from me."

Rachael knew that the paper Emma Jane signed would never stand up in a court of law. She would pray that would never happen.

"I'm gonna go see my momma," Rachael said, putting on her jacket.

"What fer?" Ben asked. "They ain't due no money. You ain't gonna tell her that Emma Jane wuz heer, are you?"

"No, she sure don't need ta know that. I just need to see her." Opening the truck door, she was startled by Joe Seminole. She had forgotten all about him.

"Is it all right for me ta git out of the truck now? I pert neer been sittin' in here for ovah an hour."

Chapter Twenty-Three

Autumn was silently moving across the mountains. Each day the tree would take on a new color and there was a morning chill in the air. The woodpile along side the house was growing and the money under Rachael's mattress was getting thicker. Rachael's occasional trip pass Mabry's store with Joe Seminole in the passenger seat seemed to quell the curiosity about Nevers. Everyone in Bent Creek now believed he was sick, but still was running the show at his house. It was almost a true statement since everything they did was controlled by the fact that they had to pretend he was alive. That meant they couldn't buy anything special with their money, or even go into Lynch for an afternoon movie. Nevers wouldn't have allowed that. Rachael and Jesse usually spent less than fifteen minutes dropping off the whiskey and picking up supplies. The temptation to buy a candy bar or a new pair of shoes was getting stronger each week, especially for Jesse.

Since Ben had made the offer to buy Violet from Emma Jane, Lily became his constant companion. She would sit next to him and put Violet on his lap. She loved to watch as he played with her or rocked her to sleep. When the baby was napping, Lily would go out to the smokehouse and sit with Ben when it was his turn to stoke the fire. Jesse was well aware of her new found interest in his brother and it was beginning to play on his nerves. He had expected by now he would be sharing Lily's bed instead of the steady snubs he got from her. He knew he had gone about courting her all wrong. He had tried to move on her too quickly. When Jesse tried to change and be kinder to her, she still did not respond. He picked flowers from the field and brought them to her, he brought butterscotch candies from town and even tried playing with the baby. Nothing seemed to work. She was simply not interested in him anymore.

Jesse watched as Lily brushed her hair until it hung down her back like strands of silk and when she put lavender in her pockets knowing it was not for his benefit. She now favored Ben's company. Jesse could not understand why Lily preferred a man with no legs to him. When Jesse complained to Rachael, she just told him that Ben was more a gentle sort and didn't make demands of Lily. Rachael only hoped that Lily's feelings for Ben was genuine and not because she felt sorry for him or that he had stood up to Jimmy Dell. Rachael did not know that when they were alone, Ben, with his limited knowledge of writing and reading, was teaching Lily what he knew. When she confessed to him that she was completely illiterate and didn't want to raise her daughter the same way he agreed to help her learn. Lily was overwhelmed with Ben's attitude towards her. He did not make fun of her or grab at her and the idea that he had paid for her to keep Violet was still more than she could comprehend. No man in her entire life had ever done anything that kind for her.

Lily didn't know that when she asked Ben for help with her schooling it made him feel he had a purpose other than keeping the fire under the still going. He looked forward to her visits. Ben would pull the chalkboard out from behind the woodpile and take out the one of the books Rachael had given him. They would sit in the glowing light of the fire, there heads close together and practice letters and reading. When Lily was able to print her name tears ran down her face. Ben looked at her and he realized that she was becoming important to him.

On a rainy day in early October, while Rachael tended the still and Jesse left to take a shipment in to Lynch, Joe headed to the barn. He said he needed a day off. Lily sat next to the stove rocking Violet while Ben finished off his second bowl of soup. Can I ask you a question, Ben?" she said, softly.

"Sure, go ahead," he answered.

"Does it bother you that I'm a soiled woman?"

Ben looked startled. "What do you mean, soiled? You ain't soiled. I'm the one that's soiled."

"You got yer legs takin' away from you by accident. I coulda have run away from Nevers before he got to me. But, I didn't."

Ben wheeled his chair over next to Lily. "Where would you have gone, Lily? I reckon you didn't have much choice. You wuz jest a kid. Kids ain't supposed to be treated like you wuz. Don't ever say yer soiled."

"I know Jesse has a hankerin' fer me. After Nevers died I knew what he wanted and he figured since I had already had done my wifely duties that I wouldn't mind doin' it with him. I know he tried hard to court me the right way, but I didn't feel anythin' for him. Ben, I want someone to love me for who I am not jest what they kin git from me. I jest don't think any decent man would ever want me." Lily sighed and rubbed her hand over Violet's soft curls.

"I want you, Lily. I mean…if'n I was a whole man, I'd want you."

"Oh, Ben, yer legs don't mean nothin' to me. I like you jest the way you are now." She reached over and kissed him on the cheek. Ben took her hand and held it close to his face. "I surely do like you, Lily. I surely do."

Violet stirred and let out a squeal. "You see there, Ben. Even my baby approves of you. I think you jest stirred my heart. Now what are we gonna do?"

"We're gonna give it some time to stir, Lily and see what happens. We got time and that's a good thing."

On that day, Lily Bains knew that she was in love with Ben Riley.

Chapter Twenty-Four

Life had taken on a rhythm that was working well for the Riley family. The moonshine was brewed, bottled and boxed in a smooth operation. It was only the trip to Lynch that made them nervous. There was always the worry that the truck may break down or a car full of revenuers might be lurking behind a grove of trees ready to spring out at them. There was also the real concern that other moon shiners had found out about their operation and were just waiting for an opportunity to move into their territory. Each time they returned home with an empty truck and a pocketful of money there was a sigh of relief.

Every Saturday, Clyde Orby was also nervous as he waited for Jesse and Rachael to bring in the load of moonshine. On this day it was only Jesse who showed up. The cases were quickly unloaded into the back room of Clyde's store and Jesse was given the money, which he stuck under the loose floorboard in the truck. His usual routine was to get back in the truck and head back home. Today he decided that a cold soda would really taste good. He had a right to treat himself once in a while. Walking across to the drugstore with his hands in his pockets and his head down, he didn't see the two men coming out the door until he ran headlong into them. "Oh, hey, I'm sorry," Jesse said. " I sure didn't mean to run ya'll down."

"Yah need ta watch whar yer goin'," one of the men said. Jesse looked into the face of a yellow-toothed, one-eyed man he had never seen before in Lynch. A deep scar criss-crossed his face. The stench of the man's breath lingered on Jesse's shirt.

"I'm reel sorry," Jesse said again. Changing his mind about the soda, he wheeled around and headed for his truck. Just as he put his foot on the running board, he felt someone standing behind him. He turned into the same ugly face again.

"What's yer hurry, Boy? Me and my friend are needin' a ride to Bent Creek. Ya'll goin' that away."

His immediate reaction was to start up the truck and take off, but he knew better. They weren't the kind of men you could run from. He stuttered, "Er...ah...yep, I'm a goin' that way. Ya'll want ta climb in the back?"

They didn't answer him and within a few seconds both men walked around to the other side of the truck and climbed in next to him. Jesse moved over as far as he could, his side pressing against the door handle.

"Whar ya from?" the one-eyed man asked.

"I live down jest pass Bent Creek. Me and my family, we got a place thar. I'm Jesse Riley," he said, hoping to find out who these two strangers were. The man nodded.

"Names Cooter, this here fella is Norvelle. You ever hear of a man named Rooster comin' round these parts? I'm a lookin' fer him. He's mah brother."

Jesse could feel his legs going weak. He hoped he wouldn't pee in his pants. "Nope, sure ain't heard of him, but I keep tah myself. I don't know too much about anything. I jest bring our vegetables into Clyde's store and then I go back on home."

"That a fact?" Cooter said, staring sideways at Jesse. "How bout Nevers Bain. Ya know him?"

"Heard of him, but ah don't know him personal like." Jesse over-corrected on a sharp turn and the truck swayed from side to side.

"That's alls the questions I got fer you. Jest stop swerving on this road and pay a mind to what yer doin'."

Jesse pulled the truck up in front of Mabry's store. "This here is Bent Creek. Ya'll kin git out now."

"Mighty grateful fer the ride," Cooter said. He leaned his elbows on the window, his face just a few inches from Jesse. "Maybe I'll be seein' you agin' sometime. You take care of yerself, yah heer?" He sauntered away from the truck with Norvelle trailing behind him.

Once at home, Jesse ran into the house and told everyone what had happened. "Yep, he's a lookin' fer his brother and he's a mean sum bitch, I kin tell you that right now. He done stunk like two wet skunks in a gunny sack and I seed a big ole knife stickin' outta his pocket."

"You don't worry about them, Jesse. They ain't gonna find Rooster so they'll probably move along in a couply days," Rachael said.

"I shure hope yer right, Rachael, I surely do. They was askin' about Nevers. They jest might show up out here. They done scared the hell outta me."

❧   ❧   ❧

Rachael pulled her coat close to her body. Her hand shook as she put the key into the ignition and listened to the grinding sound of the truck. On the third try it started. Still shivering from the cold morning she honked the horn and waited. Jesse finally appeared in the doorway and waved to her. She had to wait on him again. Ever since he had encountered Cooter and Norvelle he was hesitant about going into Lynch.

When he finally came outside and got into the truck, Rachael was fuming. "I swear, Jesse, if you don't start gettin' ready sooner I'm jest gonna leave without you. I'm sittin' out here freezin' to death."

"Well you jest go ahead and go. If'n you think you kin get this load to Lynch on yer own, do it."

"You sure are grouchy this morning," Rachael remarked.

"I got good reason to be. I'm still scart about runnin' into them men in Lynch and ta top it all off, Ben done told me last night that he and Lily have feelins' fer each other. Bad enuf that Ben's a cripple and now he's takin' my woman from me. Jest taint fair," Jesse grumbled.

"She's not yer woman, Jesse. People have a right to make their own choices and Lily chose Ben. I'm jest hopin' she's jest not feelin' sorry fer him or thankful cause he paid fer Violet. She says not."

"I done seed her first and then he comes along and takes her away from me. If'n he was standin' on two legs I'd knock them right out from under him. And I'm gonna tell you right now, Rachael, I ain't plannin' on stickin' around much longer. We got plenty of money. I'm gonna take my share and hit the road. I'm gonna buy me a truck and head up to Lexington to find me a new life. Alls we do here is work, work, work and then some more. It's time fer me to call it quits."

"I know you're tired of all this," Rachael said, trying to calm him, "But it will only be a few more weeks and then we'll all be leavin'. I promise, Jesse. Just stick it out a few more weeks for me. We'll be outta here before the first icicle hits the rain barrel."

"Few more weeks and that's it. Ah don't like this and I ain't gonna do it no more." he said. He sunk down in the seat and sulked the rest of the way home.

Jesse helped Clyde put the bags of sugar and corn into the truck and hurriedly covered them with the tarps. Clyde went inside and handed Rachael an envelope. "I gotta tell you, Rachael, I here tell that there are some revenuers lurkin' about these parts. I ain't seen them around here yet, but maybe it would be better if you come on Friday next week stead of Saturday. You know, jest in case they're awatchin'."

"I ain't gonna worry about no rumor. We'll be comin' on Saturday like usual. Now we gotta get. It's startin' to rain." As she started toward the truck, Billy Tate jumped out from behind the front bumper. She let out a scream. "I swear, Billy Tate, you don't have the sense you were born with. Why'd you go and scare me like that?"

"You're awful jumpy, Rachael. You got somethin' hidin' in that truck. Whar's Nevers? Why ain't he around anymore?" Billy asked.

"Cause he sick, that's why." She tried to pass him by.

"What you got in that truck?" he asked again. "Ya'll sure do buy a lot of supplies." Walking backward he began to lift the corner of the tarp. Rachael smacked it down with her hand. "Ain't none of yer concern what's in my truck. Now move out of the way."

Billy stood his ground and grabbed Rachael by the arm. "Don't be so mean with me, Rachael. Come on across the street to the drugstore. I'll buy you a sodee."

"I don't want a sodee. I have to get home a fore it starts raining harder. We got a hole in the floorboards and the water comes in the truck." She looked around for Jesse.

Still holding on to her, Billy whined, "Aw, come on Rachael. Have a sodee with me."

Rachael tried to pry his hand loose. "I said...I don't want a sodee. Let go of my arm!"

His grip grew tighter and as she struggled to free herself. She hadn't heard someone comin' up behind her. " The lady said to let go of her, I suggest you do so or I might have to knock out the few teeth you got left in your head." Billy dropped his hands to his sides and stared into the face of the dark haired man standing in front of him. "I know you, yer Sammy Montgomery. Yeah, that's who you are. I'll be damn, I ain't seen you since we was in school."

"That's me. And here you are, still picking on the ladies. Same old Billy Tate."

Billy threw his head back and laughed. "As I recollect you did yer share of teasin," he said, pointing at Rachael. "This ain't no lady, this here is Rachael Riley. You remember her? You used ta call her names all the time."

"I sure do remember her," he replied, grinning.

Rachael tried to tuck her hair behind her ears. She knew she must look a fright in torn overalls and a coat with no buttons. She lowered her head. "Hello, Sammy, how are you?"

He turned to Billy Tate. "Are you going to keep your hands to yourself or do I have to come after you?"

Billy grinned. "I was jest havin' some fun with Rachael. She never gives me the time of day. I got to git." He trotted off down the street.

"It's good to see you again, Rachael. How have you been?"

"I'm okay. What are you doin' here in Lynch? I thought you moved to Ohio."

"I did. I'm back here doing some work for my company. You have time for that soda, Rachael?" Sam asked.

"No, thanks, I got ta git home. I'm jest waitin' for Jesse. We come in town to git some supplies, sides I look a mess. Maybe some other time, that is, if yer going to be here for a while."

"Yeah, I'm back for a month or two. I don't think you've grown an inch since sixth grade," he said, putting his hand above her head."

Rachael laughed. "I sure have. It's jest that yer so tall. I see you grew into yer monkey ears."

"Yeah, it took a while, but my head finally grew. How about I meet you back here next Saturday afternoon and I'll buy you something to eat to go along with that soda. We can talk about old times. Say one o'clock?" Sam asked.

She stuttered for a moment. "Yes, I'd like that. Here comes Jesse. I'll see you on Saturday."

Turning her head around to watch him walk across the street as Jesse pulled the truck up next to her, she let out a low whistle. "Wow, he sure looks nice."

"Who was that you was talkin' to?" Jesse asked.

"Sammy Montgomery. Do you remember him? He went to school with us, but he left after his father was kilt in the mine. His mom and him left and went somewheres in Ohio to live with his grandparents. I'm gonna meet him next week. He's gonna buy me a sodee and something to eat. Kin you believe that? I think I have a date."

"You better be careful who yer talkin' to, Rachael. What's he doin' back here anyway?"

"I don't know, but I'll find out next Saturday," Rachael replied. She smiled all the way home. It wasn't until she pulled into the yard that it would be impossible for her to go anywhere with Sammy. She didn't even own a dress. It was Lily who came to her rescue.

"Nevers bought me this green material to make curtains for the sittin' room, but I didn't get round to it. It's real purty, Rachael and feel how soft it is. It'll make a real nice dress. I even got some white lace I can use ta trim it and I'll pull some buttons off of somewhere and fix yer coat. Here, stand on this chair so I kin measure you."

Jesse had walked in on the middle of their conversation. "I can't believe you two. Why'd you have to make a dress out

of curtain material when we got enough money hidden somewheres to choke a horse. Rachael should go buy herself a
dress."

"Not yet, I ain't buyin' any dresses yet. You go on and
git so we can get started. Take the truck and go down and give
daddy our five dollars for the week."

"And that's another thang, Rachael. Momma and daddy
need more money than five dollars to live on."

Rachael jumped down from the chair. "You look here,
Jesse Riley, if they would get off of their behinds they could
have it better. Daddy jest sits around all day doing nothin' and
so does momma. They act like they jest gave up on life. Alls
they do is wait around fer us to help them out. He coulda set
some traps or go fishin' and built a pen for them animals we
gave them instead of lettin' half of them wander off. He coulda
cut some boards to fix the house and momma coulda had a nice
little garden this year. But no, they did nothin'. They ain't crip-
pled. People shouldn't sit around and expect other people to
take care of them, even if we are their kids."

The room was silent. Even little Violet stopped cooing
as she sat on Ben's lap. Rachael folded her arms across her
chest. "Well, somebody go on and say it. Say that I don't have
no right to talk about them like that. Anybody here want to go
back and live with them?" Lily pretended to be busy measuring
the material, while Ben took Violet and wheeled himself into
the bedroom. Jesse took the five dollars off the table and
headed for the door. "Okay, now, Lily let's make that dress."

Chapter Twenty-Five

Saturday couldn't come soon enough for Rachael. One minute she was nervous as a cat just thinking about it the next minute she was laughing and enduring the teasing from the others. In her whole eighteen years no one except Billie Tate had ever taken a second look at her. Sure the boys picked on her at school, but they did that to all the girls.

Sammy was at least four years older than her. He had stayed in school longer than all the boys, but when his father died in a mining accident he dropped out of school and a few months later he moved away. She still wondered why he wanted to buy her a soda. She wasn't anyone special.

When Rachael decided to drive the truck into Lynch by herself on Saturday, she was met with a lot of grief from the others. No one thought it was a good idea, especially Ben. "What if'n the truck breaks down or what if'n somebody stops you?"

"Wouldn't be much different if Jesse was with me," she replied. "I really need to do this. I don't want Jesse takin' up my time with Sammy. I ain't been out of this house by myself not one time since we moved here." She stood her ground and Ben finally relented. He looked at his little sister in her new green dress, Lily's white sweater and polished shoes. She wasn't a kid anymore, but a full-grown woman. "You be reel careful, ya heer and you be sure not to tell Sammy anythang he don't need to know. Now go on and git."

Clyde was surprised when Rachael arrived early. He was even more surprised to see her in a dress. "You sure do look nice, Rachael. You clean up real good," he said, grinning.

"You jest shut up old man and get this stuff off the truck. I'll give you a dollar if you load up my supplies and let me leave the truck here fer a few hours. I got somethin' to do."

"Suppose I kin do that fer you. Looks like you brought me a good load."

Rachael walked through the store and came out the front door just as Sammy came around the corner. She smoothed her hair and tried to look calm, while her insides were shaking so hard she had to put her hand on her stomach to stop them.

"Hi, Rachael. Glad you could make it. I'm real hungry. Instead of a soda at the drugstore let's go get something to eat. Is that all right with you?"

She nodded. She had no idea if she could eat a bite, but he took her arm and began leading her down the sidewalk. "I thought we could go to Ruth's Café. I've eaten there several times since I've been back. They have pretty good food." Once again he asked if that was okay and once again she nodded.

He ushered her down the aisle of the restaurant to a table near the window. As she started to sit down he came around behind her and touched her shoulders. "Whatcha doin'?" she asked, in a surprised voice.

"I was going to take your sweater and hang it up."

"Oh," she replied and handed it to him.

"You look really nice, Rachael. Is that a new dress?"

"Lily made it fer me. I really don't have any nice things Sammy. That thar is Lily's sweater."

He smiled at her candor. "I wonder if I could ask you a favor, Rachael? Could you call me Sam, instead of Sammy? I

kind of gave up being called Sammy when I moved. I mean…
if that's okay with you."

"Sure, Sam. Yep, that sounds good. I think I like that
better anyway. I mean, since we're all grow'd up now."

Sam handed her the menu and she opened it to the middle page. Her finger traveled up and down, savoring each
description of the food she could choose from.

Sam watched her while she was engrossed in the menu.
He noticed how round her face was and the glow on her cheeks
even though she didn't have on makeup. A few freckles
crossed her nose and her brown hair, pulled back in a ponytail
made her still look like a young girl.

"Yer starin' at me, Sam. Do I have somethin' on my
face?"

"No, I was just checking you out. You're just plain
cute, Rachael."

"Lordy, yer gonna make me blush," she said covering
her face with the menu.

Sam laughed, "Okay, I'll be nice. Do you see anything
on the menu that you like?"

"I have. I want a hamburger on a bun, with French fries,
pickles, catsup and no onions. I want a Coca Cola to drink."
She closed the menu and laid it down in front of her. He smiled
and then ordered the same thing.

"Tell me about your family, Rachael? Billy told me
about Willie and Paul and I'm very sorry. That's terrible losing
two brothers in less than a year. How are your mom and dad?"

"Well, I reckon you know since the mine closed it been
real tough living here. Daddy jest sits around doing nothin'.
Since Jesse and I moved in with Nevers, he depends on us to
provide him and momma with money and food. Ben lives with
us, too. He jest wasn't doin' good livin' in the holler. Did you
know that Ben got his legs cut off? He had a bad accident when

he was in the army. He gits money from the government, but most times he gives it all to our parents."

The food arrived and Rachael put her napkin under her chin and took a big bite of the hamburger. "Wow, this is so good." Dipping a French Fry in the catsup, she twirled it around her plate. "Momma just couldn't deal with everythin' that's happened to her. Losin' both my brothers was jest plain arful. Then Ben comes home with no legs and Emma Jane got herself pregnant. Lily, that's Nevers' wife, is raisin' the baby. Now, Nevers is reel sick and we have to do everythin' for him." She continued on as she dunked several more fries into the catsup and put them in her mouth. "What..." she said, realizing that Sam was just grinning at her and not eating his food. "I reckon I'm a ramblin' on. I have never had a hamburger or French fries in my life. Fact of the matter is I ain't ever been in a restaurant, cept one time when I was reel little and I had to use the bathroom and mamma tuck me into a diner. We didn't eat thar or nothin'. I reckon I'm showin' my ignorance." She wiped her nose on her napkin. "I'm sorry, Sam. I'm jest as nervous as a cat."

Sam reached across the table and touched her hand. "There is absolutely nothing wrong with you. I'm enjoying your company. Just relax and enjoy your meal."

"Really?" she said, putting her half eaten hamburger on her plate. I've been so nervous about today."

"Rachael, it's just me, I'm the same old Sam that you used to call monkey ears. To be honest, I was scared to death of you when we were younger. You always knew exactly what you wanted and seemed so sure of yourself. You were a tough little kid."

"You gotta be kidding. Why would anyone be afeared of me? And yer not the same Sam that left here. You talk different like and you have on nice clothes and short hair. You probably been to high school and got a good education. I've been trying reel hard not ta talk like a hillbilly, but it's hard when everybody round me talks that a way. You ain't told me anythin' about yourself," she said, picking up her hamburger.

He leaned back against the booth. " It was tough living with my grandparents in Dayton. They had a real small house and they weren't real happy about my mom and I being there, but we had no place else to go. My mom was so grief stricken when my father got killed that it took months before she would even venture out of the house. I went to a neighborhood school and if you think you have ever been teased, you have no idea what it was like there. The kids there called me every name you can think of, hillbilly boy, hayseed, yokel, Li'l Abner and other ones I don't want to say. They pushed and tripped me in the hallways until I finally had enough. I cut my hair, got new clothes and stood in front of the mirror for hours practicing how to speak without sounding like I just fell off the turnip truck. I didn't have any friends, so I just concentrated on school and before you know it I had caught and passed most of the kids in my grade. I got out of school early and took some college courses. About that time my mother remarried and we moved to Covington, Kentucky. Her new husband works for the government and he was able to get me a job. It was pure luck, Rachael but I had to work harder than I ever thought I could to prove myself."

"My goodness, Sam, that's some story. What exactly do you do for the government?" Rachael asked.

He paused for a moment. "Surveying. I do surveying for the state of Kentucky."

The door was open for more conversation and they talked through the rest of the meal and an ice cream sundae at the drugstore. She didn't want the day to end and when he took her hand and walked her back to Clyde's store, she knew it was time to go home. "I had a reel nice time today, Sam. My truck is behind the store. I reckon I better git home."

"What about next Saturday, will you be in town? I hear they got a new picture showing at the movie show?"

"I'll try, but I can't make any promises. It depends on what kind of mood Nevers is in. If'n I'm not here by two o'clock I ain't comin'."

"I just want to tell you one last thing," Sam said. "Sometimes it not about how you say the words, but what they mean that counts. You be careful going home."

"Thank you, Sam. That's reel nice of you ta say that."

When Rachael arrived home she found everyone, including Joe Seminole, sitting at the kitchen table. "What took you so long, Rachael?" Jesse asked. "We were plum worried about you."

"We got to talkin' and I just lost track of time. You didn't all have to be waitin' fer me."

"We been havin' a talk. Sit down we have sumthin' to tell you," Ben said.

Rachael slid into a chair wondering what she had done to upset them. "What's wrong, what did I do?"

"Now this ain't about you, Rachael. It's about the whole situation. First off, we're workin' our butts off each week and Clyde is reapin' all the benefits. I hear tell from some of the men at Mabry's' that moonshine is goin' fer near a dollar a bottle right off the hill. Clyde is only givin' us twenty cents and then he turns around and sells it for two dollars to them men upstate. He don't do none of the work. Either he starts givin' us at least forty cents a gallon or we'll find someone else to sell it to. Then thars all this goins on about Nevers. It's wearin' us thin. It's time we had him dead like he should be and that away me and Lily kin git married and her family won't have nothin' to say about this place. And another thang, we need to go down somewheres in Tennessee and buy us some clothes and things. Except for that dress Lily made you, none of us ain't even had so much as a new pair of underwear in a coon's age." He stopped talking and folded his hands over his chest.

"Okay," Rachael said. "You didn't tell me that you and Lily was thinkin' bout gittin' hitched. When that all come about? I got to ponder on how we kin git rid of Nevers once and fer all and I think gettin' some new stuff sounds reel good."

"Hold on thar girl. You mean to tell me, you ain't mad about all this? Is that alls you got to say about it?"

"Yep." She left the room and four dumbfounded people sat quiet at the table. They hadn't planned on her response. She was supposed to get mad and ask them how they planned to do all those things and then they were all relying on her to have the answers. She always had a plan for everything, but not today. Rachael was lying across her bed reliving every moment of her day with Sam.

Chapter Twenty-Six

"Okay, this is what we're gonna do," Rachael said as she stood at the head of the breakfast table. If everyone does their part I think we kin git Nevers buried and you two married," she said pointing to Ben and Lily. "Thar ain't gonna be no to room for mistakes, so when I explain it all to you, be sure you understand. As usual, Rachael had come up with a plan that seemed impossible but she assured them it would work. Since none of them had a better idea they would go along with her.

Late Friday afternoon, Sheriff Donald Elbers pulled his patrol car into the parking lot of Mabry's store. He had just dropped his wife off at the church to play bingo, just like he did every week. Once inside the store he filled his coffee cup with liquor from the jug that was passed to him. Sitting down with the other men, he would stay there until nine o'clock and then leave to pick his wife up. Usually by seven he was beginning to get a little tipsy and he would stop drinking and start drinking black coffee. By nine he could walk a straight line and drive his patrol car without weaving. Everyone in the hollow knew that Sheriff Elbers was a lazy son of a gun who would get real queasy at the sight of blood. His race for sheriff was never challenged since he was the only one that was up for reelection year after year. No one was really interested in having his job. The pay was small, and the only perk was the twenty-year old patrol car that he was given to drive.

At Seven-ten, just as the sheriff poured his first cup of coffee, Jesse Riley rushed into the store and called out to him. "Oh Lordy, Sheriff, ya gotta come with me. Me and Rachael jest found Never's in the woods. He's all bloody"

Sheriff Elbers stood up, slightly swaying. "Hold on a minute, Boy. Where'd you find him? How in the hell did he git in the woods?" He had heard that Nevers had been sick and he was glad that he didn't have to worry about him for a while. Nevers was about the only one in the hollow that gave him any grief. Except for the few drunks he picked up on Saturday nights, the jail was usually empty.

"Nevers has been actin' real crazy since he's got sick and when we got up this mornin' he twernt in his bed. Lately he had takin' to rantin' like a mad man and hobblin' around the house yellin' at all of us. Most time we could git him back to the bed. That fection was goin' plum ta his head. Anyway, when he come up missin' we spent all day huntin" for him and we come across his body out yonder in the woods. It sure ain't a purty sight. Looks like he must have fell and hit his head on a rock and then somewheres in the night he got a visit from some coyotes. Half his face is gone and his arm is jest hangin' almost off. We brung him into the barn, but he's already cold as an icicle hangin' from the privy." Jesse could see the expression changing on the sheriff's face and he seemed to be turning pale. The moonshine churning in his stomach was helping to make his queasy. "Well, I reckon I better check it out. I need a witness since I can't get a hold of the coroner this late in the day. Any of you men volunteer to go with me. Artie Shoulders and his son agreed to go along with him. Jesse hadn't planned on that.

When Jesse pulled into the yard, he ran to the barn to alert the others. "Sheriff's comin' and he's got Artie and his boy with him."

With only a couple of lanterns burning, it was difficult to see in the barn. Old Joe Seminole was lying under a blanket that had been soaked with chicken blood. Rachael had wrapped a cloth across his head that covered one side of his face. It too, was blood soaked. Rachael whispered to Joe that he had to try and breathe real shallow. She was scared to death that Joe wouldn't be able to do it, but they had practiced for two days. He had protested at first, but when Rachael told him that if the plan didn't work he would have to go somewhere else to live, he relented. She prayed that he wouldn't cough or fart or do something to let them know he was alive. Sheriff Collins ducked his head and stepped into the barn, followed by Artie. His son had decided to wait in the patrol car. "Oh, Lordy, he sure is a mess. Man, he sure lost a lot of weight since he's been sick. Can't see much of his face."

"I kin uncover him, if you like," Rachael said. "I kin show you what the coyotes did to his arm." She slowly picked up the corner of the blanket.

"No! Never mind. I seen enough. How bout you, Artie? You witnessin' that Nevers Bains is dead?"

"I sure am," Artie said, rushing out of the barn.

"I'll get you a death certificate issued."

"Kin we go ahead and bury him tomorrow? His body is beginnin' to putrefy."

"Yeah, go ahead and bury him. I'll call the preacher at the Baptist Church and have him come out tamorry so you kin give him a proper burial. Sorry about this folks. I got to run." Standing outside, Sheriff Elbers took a deep breath to keep from vomiting and headed for his car.

Joe let out a loud sputtering sound and sat up. "It ain't Saturday, but I sure do need a bath."

"You all did jest great," Rachael said smiling. "I think we might jest get through this.

The next morning Jesse went into Mabry's store and bought a wooden burial box. That was something that Mabry always kept in stock. He told Mabry and all the men at the store about Nevers. By the time he returned, Lily and Rachael had dug a trench in the graveyard along side of Never's two wives. Jesse put the coffin into the hole and they waited for the preacher, while Lily had put on her white dress. Ben combed his hair and put on a clean shirt. When they saw Reverend Lewis coming up the hill, Rachael whispered, "Okay, ya'll remember what yer supposed to do."

"Ah, Mrs. Bains, I am so sorry to hear about your husband. Please accept my condolences. I see you have already put him in his grave." He seemed surprised.

Rachael stepped forward. "We had to sir, the blood was starting to seep through the coffin and..."

"He put his hand up, "I quite understand. He opened his book. "Shall we pray?"

Everyone bowed their heads and the preacher read several passages from his bible. Making the sign of the cross he picked up a handful of dirt and threw it into the grave. The others followed suit. "I suppose this is all we can do for Nevers Bains. I hope the good Lord forgives his sins. Is there anything else I can do for you before I leave?" he said to Lily. She nodded. "Yes sir, you kin marry me and Ben."

They were not sure if he was surprised at the request or the fact that Lily could speak. Whatever the reason it brought him to laughter. "Well, I do declare. I have never performed a burial and a wedding in the same hour. I know your family, Lily, so I don't suppose this is such an outrageous request." Reverend Lewis was also well aware of Never's demeanor and had even been a victim at one time. A few years earlier, Lily had come to church without Never's permission; Nevers had burst into the chapel and drug her out by her arm. When the

Reverend followed him out to protest his treatment of her, Nevers punched him in the face and threatened to burn down the church if he interfered in his life again. Afraid for himself and his congregation, the preacher returned to the pulpit with a bloody nose and a sermon about the sins of man and the fire of hell.

After the short ceremony in the sitting room, Reverend Lewis drank a toast of apple juice to the new couple. He promised to prepare the marriage license and send it to them in the next few days.

"I suppose you want to move Ben's thangs into yer room, Lily. You can move Violet in with me if'n you want," Rachael said, as she stood by the window watching Reverend Lewis drive away.

"Oh no, not yet, Rachael. Me and Ben ain't to that part yet. We both want some time to ponder on things. We love each other, but not in that way yet. Ben, is still worried about me seein' him with no legs and I ain't sure I kin be a good wife to him yet."

"I understand," Rachael replied. Both of them had broken bodies and needed time to mend. She changed the subject. "Now, all we have to do is deal with yer family, Lily and then we should be able to get back to business. I guess by now they know Nevers is dead. I expect they'll be showin' up here any day now. We all have to be on the lookout fer them. If'n they give us any trouble we'll jest call the sheriff. I'm gonna take a walk."

Today was Saturday. The day she was supposed to meet Sam in town. She wondered if he remembered and if he did, how long did he wait for her. She had to forget about him for now. Her life was in too much of a turmoil, but she sure did like him.

❧   ❧   ❧

Even in a sparsely populated valley with no telephones news traveled. Barely two days went by before Lily's family heard about Nevers' death. Her stepfather, Earl and Lily's mother, Alma, showed up in a horse drawn wagon wrapped in blankets to ward off the cold October morning. They had brought along Earl's son and his wife for reinforcement. A couple of other men, who were probably Lily's brothers, were also in the back of the wagon.

"Here they come," Lily said, when she heard the bell on the gate clanging against the post. Sure didn't take them very long. Ya'll stay in here and let me take care of this myself. If'n I need you I'll yell."

Earl climbed down from the wagon and walked toward the porch with the aid of a cane. He didn't look big and scary to Lily this time. Lily pushed open the door and stood on the porch with her arms crossed over her chest. "Lily, girl. It's good ta see ya. Sorry ta heer about yer husband. We come ta see if ya needed any halp. Look ay you, all grow'd up and purty, too."

"I don't need anythin' from you," Lily replied.

Earl gave a startled look. "Lord a mighty gal. You kin talk. Praise the Lord, it's a reel miracle. Ma, lissen ta yer daughter. She kin talk," he called back to the wagon. "The Lord works in mysterious ways, don't he now?"

"Don't you talk about the Lord ta me you old coot. Jest git back in yer wagon and high tail it out of here. You ain't wanted at my house. If'n you think that Nevers left me a passel of money, yer wrong. He done left me nothin' but this house and land and you ain't gittin' one foot of it. So go on and git."

"Is that anyway ta talk ta me, Lily," We need help reel bad. Yer momma, she's got lumbago so bad, she can't git around and ya kin see I got a reel bad leg. And Zebulon," he said, pointing to the boy sitting in the wagon, he done got three youngins and one on the way. He ain't able ta find work. We gonna be in reel bad shape with winter comin' on."

"You should have thought of that six years ago when you sold me to Nevers. You ain't never done a decent day's work in yer life. I ain't doin' nothin' fer ya. Besides I got me a new husband and he's in charge now. We done went into the courthouse and had his name put on the deed. It belongs to both of us now. He says I coulda had you put in jail fer sellin' me"

"You got a new husband, already! Yer old husband ain't even cold in his grave. Lordy, girl, that's a sin ta take a new one right off."

"You ain't one ta talk about sinnin', Earl. Ain't any of yer business so go on and git before I call the sheriff and tell him yer trespassing on my property."

Lily's mother climbed down from the wagon and hobbled across the yard, holding her ragged coat close to her body. "I'm reel sorry fer what we done, Lily, but I'm yer mother and you …"

Lily interrupted her. "You ain't no kin to me. You done give up that right the first time you let Earl touch me and you knew about it. Ain't no mother would ever do that to her own child, plus sell her away to a nasty old man." Her voice softened as she choked back her tears. "Why'd you do that to me, Momma. I always loved you. I coulda forgiven you for most anythin' til you let Nevers take me away. Why, Momma?"

"Twernt nothin' I could do about it, Lily. It was all his doin'," she said pointing toward Earl. "He said if'n I didn't go along with what he wanted he was gonna kick me and all yer sisters and brothers outta the house. What was I ta do?"

"Doesn't matter anymore. You go on and git and don't come round here no more. I'm done with you and that's alls I gotta say. " Lily turned and went into the house. She ran into her room and closed the door.

The wagon sat in the yard for about ten minutes and then slowly turned and left.

"Are you okay?" Rachael asked. Lily sat on the bed cuddling Violet in her arms.

"I'm gonna be jest fine, Rachael." Tears ran down her face as she rocked back and forth. "Yeah, I'll be jest fine. You kin jest bet on yer life I ain't never gonna treat my daughter like I wuz treated. They are evil people, Rachael. They deserve anythin bad that comes to them."

"I reckon I better go tell momma and daddy about you and Ben. That is if'n they ain't heard it from somebody else. I'll be back in a little while," Rachael said. She dreaded making this trip. She knew just how are mother was going to react and she was right.

"We buried Nevers today and then Ben and Lily got married," Rachael blurted out. She stared at her mother sitting across the table from her, waiting for her reaction.

"You mean ta tell me, that Lily ain't even waitin' til her husband is cold in the grave afore she married my son? The Lord have mercy on them."

"Oh, Momma, come on. You know that Nevers was a mean, old bastard and that he treated Lily terrible. She loves Ben and she'll take good care of him," Rachael replied.

"How they had time ta git close to each tuther lessen they wuz doin' somethin' they twernt supposed to be doin' while she wuz still a married woman. Sides, Lily done stole my only granddaughter from Emma Jane and I reckon she married my son for his army pension. Even if'n' Nevers twernt a good husband, she ain't got no right ta do this."

Rachael stood up. "Well, Momma, let me tell you what really happened. When them gypsies showed up at the house Ben bought Violet from Emma Jane and Jimmy Dell for one hundred dollars. They wanted more, but he wouldn't give it to them. I'm sure if'n we hadn't taken the baby in, they'd gone on their way and sold the baby to someone else."

"Yer lyin'!" Ida Mae screamed, putting her hands over her ears.

"No, I ain't, Momma. Ben married Lily so she wouldn't lose her house and land to her family. They've already come round tryin' to git it. Lily would be out in the cold again. She's had a hard enough life already. You jest better accept it and come down and see yer sons and granddaughter once in a while."

"I ain't never comin' to that house and she ain't welcome here. Now I got work ta do, so you go on and git." Ida Mae disappeared into the back of the house.

"Don't be too hard on her, Rachael. She's goin' through a hard time," Roy said. Rachael didn't know that her father was sitting on the porch by the window listening to their conversation. She gave him a quick hug. "Momma jest closen her head. "I'm jest tryin' to make her understand, but she won't listen. What'd you think about all this?"

"I'm, stayin' ta myself, girl. I reckon it's all true, but reel hard fer yer mamma ta swaller. I can't believe my own flesh and blood would sell her own baby. I blame it on them gypsies. They done tainted Emma Jane's head. I'm glad that the baby is safe and ya'll are doin' okay. Can't say the same fer us. Vittles are reel scarce round heah and so is heatin' wood. I reckon it's time fer you and Jesse ta come on back home and leave them be."

Rachel knew her father was once again worried about himself by not willing to do anything about it. She reached in her pocket and handed her father a ten-dollar bill. "Here, get some food. I'll send Jesse down here to cut some logs for you. Maybe you could cut a few yerself. I got to go. I ain't comin' back here til things are settled down and besides I don't think mamma really wants us back." Walking to the back of the house, she raised her voice. "I'm leavin' now, Momma. I gave Daddy some money for food. I love you."

She cried all the way home.

Chapter Twenty-Seven

"Now, this is the way it's gonna be, Rachael. You, Jesse and me are gonna take the load into town. I want to talk to Clyde Orby," Ben said.

"But, I'm the one that always does business with him, Ben. I think I can handle it," she replied.

"You done a fine job of taken care of us, but I think this is a man's job. Clyde won't cotton to doin' business with a woman when it comes ta him havin' ta pay us more. Jest let me handle it, okay?'

"What about me and Violet?" Lily asked. "If'n ya'll go off to Lynch I'll be here all alone. What if'n someone comes by? I'm scared somethin bad will happen while yer gone."

"You won't be alone," Ben replied. "Old Joe will be here. I'll give him my shotgun afore I leave. Ya'll be fine."

"I bet old Joe can't even hit the side of a barn, you better leave it with me," Lily replied.

The truck loped along the bumpy road, every once in a while leaving out a loud bark and releasing a cloud of black smoke behind them. "You heer that?" Ben asked. "It's a bad exhaust systems. I bet the spark plugs ain't been changed in this truck in yars. When we go shoppin' I'm gonna buy some parts fer this old buggy and fix it up real good. I ain't teched a motor since…well, you know…my accident. I bet I kin git her runnin' faster than greased lighten'. Then if'n them revenuers come after us, they'll be in fer a big surprise."

"Jesse leaned forward in the driver's seat. "What'd you mean, revenuers chasin' us? I ain't runnin' from no revenuers. They got guns so you can count me out."

Ben let out a chuckle. "Yeah, this old hunk of rust is gonna run like a scalded dog when I git through with it."

Ben pulled the truck behind Clyde's store and waited until Jesse brought his chair to him. Clyde watched from the doorway of the warehouse. He wondered why they had brought the cripple along. Instead of unloading the boxes as usual, the three came toward him. "Clyde, you and me have to talk," Ben said. "Do you want ta step inside yer store?"

Without answering him, Clyde turned and went back inside, followed by the Rileys. ""Okay, what's this all about? I'm a busy man."

"Well, Clyde, we have been doen some figuerin' and we decided that from now on, we want forty cents fer each gallon stead of twenty cents you were given Nevers.

Clyde let out a bellow. "Who do you think you are comin' in here and making demands on me. I ain't about to give you that much. You take the twenty cents and be glad yer getting' that."

"No, we don't have to take it. I got tuther customer that's willin' to give me forty-five cents, but since you been doin' business with Nevers fer so long, I was gonna give you a break. You know that we been bringin' you good stuff. Better than most that's around these parts," Ben said.

Clyde pointed toward the door. "Take yer kin and git out. Good luck with yer new customer."

Rachael was stunned. She had no idea that Ben was going to ask for so much. She knew he wanted more money, but forty cents, that was a lot and who was he talking about?

She knew nothing about another person wanting to buy their liquor."

"If'n that's the way you feel, we'll be leavin' now," Ben said, turning his chair and starting toward the door. Rachael and Jesse followed slowly behind him. He stopped and turned his chair around. Pointing his finger at Clyde he said, "That thar stuff you been gettin' is the best around these parts and you know it. Besides who else brings you apple and peach licker?"

"Wait! You done got me over a barrel. I got people waitin' for this load. I'll pay you forty this time."

"Then I assume you don't want any next week, that right?" Ben asked.

"Aw, I ain't got no choice. You damn Rileys are givin' me a pain in my backside. If'n yer gonna charge me more yer gonna have to start bringin' me more. Yer cuttin' me to ta bone. I want you to double yer order. Now git them boxes unloaded." He stomped off into the front of the store with Rachael right behind him.

"Clyde I was wonderin' if you have seen Sam around lately?

"Yeah, he stopped by last Saturday. He was lookin' fer you. He said if I saw you I should tell you that he had to leave for a few weeks."

"Well, why didn't you tell me?" she asked.

"I jest did," he replied.

Sam had sat on the bench in front of the drugstore for almost an hour on that Saturday before he went inside. He was disappointed that she wasn't coming.

Billy Tate passed by the lunch counter looking for an empty stool. At the end of the counter he sat down next to Sam, who was reading the paper. "Mind if I sit a spell?" he asked.

Sam looked over his paper. "No problem." He went back to reading.

After he had ordered, Billy fidgeted with the sugar jar and dumped three toothpicks on the counter. "Ya still mad at me, Sam? You know'd I was only funnin' with Rachael. She ain't been around lately. You seen her?"

Sam folded the paper when his plate of bacon and eggs were set before him. "No, I haven't. You just keep your hands to yourself and everything will be just fine. Now leave me alone and let me eat my breakfast."

The silence only lasted a few minutes. "Did you ever wonder how them Rileys are livin' out there with no income except the stuff they sell to Clyde? I been by thar place and it's lookin' real nice. I heer they been givin' money to their folks, too. Seems sort of strange. Some say that Nevers left them a pile of money. Wonder where he got it? Not from them old skins he used to sell?'

"Why don't you just mind your own business, Billy? Doesn't seem that what they're doing is hurting you or anyone else. Just leave it be." Sam put fifty cents on the counter, picked up his paper and left.

Rachael and Jesse took the sacks of dried meats and jars of jelly to the front of the store. They removed the canvas cover from the back of the truck and began stacking the brown boxes in the corner. When they were done, Jesse helped Ben back into the truck and they pulled out of the alleyway onto the main street. They had no idea that the man standing across the street had watched them pull in and now watched as they pulled away. They didn't look back to see him slowly cross the street and make his way down the alley. Clyde didn't see the man standing in the shadows of the building and watch him through the window as he funneled the clear liquid into tall brown bottles and repacked it into white boxes. Two hours later the man sat on a bench in front of Clyde's store smoking a cigarette. When the second truck arrived, he took out a piece of paper and a stub of a pencil and wrote down the license number. Sticking it into his pocket, he meandered down the sidewalk toward the café.

Ben grinned from ear to ear. "That was a lot easier than I though it was gonna be. He wants twice as much. We're gonna make a lot of money, yep a lot of money."

"That was risky," Rachel said. "He could have jest as well told us to get out. Then what would we have done?"

"Well, he didn't and now we got ta make tracks. We got a lot of brewin' to do in the next week. When we git home I want you ta break out that Sears catalog. We're gonna do some shoppin'. I want to buy some parts for the truck. With a few parts and a lot of elbow grease I reckon I can get this truck runnin' as fast as anythang on these roads."

Arriving home, the aroma of bacon greeted them. "Man, that sure does smell good. Looks like Lily cooked us up some vittles," Ben said. To their surprise it was old Joe who was cooking. He had never spent more than a few minutes in the house but today he was making a grand mess of the kitchen.

"What's goin' on, where's Lily," Rachael asked.

"She's in the bed with the baby. The baby's ailin," he answered. "I wuz hungry."

"Lily, what's wrong with Violet?" Rachael asked, pushing open the door.

"She's been cryin' all day. I can't git her ta stop. I'm real worried about her, Rachael."

Rachael picked up the wailing baby and held her close for a moment, listening to her chest. Laying her on the bed, she pulled up her nightshirt and unpinned her diaper. Everything looked okay to her. "Well, she ain't a rattlin' and it don't look like she's got a rash. Putting her finger into Violet's mouth, the baby gurgled and sucked on Rachael's finger. "I think she's just jest tryin' to cut some teeth, Lily. Look, her gums are all red and swollen. She stopped cryin' when I rubbed them. You need to let her suck on a cold cloth and see if that helps."

" I was so worried. I kept thinkin' what would I do if she died. I love her so much." Lily picked up Violet and carried her into the kitchen. Once the cloth was put in her mouth she stopped crying and soon was asleep.

"Now that we're all here, we might as well have our talk," Ben said. "Rachael go get the money box."

"Why?" she asked.

"Cause I reckon we'd all like to see how much we got now and git the catalog while yer at it."

Rachael reluctantly left the room. Reaching into the top of her dresser she uncovered the box. This was the first time that she had ever shared the box with the others. This had always been her domain. She didn't like how she was feeling. After all she was the one who had always made all the plans to keep things running smooth. They had trusted her to be in charge and now, Ben was suddenly making the decisions. She didn't like it one bit.

Putting the box on the table, Ben opened it and stared at the bills neatly bundled and tied with string. "How much you reckon we got in this box, Rachael?"

"We been takin' out about twenty dollars a week to live on, so I reckon there should be about nine hundred dollars left."

"Got dang," Jesse yelled. "Nine hundred dollars. Damn, we are plumb rich."

Rachael slammed her hand on the table. "No, we are not! I figure we need at least three times that much to git to Florida and find a place to live. We can't go spendin' any more money than we have to."

"Look, I know yer hell bent on goin' to Florida, Rachael, but right now we need to buy some things. Since Clyde is gonna pay us more, we'll make it back in no time," Ben said. "Besides, right now we kin still pass off the money we spend as cash that Nevers had stashed away if anybody has a mind ta ask us how come we got cash to spend."

Lily was the first to open the catalog. "Kin we jest circle what we want and then Rachael kin go into Lynch and call in our order? Ben pulled his chair next to hers and Jesse hovered over them as they slowly turned the pages. "What do you need, Rachael and how about you Joe? Where's Rachael?"

"She jest went out the door. I don't need nothin'. I don't spect I'm gonna be around much longer. No sense spendin' money on an old man. Lessen you see some warm long johns in that book and a big ole pack of chaw." He cackled a toothless grin. I'll be goin' out ta the barn now." No one answered. They were too engrossed in the catalog.

Joe walked slowly down the path to the smokehouse. It was time to put some more wood on the fire. Carrying three logs in his arm he pushed open the door. Rachael was sitting next to the still, her head buried in her hands. She jumped when he pushed back the wall. "Sorry if'n I scart you, Gal. I didn't know you were in here. What's goin' on with you? You cryin'?"

"I'm okay, Joe. I reckon I'm jest feelin' a little under appreciated right now. I mean, they're in the house pourin' over that book and not even thinkin' about savin' money. They don't seem so helpless now. Where were they when I really needed them? The whole idée behind my plan was ta save as much as we kin, not go off an spend it."

"You feelin' plumb sorry fer yerself, eh?"

"Yes, I reckon I am," she replied, tears filling her eyes.

"Taint unusual. Money turns people. Turned me yars ago and I paid fer it. Once I started makin' money on moonshine I got myself a whole passel of woes. Let em have thar fun. Then in a few days start makin' them feel real scart about what's ahead of em and put the fear of God in em. They'll sit up and take note and start lookin' up to you agin." Joe threw his head back and laughed.

Rachael rubbed her eyes with the hem of her shirt. "How do I do that, Joe?"

"Jest start talkin' bout the law and about other rum runners that could be lookin' ta take over this still. Git them brewin' night and day and make yer money back fast. It's a real fact, Gal, we could be out of business in the blink of an eye ball. This ain't no easy business. We been reel lucky, so far, but luck don't last forever. Hell, Gal, yer still a youngin, still wet behind the ears and yer runnin' rum. Might do you some good ta think about what would happen if ya git caught."

Rachael's eyes widened. "I reckon I jest don't want ta think about that stuff, but yer right. Thanks. I have to go back and talk to them."

They were still sitting at the table when she went into the house." So here's my idee. From now on we're gonna figure up our expenses and then we're gonna divide the extry money four ways. Ya'll can do what you like with yer money, but I'm gonna keep on savin' mine. That so when the revenuers come sniffin' round I'll have enough ta make a run for it. Good luck to you guys."

On the following trip to Lynch, Rachael counted out the money and she took her share and handed the rest to Ben.

Chapter Twenty-Eight

Old Joe was pacing back and forth across the yard when the truck pulled in. "Some fella come round while you was gone ta Lynch. I was outside and I didn't heer the bell on the gate. I reckon he come round from the back and climbed ovah the fence. When I seed him standin' on the porch I got my gun outta the barn. He said he come to see Nevers. I told him that Nevers was dead. He didn't seem none too surprised. Didn't even ask me how it happened. I knew'd he wasn't from round here since he didn't know bout Nevers. He asked who was livin' here and I told him it weren't none on his concern. He said he'd be back and then he went on down the road and I heered a car motor a little time later. He musta had someone a waitin' fer him. He was a reel nasty lookin' feller, with them little beady eyes and big ole scar that run clear across his face. Looked like somebody cut him up reel good. He had a big fishin' knife stuck in his belt loop."

Lily pulled Violet closer to her. "Do you think it was the gypsies? Do you think they come back for my baby?"

Rachael shook her head. "No, I'd think it must be some kin or friend of that fella that Never's killed."

"I know'd who that fella wuz!" Jesse said. "That thar is the same fella I give a ride to a couply weeks ago. Wonder what thar still doin' round here. They told me they wuz jest passin' through. We got some trouble on our hands. I bet they know'd that Nevers had sumthin' ta do with his brother disappearin'."

189

"I reckon we better take turns stayin' up at night and makin' sure they don't come sneakin' round while we're all asleep. I'm not reel tired, I'll stay up tonight. Jesse, you load me up another one of those shotguns."

"You wake me in a couply hours, Rachael and I'll come out and spell you," Jesse said, his voice a little shaky.

"Come on, Gal, I'll sit up with ya fer a spell," Joe said as he and Rachael headed for the barn. "Ya like a swig of moon or a chaw?"

"No, thanks, Joe. If'n I did that I'd probably fall right to sleep," Rachael replied. "Let's jest sit and talk. Tell me bout yerself, Joe. You ever been married?"

"Oh yeah, couple, three times. First time I was jest a youngin. Hell, her and me didn't even know what we wuz doin'. Then one day she jest said she was a goin' home. Second time I married a gal from town. She was sumthin', but when she got riled she liked to throw things and hit me in the head. Lawdy, she bout knocked the brains outta me. I wuz afeared ta go ta sleep at night with her lyin' next to me. One day I jest took off. I hid out in the mountains. I herd she was comin' through Bent Creek with a big ole stick a lookin' fer me, but I wuz too smart fer her." He slapped his knee and cackled. "Don't rightly know if I divorced either them women. Then thar was Silvy. Her grandpappy was a Seminole Chief. She had real dark eyes and long hair. Had some long Indian name, but I jest called her Silvy. She could cook up a mess of corn biscuits and deer stew that would git yer mouth ta waterin'."

"I thought you wuz the one with Seminole blood in ya, Joe,"

"Naw, ain't got nary a drop of injun blood in me. Ain't even been in a teepee." He let out another loud laugh. "It was jest a good story ta tell."

"You ever had any kids?" Rachael asked.

"Oh, yeah, I had a mess of youngins. Nine or ten I reckon. Some died young, whoopen cough and sech, some jest left home and a few was kilt in the mines."

"That's real sad. What happened to Silvy?" Rachael asked.

"When I went off ta prison, she jest left. Don't rightly know what happened to her or my kids."

"Didn't you ever try to find any of them?"

"Nope. No sense havin' an old codger like me hangin' round them. Thar pert near better off, I reckon." He stretched his hands over his head. "And now my time is a nearin' ta meet mah maker, so's I better go do some prayin'. Thar are things that are meant ta be. Ya can't change them. Thar jest meant to be. I jest hope I don't run into all three of them women at the same time." He let out a loud laugh.

Rachael stood up and picked up the rifle. "You get some rest, Joe. I reckon I better git ready fer a long night." She climbed up into the loft and took her position near the overhead door. She had a clear view of the yard and the path leading to the house. Ben had strung a rope across the boards of the gate. Even the slightest movement would set the bell in motion. If she saw or heard anything, she was to wake up everyone. Old Joe sat down on his cot below the loft and hollered up to her. "Mah bones is tired and I'm gonna rest, Rachael, but if'n you need me you jest let out a yell."

The house was completely dark when Lily crept silently across the kitchen with her sleeping baby in her arms. Lily pushed open the door of the bedroom and stepped inside. "Jesse," she whispered. "Jesse, get up. Go sleep in Rachael's room."

Groggy and half asleep, Jesse, clad only in his long johns, mumbled something and left the room. Crawling under the covers, Lily positioned Violet between herelf and Ben. Ben moved slightly and then turned over. "What's goin' on?"

"I need ta sleep with you Ben. I'm scart. I need ta keep Violet safe. Is that okay?"

"I reckon, since yer already here. Sides, yer my wife." He pulled his blanket closer to him, trying to conceal the stumps of his legs. Someday he would show her them, but not now. It was too soon. He lay in the darkness, his thoughts no longer on sleep.

Rachael too was staring into the darkness. *What was she doing? Sitting in a hayloft with a gun on her lap waiting for who knows what? She was just Rachael Riley, a poor girl from the holler. She had to talk to Ben in the morning about speeding things up. Maybe they could find someone else that would buy the shine from them. Two customers would make the money come in a lot faster.* She yawned. *Wake up, Rachael, you got to make it through this night. What was that! Crap, scared the heck out of me. It's just a raccoon rummaging for food. Hope he stays away from the chicken house.* She yawned again. Her eyes fluttered and then closed. She leaned back against a hay bale. *Just a few minutes rest and I'll be fine.*

Rachael was jolted awake by a rooster sitting just a few feet away from announcing that it was morning. Sitting up she looked around for a moment forgetting where she was. Rachael stood up and brushed the hay off her pants. Moving down the ladder, she saw Joe still under the covers in his bunk. It seemed unusual. He was always up before the sun. She walked passed him and into the house.

"You sleep good?" Jesse asked, stuffing a biscuit into his mouth. He brushed the crumbs off the table with the back of his hand."

"I stayed awake as long as I could. How'd you know I fell asleep?'

"Cause I come out there and checked on you. You was plumb out of it. I coulda hit you in the head and you'd been dead. You didn't even hear me. I sit up in that loft all night and you never stirred. Some lookout you are."

"Okay, okay, so I'm not a good guard. Leastwise nothin' happened."

Jesse threw his leg over the bench. "Not any thanks to you." He stomped out the door.

Rachael was in no mood to be challenged. She threw open the screen door and yelled after him. "You come back and clean up the mess you made in here. I'm not yer maid." She slammed the door. In a few seconds it flew open again.

"You lissen to me Rachael Riley, I ain't about ta die cause of this damn still. I'll be leavin' here soon and you can count on that." This time Jesse slammed the door.

A few minutes later he was back again. Not to clean up the mess, but to tell give her some bad news. "Old Joe is dead! When he twernt in the smoke house, I went a lookin' fer him. He was still in the bed. He's as cold as a cucumber, he musta died sometime durin' the night."

"Oh, Lordy, I walked right passed him, I thought he was jest sleepin'. Poor, old Joe. Me and him had a long talk last night. He's been tellin' me that his time was nearin', but I didn't pay him no mind," Rachael said.

Jesse ran his hand across his forehead. "I reckon we better bury him. We kin dig up that empty box we buried. If'n I go and buy one, Mabry will want to know who died. We can't have them comin' out here snoopin' around. I'll get started."

By afternoon, the rough-hewn box was unearthed. Jesse wrapped Joe's frail body in his plaid blanket and placed him in the coffin.

"I reckon we should all say a few words to send him off," Lily said as they all stood around the grave. "I'll go first. I want to thank you Joe for all yer help. Violet really liked you and she'll miss you. You were a nice man and I hope you go to heaven. That's all, amen."

Ben was next. "We got along reel good, you and me, Joe. I liked talkin' ta you while we wuz in the smoke house. Good-bye old friend. And I want ta thank you fer givin' us yer recipes." Ben put a handful of dirt on the coffin.

"You go next, Jesse," Rachael said.

"I ain't sayin nothin'. Jest leave me alone." He turned and ran down the hill.

Rachael stepped forward. "I remember the first time you and I met, Joe and I thought we would never be as close as we were. You were a might strange, but you had a hard life and I'm glad these last few months were better for you." Rachael bowed her head, now let's all pray."

After the coffin was covered, Lily and Rachael struggled to get Ben's chair down the hill. Once in the yard, Rachael headed to the barn. She waited a moment for her eyes to adjust to the dim light in Joe's room. She sat down on his cot and folded her hands. *God please take care of Joe. He really didn't mean to do anythin' wrong. It was me who talked him into it. Look at this place, God? Did you ever see a man leavin' this earth havin' so little? He had one change of underwear, a tin of tobacco and half a jug of liquor. I promise if I get enough money and get away from here I'll find a church and donate some money in Joe's name. That's all I have to say for right now, but I sure hope you understand. Amen.*

Chapter Twenty-Nine

"Some bodies a comin'!" Jesse yelled from the porch. "Bell is a clangin' on the fence. Stay whar you are till I find out who it is."

The bell clanged again as the gate was closed and a man in jeans and a white shirt strode up the path. Jesse recognized him as he came closer. Standing next to the open window, Jesse said, "It's Sam Bradford. I reckon he's here ta see Rachael."

"Oh, good Lord," Rachael said running toward the bathroom. "I look a mess. Give me a minute to get presentable. She pulled her tee shirt over her head and grabbed a blue blouse out of the closet. Tucking the blouse into her pants, she ran a brush through her hair and pulled it back into a ponytail. That was the best she could do. Trying to remain calm she walked outside and greeted Sam. "Well, hi there. What brings you out to these parts?"

Sam grinned. "I came to see you and make sure everything was okay. I just stopped by and saw your parents."

Rachael was annoyed. "Why did you stop there? I told you I was livin' here."

"I had a letter for them. I stopped in Mabry's store and he said he had mail for your parents and they hadn't been into the store in over a week. I told him I would take it to them. I hope that was all right."

"Oh, sure that's fine. I wonder who it was from?" Rachael said, her voice softening.

"It was from the Department of Defense. They sent your parents a check for twenty dollars that was left over from an account Ben had started when he joined up. Your mom had me read it to them. Needless to say, they were pretty happy about it. You may want to make sure they get to the bank and get it cashed."

Rachael nodded. "I surely will. Thank you. Would you like to stay fer dinner? I got green beans and ham on the stove. It's already made."

"Sounds good to me. That's my favorite meal."

The conversation flowed during dinner with Sam doing most of the talking. Jesse and Ben both seemed relaxed around him after a few minutes and had lots of questions. Lily just smiled, knowing that he had come to see Rachael. That made her happy to think that someone was interested in Rachael.

After dinner, Sam went outside and sat down on the porch swing. Rachael was glad he had decided to stay. While she filled the glasses with lemonade, Lily stood on her tiptoes looking out the kitchen window.

"He sure is cute, Rachael."

"Shush, Lily, he might hear you. He is cute, isn't he?" She could feel her face getting red.

Before long, everyone, including Violet was occupying the porch. The last warm evenings of Indian summer were coming to an end. There was a lot of discussion and laughing about when they were all children and then a serious moment when Ben told Sam about losing his legs.

"Well, don't you worry, Ben, with all these pretty women around to take care of you, I don't think you'll ever go hungry." Rachael blushed and Lily giggled. Trying not to be too obvious, Jesse and Ben had to leave to tend to the still and Lily said it was Violet's bedtime.

"I like your family, Rachael. I guess it's good to be a part of something. That's one thing I miss being away from home. "

They walked along the path leading to the creek. "I'm sorry you missed our picture show date. I waited for you, but then I heard about Nevers. The next day I had to go back to Ohio for a few days. Did Clyde give you my message?"

"Kind of. He didn't tell me that you had gone off. Is that what it was...a date. I mean, why would you want to date me?"

"Well, let's see. You're easy to talk to, we have a lot in common and besides that you're kind of cute," he said grinning.

Rachael knew she was blushing again. "You go on, I'm not at all cute, not one bit." A brilliant, orange butterfly skimmed close to Rachael's face and circled around her head. "Watch this, Sam, my daddy taught me this." Licking the back of her hand, she extended her arm out and stood quietly while the butterfly glided closer to her and landed on her hand. "It's a Monarch," Rachael whispered. She's after the salt in my saliva. That's called a butterfly kiss." A few seconds later the butterfly took flight.

"Can I kiss you, Rachael?" Sam asked, as he stepped closer to her.

Rachael smiled and moved toward him. "You sure can."

Sam drew her into his arms. His lips softly touched her cheek and moved across her face catching the corner of her mouth. His hand circled her head and pulled her body into his. It was slow and deliberate and Rachael could feel her knees going weak. When he finally released her, she stood with eyes closed not really wanting to move away from him.

"That was really nice, Sam. Thank you."

Sam began to laugh. "I'm not making fun, but I never had a girl thank me for kissing them."

"Maybe because that wasn't the girl's first kiss. That was mine. I'm nearin' nineteen and you were the first one to kiss me, Sam. Gosh, most girls my age are married and havin' kids."

"Let's fix that, Rachael. He kissed her again and then again. "Now, you've been kissed more than once. And now, it's getting dark, we better get back to the house." He took her hand and they slowly walked up the path. "Try to get into Lynch on Saturday around two, Rachael, and I promise you I'll take you to the movies."

"I promise, I'll be there." He kissed her again and turned to leave. She stood on the porch until she heard the clanging of the bell on the gate.

Lily was listening to the radio and rocking Violet. "Lily, I think I'm in love," Rachael blurted out and then went to her room to relive every minute of the evening.

The following Saturday, Rachael and Sam went to the movies and on Sunday they went fishing. On Monday, Sam took Rachael to see her parents. She wanted to make sure that the twenty dollars check was cashed and that her father was given the right amount of money. She sat close to him in his car and he held her hand.

"There's Daddy," Rachael said as they pulled into the yard. "He's playin' that dang card game again."

Roy looked up and then yelled for Ida Mae. "Some body is a comin'. Well, lookee there, it's Rachael gettin' out of that fancy automobile with Sam."

"Hi, Daddy. You remember Sam. He brought you the letter the other day."

"Course I do. I ain't fergettin' things yet. Why you comin' around today? We twernt expectin' you."

" You might as well wait in the car, Sam. I reckon this is gonna be a short visit," Rachael said as she stepped on to the porch. "I come to see if you need me to take yer check to the bank in Lynch and cash it for you."

"Ain't necessary. Done got it cashed two days ago. Mabry done it for me. Give me back a whole mess of five dollar bills."

Ida Mae stood with her hands crossed over her chest, not saying a word. "How are you, Momma?' Rachael asked.

"Doin' jest fine, as if'n it matters at tall to you. Ya'll want some water. Ain't got no coffee. Can't get to the store on foot."

"I'm sorry, Momma. I'll come by in the truck tomorrow and take you to Mabry's so that you can get some supplies. About nine okay?'

"I reckon it will have ta be." Ida Mae turned and went into the house.

"That thar fella yer boyfriend, Rachael?" Roy asked.

Rachael could once again feel herself turning red. "No, Daddy. He's not my boyfriend. We're jest friends."

"Then why's he hangin' round. Seems to me you were sittin' mighty close to each tuther in that car."

"We have to go, Daddy. Tell Momma I'll see her in the morning." Rachael hurried down the steps before her father could say anything else. She was quiet until the car pulled out onto the road. "I'm sorry, Sam. My daddy jest says whatever he's thinkin'. He really has no couth at all."

Sam laughed. "I thought it was real funny. By the way, who is your boyfriend? If it isn't me who is it?"

Rachael was silent until they reached the road leading to the gate. "Did I say something to make you mad, Rachael?" Sam asked.

"No, I was just thinkin' about us and wonderin' if maybe I'm gettin' too attached to you? I mean, I know you probably have had a lot of girlfriends and…"

Sam put his finger to her lips. "You really think too much sometimes. He pulled the car to the side of the road and took her into his arms. "I've had other girlfriends, but that doesn't make any difference. Right now, I'm with you. He kissed her tenderly. She laid her head on his chest. She didn't want to leave him. "I put on a pot of ham hocks and green beans before I left, I know it's yer favorite. Would you like to come in and eat?"

"I'd love to, Rachael, but I have to get back to Lynch and pack. I'm going to be gone for a few days."

"Whar you going? When will you be back?"

"I'm just going up to Pine Ridge to take a look around."

"Why would you go up there? Who would build a railroad on the mountain?" she asked.

"I'm not suppose to tell anyone what I am going to tell you, but I like you too much to go on lying to you. I'm not a surveyor, Rachael. I'm a Federal Agent. I work for the Department of Alcohol, Tobacco and Firearms."

She could feel a cold chill running down her back. He had to be kidding her. "Yer not, yer joshin' me, ain't you?"

"No, I joined the agency two years ago. They sent me here when they found out I was familiar with this part of the country. Seems there's a pretty big moonshine operation working somewhere in this area. I figured it was coming out of Lynch, but I haven't been able to find anyone there who knows anything and if they do know, they're not talking. Whoever it is, has been sending it by truck to Chicago. It's being sold to clubs in Chicago and causing a big criminal element to operate there. Ordinarily we don't mess around with the little stills that the hollow people have in their sheds. It's only when it gets this big that the government steps in. They want this operation shut down and soon. I'm going up to the mountain and see if I can find any signs of it. I know everyone in these parts is tight-lipped when it comes to giving out information. I just can't figure how whoever is doing this is getting it passed me. I'm sorry I didn't tell you the truth, but this is got to be kept between you and me."

Rachael nodded her head. "Sure, I mean…I won't tell a soul. I'm jest surprised." She kissed him quickly and opened the car door. "I'll walk from here. You better to git a goin'. I'll see you when you git back." Before he could protest she ran to the gate and climbed over it and headed for the house. "No, dammit, dammit, dammit!" She kept repeating. "An agent, he's a friggen revenuer, dammit."

Rachael jerked open the screen door and stomped in. "Yer not going to believe this. Sam ain't no surveyor, he works fer the government. He's a revenuer. He's here ta find out who is runnin' moonshine. Sam is a lookin' fer us!"

Ben put his spoon in his bowl of beans. "Well ain't that jest a whippin'. So that's why so many round here are gettin' raided. It's Sam. He's a turnin' everyone in to the law."

"Naw, I think that's jest the sheriff doin' that. Those are jest piddly moon shiners. Sam's lookin' fer the one that's sending all the liquor up North. That's us!" Rachael said.

"Ya know, Rachael, this might not be a bad thang fer us. I reckon he don't suspect you at tall. That means he'll jest keep on lookin' somewheres else until he finally gives up and leaves."

"Ben Riley, you can't mean that. I like Sam. I like him a lot. Am I supposed to pretend that everythin' is jest fine?"

"Look, girl, we need four more deliveries to meet our goal. The minister at the Baptist church in Lynch is interested in this place since we got lectricity and indoor plumin'. With the money from the sale of the house and land and what we got already we should be jest fine. You need ta hold on a while longer."

Rachael bit her tongue. What she wanted to say is that if all of them hadn't spent so much money on stuff, they would have enough right now. Instead she blurted out, "I don't know if I can do that."

Jesse wiped his mouth on his sleeve and pushed back his chair. "What makes you think that once Sam was done with his job here he was gonna stay. You think he's gonna give up his job with the government and come live here with you in Bent Creek? I sure don't think so."

She hadn't even given that thought. She hated the idea that Jesse was probably right. "All right, four more deliveries and then we're finished bein' bootleggers and we kin moved ta Florida. It ain't gonna be easy, but I'll do it."

"These beans you made are real tasty," Lily said. "You want some?"

"No thanks, I'd probably just choke on them." Rachael headed for her room to have a good cry

ॐ   ॐ   ॐ

Sam checked his backpack to make sure he had everything he needed to spend the night in the mountains. It would be the first time in many years he would go up to Black Mountain. Slowly driving through the meandering trails that had been there for hundreds of years, he parked his car under a canopy of trees. After trekking through the woods for most of the day without finding any clues that would lead him to a still, Sam stopped to make camp. He spread his blanket on the ground and gathered up enough firewood to keep him warm and safe from predators through the hours of darkness.

As a kid, he had spent many nights camped out with his father on the rim of this mountain. It was the only thing he and his father ever were able to do together that didn't cost money. With most of his father's time consumed with working in the mine and taking care of his family, the hours spent alone with him were precious memories to Sam. Tramping through the woods his father pointed out trees and bushes that provided nourishment enough to live on for days. He taught Sam how to make a shelter of pine branches to protect him from the cold and how to start a fire from flint rock. During the day they would fish in the icy cold streams that rambled through the woods. At night they would sit at a campfire and cook the day's catch on a sharpened stick. His father would tell him stories about bear hunts and the legend of Seminole Joe. He would lay close to his father, rolled up in a blanket until the call of the morning doves awoke them. Sam never forgot those times or the many times he was told that he should never go to work in the mines. It was his father's death in the tunnel and Sam's move to Ohio that kept that from happening.

After high school it was his uncle's persistence that made him join the police force and in less than two years take a transfer to the Department of Alcohol, Tobacco and Firearms. It seemed strange that he would now be tracking down moonshine stills that were once a common sight in almost every yard in the hollow. Moonshine ran as easy as water to the hill people. It was their way of easing the pain that engulfed them every day of their lives. It didn't seem like a very big deal to him at that time.

He wasn't prepared for the briefing sessions that outlined the bootlegging industry that was producing large volumes of distilled spirits and then shipping them up north. The shiners he was now encountering were mean men, serious as hell about their business and not happy about anyone putting a stop to it. A list on the wall of the bureau named all the agents killed in moonshine raids. Sam had no idea that he would be involved in gunfights and chases. It was all part of his job, now and he wasn't sure he liked it one bit.

And now there was his relationship with Rachael. That was something he hadn't planned on. He liked her a lot. She was funny and smart in her own way. He liked her assertive attitude and the easy conversation that flowed between them. He also liked her soft lips and the way she smelled of lavender soap.

What in the world was he going to do about Rachael?

Chapter Thirty

To keep Sam from getting suspicious, Rachael told him it would be easier to meet him in town on Saturday. Keeping him away from Clyde's store was critical. Once in town, she would run down the street to the café to meet him. She kept him busy for about an hour until she was sure that the truck had been unloaded. Twice Rachael had invited him to her house for supper. Everyone treated him like he was an old friend and she could see that he felt really comfortable around Ben and Jesse. She hated what she was doing, but she had convinced herself that it was for the best. Even if she cared for him, she knew he would probably be leaving soon. It was only when they were alone and they were wrapped in each other arms that she wanted to scream out loud and tell him the truth. She was totally in love with him.

Just about the time she decided she couldn't keep up the charade and tell him the truth, the decision to confess and stop moon shining was made for her. It was another Saturday and time for a delivery to Clyde's store. Jesse wasn't feeling well and even though she hated going alone, Rachael had no choice. It was one of their largest deliveries and would make them a lot of money. Today was also the day she was going to tell Sam the truth.

It had started raining that morning, a cold, steady rain that put a chill in her bones. By the time the truck was loaded, Rachael was soaked to the skin. She didn't have time to change. She was running late already. Shivering, she got behind the wheel and slowly pulled out of the yard, trying to avoid all the rain-filled ruts. She glanced at herself in the mirror. Her hair was a mess and her clothes were wrinkled and muddy. How would she explain her appearance to Sam?

While Rachael was on her way to Lynch, Clyde already had company in his store. Two men had entered the store. They stood around pretending to look at some of the hardware until all of the morning customers had left. Clyde called out to them, "Kin I hep ya?"

"Yeah, ya sure kin. I got a business proposition fer you," the largest man said.

"Sorry, I ain't buyin' anymore merchandise right now. Got too much stock as it is," Clyde said.

"Oh, I ain't a sellin' anythang. I jest want you to give me all yer money, that load of shine that'll be comin' round soon and then I'll let you stay alive. Now, that sounds like a pretty good proposition ta me," the man said.

Clyde backed up against the glass case, slowly reaching behind the counter for his pistol. His heart was thumping in his throat. One of his worse fears was coming true.

"I wouldn't do that if'n I wuz you." The man pulled a knife out of his belt and stuck it into the counter. The other man put a gun in Clyde's side and pushed him toward the back of the store. Clyde began to pray.

Rachael had made it to town and maneuvered the truck down the narrow alleyway next to Clyde's store. Pulling as close to the building as she could, she jumped down and pushed open the heavy door. Assuming that Clyde was in store waiting on a customer, Rachael began to unload the truck, stacking the heavy boxes on the wooden landing. After three trips, she decided to wait for him. Her back was already beginning to hurt from the weight of the boxes. Five minutes went by and still no Clyde. Getting impatient, Rachael walked to the door leading to the store and opened it just a few inches. There was no sign of him. Suddenly, without warning, someone came up behind her and jerked her away from the door, a hand covering her mouth. She struggled as her assailant dragged her backwards, her hands trying to pry his fingers loose from her face. Twisting just enough to turn her head a few inches, Rachael chomped down on the finger that was now almost all the way in her mouth. Her attacker let out a loud yowl and pushed her to the floor. Landing almost on her face, Rachael looked up to see Clyde's feet, tied to a chair in the far corner of the room. As she raised her head, she looked up and into his eyes. Clyde was bound with a horse rope, a rag tied across his mouth. She could see the fear in his eyes. "Git up, girl. I outta beat yer head in, you done near bit my finger off," the man, growled.

Rachael slowly sat up and faced him. She had never seen him before. He was short and stocky and dressed in coveralls. He held a red kerchief on his finger. "I outta smash yer head fer bittin' me," he snarled. Just as he moved toward her, another man entered the storeroom. A straw hat pulled down over his eyes covered most of his face. As he raised his head, she knew she was in trouble. It was the man with the scar running across his face, the mean looking bastard that Joe had described to her.

"We ain't got time fer all this crap, Norvelle. Leave her be."

"But, she done bit my finger, Cooter," he whined.

The man called Cooter pulled Rachael up by her arm and sat her down on a wooden stool. "Now, heres the way it's gonna be, Gal. You're gonna tell me where yer still is and where you got yer money hidden. Clyde, here, was nice enuf to pay us fer the shipment outside, but we want the rest of it. Now you jest tell me where it is and you kin go on yer way." He pulled a roll of bills from his overall pocket, which Rachael knew was the money that Clyde was going to give to her. "Cat got yer tongue, Girl. Ya better fess up I ain't got all day."

Rachael's mind was racing. She couldn't tell them where the still was. If they came out to the house they would probably kill all of them and take everything they owned. And what about Clyde? Were they going to kill him, too? She had to think fast.

"I don't know anythin'. I jest meet some man on the road and he puts this stuff in my truck and I bring it here. He pays me a few dollars for deliverin' it."

"Well ain't that jest a pack of lies. We been watchin' you fer over a month. We know'd fer sure you and yer family is runnin' a still. We been out ta yer house. Somethin' is a goin' on, you jest better fess up." His hand squeezed her face. "I ain't a patient man, so you jest speak up. Sides, Nevers done kilt my brother. I'm pert sure of that. I'm sorry Nevers done died, I wanted the pleasure of killin' him myself."

"It's up on Black Mountain, by Pine Ridge," she blurted out. "It's up where Nevers put it. It was too heavy fer us to move it. The money is a hidin' up there, too. We make the shine up thar and then haul it down each week and bring it here ta Lynch."

"That a fact? You tellin' me the truth, cause if'n you ain't you jest might be in a heap of trouble."

"That's the truth. I swear," she yelled out. "On my momma's grave, that's the truth."

"Well maybe you jest better take us up that thar mountain and show us where it is."

"What about Clyde?" she asked. "Why don't you let him go? He won't do you no harm."

" I was thinkin' on takin' him with us." He ran his finger over the blade of his knife. "Maybe I'll jest do him in right now and git it over with. Gimme the keys to yer truck."

"We won't all fit in the truck and if'n you don't unload it, ya'll lose half them cases going back up that steep ole mountain. You need ta leave it here and take yer car. That a way, Clyde kin stay here and make sure everythin' looks okay and watch over the cases. If'n you kill him and he's not here in the store people will wonder what happened to him. They may get suspicious, and start snoopin' around. If they find the liquor they'll probably take it or worse yet call the sheriff. That's a powerful lot of money in those boxes. You won't say anything, will you, Clyde?" Rachael looked at him with pleading eyes.

Clyde made a gurgling sound and shook his head the best he could. The scar faced man moved closer to Clyde and pulled his knife out of his belt. He placed it under Clyde's chin. "Now, this little girl thinks you kin keep yer mouth shut till we get back." He pushed the knife deeper into Clyde's throat and a trickle of blood began to run down his neck. "If'n we let you go, you ain't gonna say a thing are you, Clyde. Cause if'n you do, I'll come back and slit yer throat from ear to ear and the girl, too." He ran his hand over the scar on his face. "Yer gonna keep that truck full of shine safe fer us, ain't you, Clyde? Don't be thinkin' bout runnin' off in that there truck, cause I'll find you and I'll come back and kill this here girl right in front of you and ya'll have her blood on yer hands."

The fear in Clyde's eyes was a good enough answer. He nodded his head vigorously. His gag was removed from his mouth and with one quick movement the ropes binding him were cut. Clyde was in tears.
"I won't say nary a word, I promise," he said, choking back the sobs in his throat.

"Okay, come on gal, let's get a goin."

"Wait! Let me get my hat," Rachael said, as she bent down, she hurriedly whispered to Clyde, "Get Sam, Pine Ridge." It was all she had time to say before she was dragged outside and shoved into the backseat of Cooter's car. She thought to herself that Cooter was dumber than she imagined if he believed that Clyde was just going to go about his business as if nothing had happened. Cooter was really a stupid but very dangerous man.

She had to pee, her mouth was dry, her heart was ready to jump out of her chest and she had no idea what she was going to do to get out of this situation. Rachael was just buying time. Time for what, she had no idea. Sitting close to the window, her eyes darted from side to side. Maybe Sam was walking down the street to meet her. She prayed that Clyde wouldn't be too scared to go find Sam. Maybe he would just get in the truck and take off without looking back. As the car moved further down the street and toward the country road she knew it was all up to her to figure out how to get her out of this mess.

"Okay, you be tellin' us which a way to turn when we git near the mountain road. We ain't too familiar with these parts. You jest make sure you don't try nothin' funny. I ain't above throwin' you outta this car," Cooter said.

"It's been a time since I've been up here. I don't take care of the still," Rachael replied. "I might have to figure on it a bit, so don't drive too fast."

"It's gonna be dark soon, so you better make sure you git us there, girl a fore we can't see where we're a goin'."

That's what she was hoping for. Night in the mountains was darker than the inside of a coalminer's boot. She needed all the help she could get.

Chapter Thirty-One

Clyde sat frozen to the chair. He was afraid to move. His mind was racing. *What if'n they're really not gone? What if'n their waitin' fer me to get up and run outta here? Oh, Lordy, I knew somethin' bad was gonna happen some day, but not this bad.*

Clyde's biggest fear was that the revenuers would come some day and arrest him, but as the years passed and nothing happened he had gotten cockey. Today was far worse than that.

"Hey, is anybody here? Clyde where are ya?" Clyde was jolted back to reality by the sound of someone calling from the front of the store. Putting his hand on his neck, he could still feel the point of the knife piercing his skin. "I'm a comin', hold yer horses," he yelled.

Billy Tate leaned over the counter. "Where ya been, Clyde? I been waitin' fer about ten minutes. You don't looks so good. You got blood on yer shirt. You cut yerself?"

Clyde stammered, "Yes...No...I don't feel too good. I gotta run down the street for a minute. Watch the store fer me."

Billy's eyes widened. "You kiddin' me. You mean it, you gonna let me watch yer store? Kin I come behind the counter?"

Clyde didn't answer he was already on his way out the door. Still holding his neck, he ran the two blocks to the boarding house. "Sam here?" he asked the woman sitting at the desk, reading a magazine. She nodded without looking up and pointed up the stairs.

"Room two, second door on left. You wait, I'll get him," she said. Clyde was already half way up the stairs.

"Sam, Sam, you in thar, open the door," he hollered, his fists pounding on the door.

Sam opened the door, shaving cream dripping from his face. "What in the hell are you yelling about?" He wiped his face with a towel.

"It's Rachael! They got her. A couply of moon shiners done carried her off. One of thems called Cooter. He's a mean bastard. She needs you. She said Pine Ridge. Lord, it's a mess. You gotta find her and real quick a fore they find out she's a lyin' to them."

"What the hell are you babbling about? Start at the beginning," Sam said, as he dried his face and pulled his shirt over his head. Sit down for a minute and catch your breath."

Clyde plopped down on the side of the bed. "We ain't got but a few minutes. It's a mess, a real mess." Clyde began to talk faster and faster. " Nevers was a moon shiner. For yars he's been bringin' me his whiskey and I been sendin' it up North. When Nevers died, Rachael and her family took over. They set up a still in the smoke house and made some fine hooch. Nevers killed Cooter's, brother, Rooster and now Cooter wants everything. He come to town and took my money and then when Rachael showed up he wanted to know where the still and the rest of the money was. She said Pine Ridge. That's whar they're headed. But it ain't up thar and when they find out they'll most likely kill her. She saved my life, Sam. They was gonna kill me, but she talked them outta it. You gotta help her."

Sam pulled his jacket off the hook on the back of the door. He opened the nightstand drawer and took out a gun. Putting a box of bullets in his pocket, he said to Clyde, "You better not be telling me this just to get me out of town. Let's go."

"What should I do, Sam? You ain't gonna call the law on me, are you?" Clyde asked, following Sam down the stairs.

"Go back to your store. Stay there. Don't leave the store tonight, but if I'm not back by morning you go down to the sheriff's office and tell them they need to keep you in a cell. Tell them you're my witness and I want you safe. So, that's all Rachael said was Pine Ridge?"

"That's all she had time to say afore they drug her off. I'm jest gonna be yer witness, right, Sam. You ain't a gonna send me to prison are ya? I know'd yer family before you was born. I gave yer papa credit in my store when he was short of money. So, I'm jest yer witness, right, Sam?" he asked again.

Sam opened his car door and got in. "Do what I said, Clyde. Stay put and if Rachael's family comes looking for her, you just tell them that she is with me. That's all. They don't need to know what's going on." Clyde watched as Sam drove off and then headed back to his store. Once on the road, Sam opened the glove compartment and took out his flashlight and a boning knife in a leather sheath and stuck them in his jacket pocket.

Just on the outskirts of town, Sam turned left and headed up a wide trail winding through the woods. He had known about the old logging road ever since he was a kid. He and his brother would go pass the lumber camps to hunt rabbits and squirrels. Sam knew that Rachael was smart enough to have taken the long way, by passing up the logging road Cooter would have to drive another twelve mile to Post Fork Pass. If he could get up to the ridge before it got too dark he may have a chance of finding out where she was leading them. He rolled down the window even though the evening air was turning colder by the minute. The sound of a car engine traveled for miles on the overgrown one-lane paths leading up to the top of the ridge. Several times he stopped and listened for the sound of a car engine. Just a mile or so pass Caden's Fork, he picked up a clattering sound. It had to be them. No one else would be stupid enough to travel these roads after dark. He still hadn't even had time to process what Clyde had told him. All he knew was that Rachael was in big trouble. Parking his car as close to the side of the road as possible, Sam opened the trunk and took out a coil of rope and headed up the trail on foot. He couldn't take a chance of them hearing his car. Picking his way along the road he knew he only had about fifteen more minutes of light. Finding a sturdy tree, Sam tied the rope securely around it and began to repel down the side of the steep ravine. Once at the bottom he crossed over the narrow creek bed and started his assent up the other side. Grabbing hold of rocks and branches he pulled himself through the thicket. His throat was burning and his breath coming in short pants, but he had to make it to the top and find Rachael. Once on the ridge, he positioned himself about a hundred feet away from the lean-to. He lay down in the underbrush to conceal himself and he waited.

Driving slowly through the mountain turns; Norvelle leaned over the steering wheel trying to see the road ahead with only the help of two dim headlights. "I can't see a damn thing. I ain't even sure if'n I'm in the middle of the road or near the edge." The words were no sooner out of his mouth than the front wheel of the car slide into a deep rift, just inches from a sheer drop off. "That's it! I ain't a goin' another mile on this road. I think this gal is leadin' us on a wild goose chase."

"I ain't. It's up here. There's an old shack just up yonder where Nevers used to stay. The still is a little ways passed there." She prayed that they would suggest stopping there until daylight, even though being alone with them would put her into further danger. She prayed that Clyde had found Sam and given him her message and he was on his way up to save her. She knew by now, Jesse and Ben would know something was wrong and would be on the road to Lynch to look for her. She prayed that they would all be safe. Right now, praying was the only thing from keeping her from falling apart. She had to stay strong so that they would believe her. "Thar it is, thars the shack. See I told you so," she said pointing to the remnants of Old Joe's cabin.

"Git outta the car. You go on ahead, I'll follow you in the car," Cooter said. He opened the door and pushed Rachael out. Norvelle grabbed her by the arm and started up the incline.

"I'm plumb tuckered out and I'm hungry," Norvelle whined. "Let's light a fire and at least warm up a bit. Come on, Gal, whars that still?"

"It's too dark," Rachael said. "That still is so well hidden, even in the daylight you can be a couply feet away from it and you couldn't see it. It's gonna be too hard for us to find in the dark."

Cooter followed slowly behind them in the car and maneuvered up the steep incline within a few feet of the shed. Pulling as hard as he could on the emergency brake, the car still rolled backwards a few inches. "Damn hunk of junk. Soon as we git clear of this town I'm buyin' me a new car." Putting a rock under the front, right wheel, he turned off the lights and got out. Norvelle pushed open the door to the shack and shone his flashlight inside. He jumped when a raccoon rushed passed him and headed for the brush.

"Damn, this place smells like crap. I ain't sleepin' in here. Git in thar, Girl," he said to Rachael as he shoved her into the narrow opening. Once inside, he tied her hands behind her back and shoved her down on the rusted, metal bed frame. "This'll hold ya," he said tying the end of the rope to the center pole.

"Norvelle, you sit outside that thar door and make sure she don't go nowhere. I'm gonna lay down in the back seat til it gets light."

"Ya mean I kin go on in with the girl?" Norvelle said grinning.

"You leave her alone fer now. I don't want no ruckus tonight. They'll be a plenty time for that in the mornin' after we find that still."

Norvelle let out a grunt. "Pokin' her one time taint gonna hurt anythin'."

"Jest sit down and shut up and do what I say," Cooter said in a whining voice as he climbed into the car and pulled the door shut. If anyone was going to poke her, he wanted to be first, but he was too tired at the moment to fight with her. If she resisted he may have to kill her and then he would never find the still.

"Why ya always tellin' me what ta do? Why can't I sleep in the car?" Norvelle grumbled, knowing that if he kept it up too long, Cooter would surely punch him in the face like he had done many times before.

Sam heard it all. Still laying in the brush he had ducked when the headlights of the car almost zeroed in on him. He was primed to make his move if Cooter had turned Norvelle loose on Rachael. As it was, he had time to devise a better plan to get her out of the windowless shed. There was only one way in and one way out.

Sam waited as the night settled in and the woods began to come alive with the second shift of animals living on the mountain. The hoots of the owls judging the distance between themselves and their prey started first. Then came the hum of insects and the fluttering of wings from the swarm of bats leaving their resting places under the ledges. Crunching leaves signaled the arrival of rabbits and coons and other small mammals skittering around on the forest floor. They nervously looked around for anything edible always aware of the fox and coyotes on their trail and the owls waiting to swoop down on them.

It was only the fear of the cougars, bears and the poisonous snakes that made the mountain seem perilous to humans and of course, the trepidation of getting lost in the vast wilderness. Even the people born and raised in the hollows had a deep respect for Black Mountain. There was always the warning, "You go up that thar mountain, you best better know yer way back. Plenty to eat and drink up thar, but it gets mighty cold in the night and them critters prowlin' around would love ta find an easy meal." Sam wasn't afraid of the mountain tonight. He had to find a way to get Rachael out of the mess she had created.

Hearing the unharmonious snores of both Cooter and Norvelle, Sam began to slowly move out of the brush and into the clearing. Staying low to the ground he crawled over to the car and quietly pulled the rock out from under the right front tire. When it was clear of the car, Sam put his shoulder against the front bumper and pushed as hard he could. The car began to slowly move backward. Rolling away from the car, Sam quickly stood up and ran to the side of the shack. He tapped on the wall and called softly called Rachael's name. She answered him right away. "Sam, oh my gosh yer here. I'm all tied up."

The car was now beginning to pick up momentum. When the first branch cracked across the windshield, Cooter sat up with a start. "Holy shit!" he screamed and tried to open the door. Getting knocked into the back seat with his feet sticking up in the air, the back bumper of the car crashed into a pine tree and stopped. Cooter pulled himself up, fighting off the pine branches that had come through the window. Reaching over into the front seat, he laid on the horn. Norvelle opened his eyes and jumped up and began running down the hill.

With his distraction in place, Sam crashed into the door of the shed and with one swift slice cut through the rope tied to the pole. With her hands still bound, Sam grabbed her by the arm and pulled her out of the shed and across the clearing. "Get down, stay low," he said when they reached the brush. Crawling a few feet into the thicket, Sam stopped long enough to cut the rope on Rachael's hands. "Lay still, they can't see us."

Still cussing, Cooter kicked at the car door that was jammed against the tree. When Norvelle finally got to him, Cooter had climbed out the window. "Got damn, sum bitch, didn't you hear that car a movin'? Are you plain deef?"

Norvelle shook his head. "Naw, I didn't heer nothin' till you was honkin', sides what could I do till it stopped?"

"Aw, shut-up. I'm wide-awake now. Let's go get the girl. Might as well have a little fun."

"Sound like a good idée, Cooter. A real good idée," Norvelle agreed.

Nearing the lean-to Cooter yelled," Well, I'll be a sum bitch, that door's been done busted open." Cooter ducked as he went in side. "She's gone! Been cut loose from the pole. Got damn, that twernt no accident that my car rolled down the hill. We got company, Norvelle. Sure nuf, we got company."

Norvelle looked around, nervously. "Who'd ya think it is, Cooter? Ya think its Clyde?"

"Hell no. That coward woulda called the sheriff and they woulda come up heer guns a blastin'. Nope, I ain't sure who it is, but don't you worry none, we're gonna find em. And when I do, whoever it is and that girl are gonna be dead meat. Nobody makes a fool outta Cooter."

Cooter cupped his hands around his mouth. "We know'd yer out thar. And we are a comin' after ya. Be best jest to show yerself and maybe we kin work somethin' out."

Sam felt around on the ground until he found a good size rock. Hurling it over his head with all his might he grabbed Rachael's hand and they quickly ran across the small clearing to the side of the ravine."

Norvelle whirled around and fired off three shots in that direction.

"What in the hell is wrong with you," Cooter said. "What are you shootin' at?"

"Didn't you see that, Cooter?" Norvelle asked.

"See what, dumb ass. Ain't nothin' to see. Probably some critter jest got the hell scart outta him. Now put yer damn gun away a fore you shoot yer foot off and let's go after that gal."

Norvelle trotted behind Cooter. "What about the still, Cooter? What about the money they done buried up here?"

"Listen dumb ass, thar ain't no still and thar sure as hell ain't no money up here. We been led on a snipe hunt."

The sound of the gunfire and the squabble between Cooter and Norvelle gave Sam and Rachael the chance to descend a few feet down the steep incline.

"I'm gonna fall," Rachael whispered. "I can't get my footin'."

Sam put his fingers to his lips and pulled her to his side. "Hold on to my hand and don't let go, no matter what, don't let go," he said in a low voice. He began to inch his way grabbing hold of branches and rocks to keep them from tumbling straight down. Every once in a while they would have to sit down and just scoot on the slippery leaves still damp from the evening dew. Half way down, Sam stopped and positioned himself and

Rachael behind a fallen tree. "Let's wait here for a minute and see what they're up to," he said softly.

A beam of light from Cooter's flashlight skirted across the log and around the trees. Sam and Rachael ducked down lower. "Can't see em, but I reckon whoever it is with the gal musta taken off down the gully. Come on Norvelle, let's go." Taking just a few steps, Norvelle lost his footing and began to slide down the incline. "Crap, we're gonna kill ourselves goin' this a way. Let's jest go down the road. They gotta come up outta thar sometime," Norvelle whined. Cooter grabbed Norvelle by the back of his shirt, "Lissen you little weasel, if'n ya want yer share of the money, ya better git yer ass down this here hill. They ain't that fer ahead of us."

Sam and Rachael began to descend further down the ravine knowing that Cooter was getting closer to them. Their movement caused a small rockslide, with the sound of gravel falling into the creek below them.

Two shots rang out. The impact of the bullets hitting a tree caused a shower of splinters to rain down on Sam and Rachael. "Damn, that was close," Sam said. Rachael could feel her heart thumping in her chest. She had never been shot at before.

Coming to a stop at the edge of the creek, Sam began to run along the rocky bank, still holding Rachael's hand. "Wait, I can't go anymore. Stop a minute," she said, panting.

"Can't stop, Rachael, they're right on our heels."

The moon was now directly overhead, throwing glimpses of light between the trees. Sam scanned the ridge looking for the rope he had left hanging there. "There it is," he said. "Take hold of the rope and start walking up the rocks. Lean back and let your legs do the work. Go hand over hand."

"I can't do that!

"Oh, yes you can, and you will. Sam picked her up and she grabbed hold of the rope. "Now go, I'm right behind you."

Each time she moved her hand up higher on the rope, she closed her eyes, knowing that at any minute she might fall backwards.

Grabbing for the large tree root that signaled the top of the ridge, Rachael could hear the sounds of water splashing. It was Cooter and Norvelle running through the creek just below them. She rolled over onto the ground just as Sam reached for the tree root. Two more shots deafened her ears as Sam fell on top of her. He grabbed his arm and let out a low moan. "Oh, my God, Sam, you been hit," she yelled, forgetting to be quiet.

"I done heard her," Cooter said. "I shot somebody, but she's still up thar. Git up that rope, Norvelle, We're on em now. Git yer ass up that rope."

"Lay still. I'm okay. It just grazed me," he said. Reaching into his pocket, Sam pulled out the boning knife and scooted close to the edge, watching as Norvelle shimmied up the rope like a monkey on a stick, while Cooter still waited at the bottom. He wanted them both on the rope, but it wasn't going to happen. With one sharp flick of the knife the rope fell to the ground taking Norvelle with it. Screaming all the way down as his body bounced off the rocks and tree limbs, he landed with a splash in the creek. "Ow, ow, my leg is broken. My damn leg is broken. Sum bitch I'm gonna die. Help me."

Cooter bent down and surveyed the damage done to Norvelle. His pants were torn away and blood ran down his thigh. He sat in the water cradling his bent knee. "See if'n you kin git up," Cooter said.

"How in the hell am I gonna git up, my damn leg is broken," Norvelle whined. With one jerking motion Cooter pulled Norvelle out of the creek and stood him on his feet, while Norvelle continued to howl.

"Yer leg ain't broken, it's jest busted up a little." He cupped his hands around his mouth and yelled,

"We're a comin' up after you and when we git up thar you gonna be reel sorry and then we're gonna go git the rest of yer family and take care of them, too. It ain't over. You jest don't know who yer messin' with yet." Cooter was on fire. No one ever got the best of him and he wasn't going to let it start now.

Sam slowly sat up and looked over at Rachael. Both of her hands and knees were bleeding. She was crying softly. "Are you hurt?" he asked.

She wiped her nose. "Just a little scraped and bruised. How's your arm?"

"It's all right," he answered. "Let's go. My car is parked right around this turn."

Once in the car, Rachael said, "Do you think they gave up and left?"

"No. Cooter wants us dead. I figure with Norvelle having a bad leg, they probably went back up the ravine to get their car. If I can catch them before they get off the Post Fork road maybe I have a chance of stopping them."

The car began to pick up speed making for a jolting ride down the old, logging trail. Once on the main road, Sam turned left and drove the twelve miles to Post Fork Road. He turned up the road and stopped. "We're gonna wait right here for them. They can't get passed me. When I see them coming I want you to get down on the floor and stay there until I tell you to get up. Do you understand?" Rachael nodded her head.

The gray dawn turned into a blue-sky day as they waited. She wrapped her arms around herself and shivered from the cold. She wanted to talk to him and tell him how sorry she was but he didn't seem to be in any mood to make conversation. She sat quietly with her sore hands in her lap. Sam got out of the car and paced back and forth across the road. "Somethings wrong. It shouldn't take them this long. I'm gonna chance it and go on up to the ridge."

Passing by the shack where Rachael had been held captive, there was no sign of Cooter or Norvelle. Sam took his gun out of his holster and ducked low behind the car looking toward the spot where the car had crashed into the trees. Still nothing. A break in the trees drew his attention. Walking toward the edge of the ravine, he could see a path of broken limbs and deep ruts in the soft dirt. At the bottom of the ravine the black car laid on it's back, a small trickle of smoke coming from the engine. There was no sign of life from the mound of twisted metal.

He called back to Rachael. "Looks like they must have got the car started and then tried to turn it around. It must have caught the soft dirt and it rolled right off the ridge. I'm gonna climb down there and see if either of them are alive. You stay put. Keep the cars door locked. Here," he said, handing her his pistol. You hang on to it. Anybody shows up you just fire off two shots in the air, that is unless you want to take aim at some-body." She detected a small grin on his face.

She waited for over an hour for him to return and grew more and more worried as each minute passed. When she saw him coming toward the car she let out a sigh of relief. "Well, that's the end of that. They're both dead. That only leaves Rooster to deal with. I wish I knew if Rooster was around these parts. I'd go after him before he comes looking for you."

"He's dead, too," Rachael said.

"What! How do you know that?" Sam was surprised at her statement.

"Cause Nevers killed Rooster and another man when they tried to jump his claim up on the ridge. That's whar Nevers had his still. They shot Nevers in the gun fight and he died the next day of his wounds and we buried em all."

"When did all this happen?" Sam asked.

"Back in the spring. We found Rooster and another man dead and we brought em back to Never's place and buried em in the cemetery. A fore he got shot, none of us had any idée that

Nevers was a big time moon shiner. We wuz still believin' he wuz a trapper."

"Whoa, wait a minute. I was told that Nevers just died a couple of months ago. That doesn't make any sense." He was completely confused.

"We had to pretend he was still alive so Lily could keep the house. Then when it was safe and we had the still up and runnin' in the smoke house, Old Joe Seminole pretended to be Nevers and we covered him with blood and the sheriff thought he was dead, so we jest buried an empty coffin cause he really wasn't dead. With Nevers really dead, Lily was free to marry Ben."

"Old Joe Seminole! How...damn this is getting more confusing. So, Old Joe was living at the farm? I thought he died years ago."

"Nope, he was still livin' up on the ridge. I went up thar and fetched him. That's another story. Anyway, Old Joe died coupley weeks ago. It was natural causes. He must have been close to a hundred years old. So we dug up the empty coffin and buried him in it."

Sam laid his head on the steering wheel. "How many people are buried in that cemetery, Rachael.

" Jest the four we buried, and Nevers' first two wives, but we didn't have anythin' to do with them. You got to believe me, Sam. We never killed nobody." Rachael decided she might as well tell him the rest of the story and get it over with. "We brought the still down from the ridge and that's when we built the smoke house. It was our only chance to make some real money and leave the hollow forever and make sure Lily could keep her house."

"You knew it was against the law, Rachael. I can't believe you thought you could get away with it," Sam said.

"I reckon it really didn't matter much ta me. Prison couldn't be any worse than livin' here the rest of my life.

Should be agin the law for men to suffer a slow death from black lung and their wives widowed with a bunch of kids they can't afford to feed. Most of them youngins will die before they're five, the rest will grow up illiterate because they don't even have a coat to wear to school. Life ain't always jest about livin', Sam. It's knowin' what you want and going after it. It's thinkin' about yer future and not worryin' each day if'n yer gonna get caught. If'n yer daddy hadn't died in the mine, who knows you may have been doin' the same thing that I am," she let out a deep sigh. "Are you gonna take me to jail? If'n you are, kin I stop by the house and tell Lily, Ben and Jesse that I'm safe? Please don't arrest them. This wuz all my idée. Cause if'n you do I reckon momma will have to raise Violet. Poor little kid, she won't have a very good life ahead of her. Do they have places for people in wheelchairs in prison? Maybe Lily and I could be together in the same cell." She hung her head trying to look as pitiful as possible.

"Lord, Rachael, take a breath. No, I'm not taking you to jail. We're going to drive into Lynch so I can tell the sheriff I found the bodies of Cooter and Norvelle. Then you're going to get in your truck and go on home. I want you to dump all that shine on the truck and wash them jars. Then all of you get busy and dismantle that still. I don't care what you do with it. Bury it up on the hill with everyone else. You might want to think about what you're going to do next, because your bootlegging days are over."

"I guess you're really mad at me?' she asked.

"What do you think? All that time we were together you were running a still and lying to me." He shook his head.

"That's not entirely true cause you never told me you were a revenuer until a couply of weeks ago. I know yer not goin' to believe me, but I only had one more run before I was goin' to leave here forever. Besides, I knew once yer work was finished here you wuz goin' to go off and leave me even though you knew I loved you." She had to say something in her defense.

"How do you know that I was going to leave you? Maybe I was going to ask you to go away with me?"

Her eyes widened. "Were you?"

"That doesn't even matter right now, Rachael. We have to get this mess cleaned up first."

Once in town, Sam stopped his car outside of Clyde's store. Clyde came running out the door. "Oh, mah Lord am I glad to see you two. What about them men? Did you git em?"

"Everything is okay, Clyde. Just stay put." Sam turned to Rachael. "Get in the truck and high tail it for home. Clyde, you and I need to talk."

Rachael hesitated for a moment before she started out the side door. "Rachael," Clyde said, " I sure do want ta thank you fer savin' my life. That was reel brave of ya. Yer brother come in here last night lookin' fer you and I told him what happened. He wanted ta go up to the ridge, but I talked him outta it. I told him that Sam could take care of it and he would bring you back safe. Thanks agin, Rachael. Thar gonna be reel glad ta see ya."

"That's okay, Clyde," Rachael said as she got into her truck. She would have liked to stuck around and find out what Sam planned to do with Clyde, but she didn't want to press her luck.

"Okay, Clyde, here's the deal. I'm not going to arrest you but when your customers from up north stop getting their deliveries they'll probably come here looking for you. I've seen what happens to bootleg suppliers when they don't deliver and it's not pretty. The lucky ones were dead; the others were missing body parts. I suggest you leave here for a good long time. Maybe in a year or so you can come back to your store. Are we clear?"

"I'm clear, Sam, reel clear. I've already got the beejee-zus scart outta me."

"And no one is going to know anything about this, are they, Clyde?"

"Nope, no sir, no one is gonna know one thing. Thank ya, Sam. Thanks a lot." Clyde grabbed Sam's hand and pumped it up and down. I'll be leavin' here in jest a few minutes. I got a cousin livin' in Sevierville. I reckon I kin go stay with him for a spell."

Clyde opened the front door and looked up and down the street. As usual, Billy Tate was sitting on the bench in front of the pharmacy. Clyde let out a shrill whistle, which caught Billy's attention. Loping across the street, his curiosity still peaked about all the goings on in the last few days, he was sure that Clyde was going to fill him in. Instead he got the surprise of his life.

"I got a deal fer you Billy. I'm fixin' on leavin' town fer a spell. Could be about a year or so. I wuz wonderin' if'n you would like to run the store fer me while I'm gone. You kin keep all the profits you make so long as you keep the store open and the shelves full. I want it to be jest about the same when I git back. You think you got enough smarts ta do that?"

Billy wore a grin from ear to ear. "You bet I kin. I kin sure do that. I'm real smart in figurin'. I'd be might proud ta run the store fer you, Clyde."

"Good, here's the keys to the front and back doors, the combination to the safe and a list of people I buy stuff from. I'll see you later." Clyde stepped off the porch and headed down the street leaving Billy standing with his mouth open and hand full of keys.

Bent Creek

Sam entered the sheriff's office and made his report about Cooter and Norvelle. He gave the sheriff directions to the area where the car went off the road. "I guess that's the end of them," Sam said. "I found their still and destroyed it. I'll put it all in my report to the bureau. I guess I'll be leaving here sometime tomorrow." The sheriff seemed satisfied with Sam's story. He was just glad he hadn't got involved with the likes of Cooter and Rooster.

"You done a reel good job, Son. You better get that arm looked at," the sheriff said. Sam had forgotten all about being shot in the arm. Suddenly it began to hurt.

Chapter Thirty-Two

Rachael pulled into the yard and jumped down from the truck. She let out a moan as the realization that the bruises and scraps all over her body were beginning to ache. Jesse and Lily came out of the house and ran to her.

Jesse grabbed her by the hand." Yer all beat up. Come on let's git in the house. Rachael, damn we have been so worried about you. I waited till it was almost dark and then I went into town and Clyde told me what was goin' on. He tried to tell us some cock and bull story, but we knew'd somethin' was wrong. When he told us about Cooter I wanted ta go after you, but Lily said we better wait, jest like Sam said. What happened?"

Rachael sat at the kitchen table while Lily washed her arms and hands. Putting salve on her scraped knuckles and cuts she wrapped them in long stripes of white cloth. Lily washed off Rachael's face while Ben and Jesse waited patiently to hear the story. "Git her somethin' to drink. Don't jest sit thar and stare at her," Lily said. "She'll tell ya in due time."

Her bandaged hands shook as she sipped the hot coffee; she began to talk in a shaky voice. "Well, it all started when I pulled into Clyde's store…" She grimaced as Lily dabbed salve on her knees and continued telling them what had happened. "And then Sam told me to get in the truck and come home. He said we needed to destroy the still and wash all the jars and get rid of the rest of the mash. We need to do that right now in case the sheriff would happen to come out here and ask us some questions. I have no idée what Clyde might have told him."

"Are we all goin' ta jail?" Lily asked.

"No. I don't think Sam is going to do anything to us, but he has to make sure that the still is gone and that we never make moonshine again. He put himself on the line ta save our skins and for that we have to be reel grateful. We could have ended up in the pokey. It's time for us to pack up and get the heck out of Kentucky. We've got enough money. Ben, you kin call that minister tomarra and tell him he kin buy this property and then we'll go get momma and daddy. They're going with us whether they want to or not. I'm not leavin' them here alone. Right now I need to get some sleep. Jesse, you and Lily kin start takin' down the still. I'll help you in a few hours," Rachael yawned.

"What about you and Sam?" Lily asked. "I reckon he was kinda mad at you."

"You're not even close, Lily. Anything that me and Sam had is over. He hates my guts." She disappeared into the bedroom.

Jesse, Ben and Lily dismantled the still while Rachael slept. They washed all the jars and packed them in boxes. After Jesse carried bags of mash and sugar up the hill and buried them in a deep hole, he put all the pieces of the still in the truck, drove it up to the quarry and threw it in the deep water. Lily swept up the debris in the smoke house and helped take down the false wall. All the signs of ever running a still were gone and Rachael still never woke up. Lily checked on her twice just to make sure she was all right. Five o'clock the next morning, she awoke with a jolt, for a moment not remembering where she was. Every inch of her body ached.

A few minutes later, Lily poked her head in the door. "Thar's someone here ta see you, Rachael. It's Sam. He's a waitin' fer you out on the porch."

Rachael poured herself a cup of coffee. She had to get her thoughts together before facing the man she loved. Pushing open the screen door, she meekly said, "Hi."

"Hi to you, too," he replied.

"How's yer arm?" she asked.

"It's okay. How about you? Are you all right?"

"Jest a little sore, but nothins broken." She had no idea what to say next.

He patted the seat next to him on the swing. "Come sit with me. I need to talk and you need to listen without interrupting me. I had a long talk with Ben while you were sleeping. He told me how you saved his life when he wanted to end it all. He also told me how you have fought to keep this family together along with taking care of your parents and trying to make a better life for yourself. I just wish it could be some other way, Rachael, but you and I are on opposite sides of the law. I wish I never took this assignment. I should have known that someone I knew might be involved, but I never thought it would be you. That's why I was so darn mad at you."

"Kin I talk now?" she asked. "There ain't much I kin do to explain away what I did. I knew it was against the law, but I really didn't care. Sometimes I'd get so down them buzzards would be cirlin' my head, but I never gave up. I knew somehow, someway I was gonna git outta here. I never planned on meetin' up with you and havin' the feelins' I have for you. It jest makes my heart ache. I reckon you know I'm real fond of you."

"That's the hard part, Rachael because I care a lot about you, too. I have to go back to Ohio and make a full report on everything that has happened. Of course it will be riddled with

231

lies. I don't think I want to continue working for the agency. I'm going to look for a different job."

"Account of me yer losin' yer job. I'm sorry."

"It wasn't want I wanted anyway. I kind of got pushed into it. It was a lonely job and not very rewarding. Most of the people I turned in were just like you, just trying to make a better life for themselves. There was really only a few, like Clyde that was making big money on bootlegging."

"You got any plans fer yer future, Sam?"

"I think I might look around for a business I can buy. My father always dreamed of owing a hardware store. I think I might like something like that. How about you, Rachael what are you going to do?" he asked.

"I'm going to pack up all my things and git the heck outta here. We're gonna move to Florida and start a new life. Ain't nothin' here fer me. I reckon I won't be seein' you any time soon. Heck, maybe never."

"I wish I could sit right here and tell you that I might see you again, but that would be a lie. I have to get things straight in my head and make some decisions about my life." Sam stood up. "I guess I'd better be going. I'm going to stop back in Lynch and make sure everything is okay with Clyde. Walk me to my car."

Rachael tried to hold back the tears that were just about ready to flow down her face. She took a deep breath and followed him out into the yard. Sam put his arms around her and she buried her head in his chest. "You take care of yourself and have a good time in Florida. He tilted her face up with his two hands and kissed her."

"I want ta thank you fer savin' my life, Sam and I want to tell you jest once that I love you." He turned quickly and got into his car before she could say anything else.

As he pulled out of the yard, she said "Goodbye Sam. I love you," and then she let the tears fall.

Chapter Thirty-Three

The next few days were spent trying to get over what had just happened to them. Lily still worried that the revenuers would return and maybe even take Violet away from her. Ben reassured her it would never happen, but Jesse was on edge and wanted to leave. He was afraid Rooster and Cooter may have some more brothers that may come looking for them. Rachael didn't care about any of that. Her heart still ached over losing Sam. She wanted to leave Kentucky and head for Florida, but every time she brought up the subject no one wanted to talk about it.

On Sunday evening, Rachael set the table and put the soup pot on the table. She called out for everyone to come and eat. The clink of spoons on metal bowls and the slurp of soup was all that could be heard in the usually noisy kitchen. Pulling his napkin out of his shirt, Jesse pushed his chair back. "That was good soup, Rachael."

"Don't you go runnin' off, Jesse Riley, jest sit back down. We got somethin' we need to talk about," Rachael said. It's time we start gettin' ready to go ta Florida. I'm gonna go down to momma and daddy's house tomarra and tell them our plans. If'n they want to come along I'll help them get ready." The room was silent. "Well ain't any of you got anythang to say?" Rachael asked as she took the bowls off of the table. You all are sure being tight-lipped." She began clearing the dishes from the table.

Jesse plopped back down and stared into his empty bowl. "We ain't a goin' to Floridy, Rachael. We all decided to stay here."

"What! You have got ta be kiddin' me. We had it all planned. Why do you want to stay here?" Four bowls crashed to the floor with remnants of soup splashing on to the floor.

"Now hear me out, Rachael. Goin' to Floridy was yer idée. We'uns are mountain folk, not ocean folk. You got this big idée of sellin' oranges and shells. Well I betcha jest about every dumb hillbilly that went to Floridy had the same idée. We can't make no livin' doin' that. What happens when our money runs out? What then?"

"We'll worry about that when the time comes," she replied.

"We ain't never been too keen on that plan anyway," Ben interjected. " I reckon none of us ever thought it would come to pass. I made mah decision and I know fer sure I'm a stayin' right here. Least wise we got a roof over our heads. Me and Jesse done talked to Mr. Mabry yesterday. He's gonna rent us that empty buildin' next door ta him. I reckon with our share of the money we got we kin buy some equipment and open a car repair garage. I kin teach Jesse how ta work on engines. Times is changin' and thars more and more traffic on our road. We saw leven cars pass by in the time we was thar. Ain't no place to git gas or have yer car fixed between here and Lynch. I'm thinkin' we kin make a go of it."

Rachael was livid. "Is that so. Ya'll planned this without tellin' me and then you go ahead and talk to Mr. Mabry behind my back. Well that's jest fine with me. Ya'll kin stay here, but I'm goin' to Florida. And what about momma and daddy? Who's gonna take care of them?"

Lily spoke up. "We are, Rachael. We're gonna ask them ta come here and live."

"Of course, you kin give them my room." She marched across the hallway, returning with the tin box that held their money. She dropped it down into the middle of the table. "Okay, let's divvy up so I kin start packin'." She opened the box and dumped the stack of bills onto the table and began counting them out. "I divided it into four equal parts. Ya'll kin go ahead and recount it if'n you want to."

"Maybe you should take a little bit more fer yerself, Rachael. You did most of the thinkin'. And if'n it wasn't fer yer thing with Sam, we'd all be in jail right now," Ben said.

Rachael picked up a stack of money and wrapped a rubber band around it. "No thanks." She turned and stomped off. Pulling open her dresser drawers she threw her underwear and one nightshirt onto the bed. Opening the closet she took out her other pair of jeans, two shirts and the green dress Lily had made her. Stuffing all the items into her pillowcase, she sat down on the bed and sobbed. She didn't hear Lily come into the room, until Lily put her arm around her. Rachael moved away. "Leave me be, Lily."

"I can't stand fer you ta be mad at us. You know how much I love you. Yer like a sister ta me. You done so much fer me, I kin never repay you. Ben's my husband, I gotta side with him. We wuz plannin' on tellin' you, but then everythin' happened so fast. We sure didn't mean ta hurt you. You've been so good ta me and Ben, it jest breaks my heart ta see you leave. Can't you stay here with us?"

Rachael wiped her nose on her sleeve. "And do what, Lily? Ain't nothin' here for me. You see this," she said, pointing to the pillow case, "Everythin' I own is in here and I could throw it in a trash pile and it wouldn't make no difference. This is you and Ben's house, not mine. And Jesse, he kin do what he wants, but I want more fer myself and damn it, I'm gonna get it."

"I'm gonna miss you a whole lot and so will Violet and thars one other thing I've been fixin' ta tell you. I'm pregnant. Me and Ben are gonna have a baby of our own. Ben's reel scart about bein' a daddy. That's one reason why he didn't want ta move away. He was afraid he couldn't make a livin' fer his family. Don't be mad at us, Rachael."

"Why didn't you tell me sooner?"

"Like I said, we wuz plannin' on tellin' you everythang and havin' a little celebration but than all hell broke loose and everythang happened faster than we thought. Please don't hate us."

Rachael put her arms around Lily. "I won't hate you. I could never hate my family. I reckon I'm jest pissed off right now, but I'll git over it. I'm jest disappointed that our plan didn't work out. I need to go see momma. I have to tell her I'm leavin'."

Rachael parked the truck into the front yard of her parent's house. She sat for a moment trying to get her thoughts together. The place looked worse than ever. The roof was sagging on the left side and one of the front windows was boarded up. She couldn't understand how they could live in such a horrible place. She made up her mind what she had to do. She jumped when she heard her mother calling her name.

"You jest gonna sit out thar all day?'

"I got somethin' to tell you, Ma. I'm leavin' in the mornin'. I'm goin' to Florida. I done picked out a place thar. It's called Destin." Rachael unfolded the map she had for over a year on the kitchen table. The creases of the paper were beginning to rip from being folded and unfolded many times. She pointed to a small red circle. "That's Destin. That's whar I'm goin' and both of you are comin' with me.

"Rachael girl, I don't know much and I ain't smart like you, but I always know'd that you were too good for this place.

236

I always know'd that someday you would leave here and I would never see you agin."

"That's not true, cause like I said, Momma, you and daddy are coming with me."

"You go on. I ain't a goin' with you. I jest can't fergit that you got that money by doin' wrong. You didn't earn it."

"What do you mean I didn't earn it, Momma? Me and Jesse had to live with that mean old Nevers. I got captured by them bootleggers and got shot at twice, I worked my tail off, took chances that I never thought I'd do and lost the man I love. Now don't you tell me I didn't earn it. I never harmed a soul, and now I'm done, Momma. I got enough money fer us ta live really nice. Please momma. I want you and daddy to come with me." She took her mother's hand. " Come on Momma, come with me. You and daddy deserve something better than livin' in this run down shack."

The door to the bedroom opened and Roy Reilly stepped out clad only in his red, long johns. "I want ta go to Floridy," he declared. "I want ta go somewheres warm and pick oranges off the tree in my yard. Kin you make that happen, Rachael?"

"I'll surely try, Daddy."

"Yer plumb loco, Roy Riley. You ain't goin' any-wheres," Ida Mae said.

"You jest watch me, Ida Mae. If'n you don't want ta go, you kin stay here and go live with Ben and Lily. I ain't spendin' one more winter in this place. Hell, it'll likely fall down on our heads a fore the snow comes."

"I'll make you a deal, Momma. You come with me to the beach and if'n after a month you jest plumb hate it thar, I'll buy you a bus ticket and send you home directly."

Ida Mae folded her hands across her chest. "Well, I reckon I could try it fer at least a month."

Rachael threw her arms around her mother's neck. "I love you, Momma. We're gonna have so much fun."

❧ ❧ ❧

Jesse pulled the truck up to the bus station and everyone piled out. Ida Mae wore her Sunday church dress and Roy had on the only pair of good pants and shirt he owned. Rachael took their box, which was tied with a string, along with her bag out of the truck and set them on the platform.

"I still can't figure how you talked them into goin' with you, but I sure do hope it all works out. If not you kin send them on back to us," Ben said.

The Greyhound bus pulled in and a few passengers got off. After a few minutes the driver announced that it was time to board. Rachael hugged Jesse and Ben. She took Violet from Lily's arms and after kissing both her cheeks she handed her to her mother. Ida Mae cuddled the baby close to her. "I know'd I ain't been a reel good granny to you baby, but I want ya ta know that I love you." She turned to Lily. "I'm sorry I ain't been sociable to you, but I didn't know the whole story fer a long time. I think ya'll be a reel good wife ta Ben."

"I can't tell you how much I'm gonna miss you," Lily said. You be sure and write us as soon as you get settled. Ben says if things goes okay we should have a telephone in a couply months and then you kin call us. I'm gonna hug you real quick cause I'm gettin' ready to bawl."

The driver announced again that it was time to go. With the last flurry of hugs and kisses, Rachael and her parents got on the bus. They were actually leaving Kentucky.

"Lordy, I think I'm gonna fall right apart," Ida Mae said, holding tight onto Roy's hand.

"You jest hold on to me and everythin' will be jest fine," he said, although his hand was shaking.

Chapter Thirty-Four

Dear Family

I'm hopin' ya'll are fine. We miss you. It was a real long ride to Florida. I thought we would never git here. Momma complained the whole way. When we got off the bus I couldn't believe how warm it was. It is jest as nice as I thought it would be. We stayed in a motel fer a couply days and then I found us a real nice little house on the beach. Well, it ain't really much cause it needs some fixins' but we got inside plumbin' and even a porceline bathtub. We bought some furniture from a couply sales in people's yards and some from the Goodwill store. The house is startin' to look right nice. I got me two orange trees growin' in tubs on the porch and I pick up shells off the beach everyday. I got me a whole pile of them by my front door. See I told you. Ha ha.

At first Momma hated it here. She was reel homesick. She hated the ocean and the sand. She won't even go near the water and she kept thinkin' them waves were gonna come right over the house. She cried a lot and I was jest about ready to send her back to ya'll when she found a church in town that had bingo three nights a week. She's even got her own dobber. She said she wasn't gamblin' cause it's in a church and when she won she always gave the church part of the money. She also joined a quiltin' club at the church and thar are some women thar from Tennessee. Fer a while I hardly saw her, but I was glad she wuz happy. Me and momma went shoppin' and got some new clothes. I swear it makes me all choked up ta see how young momma looks in new clothes. She ain't an old lady at all. I took her to a picture show and she jest sat there with her mouth open. She talked about it fer three days til daddy said he heard enuf bout them movies stars.

Daddy, well…he's was a different story. Soon as we got to the house he tuk off his shoes and marched right into the water. He jest stood thar with his hands on his hips starin' at the ocean. He said it was the damdest thang he ever seen. He found a fishin' pier about half mile from our house and started goin' down thar everyday after breakfast. He spent so much time sittin' thar talkin' to all the old codgers that fish off the pier that the owner offered him a job. Daddy keeps fishin' line and bait on all the poles and untangles nets. Sometimes he sweeps up the place. He's makin' a dollar a day and he was in hog heaven fer a while. He walked round the house with money in his pocket and every now and then he'd pull out the bills and jest looks at them. I was reel glad they both are adjusten to things here.

And me, well, I got me a job and a car. It ain't much of a car, jest an old rust bucket but it runs real good. I went ta work cause a person kin only spend so *much time workin' around the house and goin' ta the beach. Besides I wanted ta make sure I don't spend all my money. I still got a sock full in my dresser drawer. I'm workin' at a restaurant jest a few blocks down the road. They serve country cookin' and lots of grits. I jest can't believe that people eat grits when they don't have to. They like the way I talk but if you ask me, I think it's the people here who talk funny. I'm thinkin' that sometime in the future I'd like to buy me a little restaurant. You know, fix some of the thangs me and momma used to cook back home. I surely hope things are goin good at home fer all of ya'll. I love ya'll a bunch and miss you reel badly. Write to me if'n you git time. Oh, by the way, have you heard anything from Sam?*

Love Rachael

A few days after sending off the letter, Rachael was surprised when her father made the announcement that Ida Mae wanted to go home. She said the month was up and it was time to leave and he was thinking he would like to go, too. He missed the tall pines of the mountains and the quiet of the hollow. Roy said that Ida Mae was tired of playing bingo and she really didn't like the church that much. She missed her old church in Bent Creek.

Rachael was stunned by his announcement. "But, Daddy, how kin you say goin' home would make you happy. Thar's nothin' thar fer you. You'll jest be miserable agin as soon as you git back."

"Naw, don't reckon I'll be miserable. I reckon it won't be too long a fore the mine opens."

Rachael threw her hands in the air. "I jest can't believe you two, but if'n that's what you want, I'll write to Ben and try to make some arrangements."

"I sure do hope you ain't mad at us, Rachael," her momma added. "It ain't that we ain't grateful fer all you did fer us, but I need ta go back ta Bent Creek. Floridy jest don't feel right ta me. I jest can't believe thar ain't no winter here. We may be miserable back home, but we're miserable here so it don't make a whole lot of difference, ceptin' I'll have my grandbabies and my church. I'm right weary of playin' bingo and I know fer sure yer pap is ready ta leave this place.

Rachael wrote another letter to Ben,

Dear Ben,

After tellin' you in my last letter bout all the good stuff happenin' here, thangs have changed agin. Momma reminded me that the month was up and she and daddy are ready ta come home. They don't like the idée that thar are no woods or fishin' holes round heer. Momma says it's way too hot and she's a missin' ya'll and daddy has jest started sittin' round in the evenin' and listens to the old hillbilly programs on the radio. I reckon I shoulda know'd it wouldn't last too long, thar jest too old to change thar ways. Bent Creek is all they ever know'd. I'm reel glad I got ta spend this time with them, but I don't want them to be unhappy. Thang is, I don't know whar they will go to live and I sure can't send them home to nothin That is lessen ya'll are still willin' ta take them in. I'm sure by now thar old house has fallin' down. If in you got any idees let me know. I still miss ya'll and wonder fin ya heard

*anythin' from Sam. Give Violet a kiss fer
me. I will write soon.*
Rachael.

Ben's reply came four days later. He said they had
plenty of room. He and Jesse had their business up and running
and it would be nice for Lily to have someone home with her
during the day since she was expecting a baby. Jesse had
decided to move out and he was living in the three rooms above
the garage. They would meet Ida Mae and Roy in Lynch on
Saturday.

With everything they owned packed in two proper suit-
cases, Ida Mae and Roy stood outside the bus station with
Rachael just as the sun was coming up. Ida Mae swished a
paper fan back and forth across her face, while Roy fidgeted
with the tickets. "Gonna be another scorcher here, Rachael,"
Ida Mae said. "Are you still mad at us?"

"I ain't mad at you," Rachael said, putting her arm
around her mother. "I want you to be happy and if goin' back
to Bent Creek is gonna do it, then I'm glad fer you. You take
care of yerselves and give everyone a kiss fer me. I'm gonna
git. Here's some travelin' money." She tucked a twenty-dollar
bill into her mother's pocket and kissed her on the cheek. She
hugged her father and whispered into his ear, " You take care of
momma and don't you dare go back to that mine, even if'n it
opens and they beg you to come back." Rachael turned and left
the depot without turning around. She didn't want them to
know how really disappointed she was.

         જ   જ   જ

It was Friday. A week had gone by since her parents had
left. Rachael swept the floor and washed up the few dishes in

the sink. She made her bed and shook out all the throw rugs. Pulling her hair back in to a ponytail, she slipped off her shoes and headed for the beach. Walking through the foamy waves that washed up on the sand she was in deep thought. She had to make some decisions about her life. It was really hard to admit to herself that Florida wasn't the answer for her. Her life had improved tremendously, but she still wasn't happy. Things were a little better when her parents were with her. At least she felt like she was needed and had someone to talk to. Now, it was just her, all alone in a house bigger than she shared with seven people when she was a child. There was plenty of food, new clothes, electricity, inside plumbing, a radio, money stashed away in a drawer and her job. None of it seemed to matter right now. She had never been alone in her life and she was finding out that it really wasn't much of a life. She needed someone to talk to, to be with and to care for. What would it be like when Thanksgiving came and oh my gosh, Christmas. There would be no snow, no family, just her, all alone with a lot of sand and water.

Turning around at the pier she headed back to the house. She had to be at work at ten. Washing her feet off in the bucket by her door, Rachael pulled off her dress and replaced it with her uniform. Today wasn't going to be a good day for her.

She hadn't really paid much attention to the time and when she arrived at the restaurant, Rita, one of the other waitresses smiled at her. "You're early, Rachael. It's only nine thirty, you're not supposed to be here until ten."

"That's okay. I'd rather be workin' than sittin' home alone."

"You need to get out and find yourself a boyfriend instead of moping around like a lost puppy. There are plenty of good looking guys on the beach."

"Ain't interested right now. Still got some things to work through."

Rita removed her apron. "Well if you're ready to start work, I think I'll head home, my feet are killing me. That okay with you?"

"Sure," Rachael replied as she began to fill her tray with napkins and silverware. After her station was set up she was ready to go work. It would be good to get her mind off her on problems for a while.

Placing a menu in front of the man sitting alone in a booth, she asked "What kin I git you to drink, Sir. We have the best sweet tea in the south." She took her pencil from behind her ear and pulled out her order pad.

"That's sounds good and do you have any green beans and ham?"

Looking down, her eyes widened and her order pad dropped to the table. "Sam! Oh my gosh, it's you." Without thinking she sat down and slid over in the booth. "What are you doin' here? How'd you know I worked here?"

Sam just kept grinning. "Slow down, Rachael. I was in Lynch a couple of days ago. I half expected to find you there, but when your family said you had actually moved to Destin I knew that had to be my next stop."

"Oh my gosh, I think I'm gonna bawl," Rachael said, covering her face with her hands.

"Don't do that. Look, I think your boss is giving you dirty looks. Just get me some iced tea and a hamburger. What time do you get off?"

"Five, I'm finished at five. You come back then, okay?"

"I'll be here. And by the way, you look great."

Rachael could feel her self blushing. "Oh, you go on Sam Montgomery."

It was the longest workday of her life, yet she couldn't stop grinning.

Taking five minutes to wash her hands and comb her hair after her shift ended, Rachael stared into the mirror in the ladies room. Her whole body was shaking. It was Sam and he was here and she knew she still loved him as much as ever.

Sam was leaning against a post on the porch when she exited the front door. He stood up straight and smiled at her. "Come on, I want to see your house."

"We kin walk to it. I got a car, but I walk to work cause it's so close." Walking down the beach, Sam reached over and took her hand.

A few minutes later she opened the door to her house. "Well, this is it. It ain't much, but it's all mine."

He walked around the room and then stood looking out the window at the ocean. "This is nice, Rachael. You got a heck of a view. Right on the ocean just like you wanted. Are you happy here?"

"Oh, Sam, I'm so miserable I could jest die. I ain't never liked it as much as I thought I would and when momma and daddy left, it got even worse. I guess Florida was jest a place, a name on the map that kept me goin' all those years. Hell, it jest might as well have been North Carolina or Alaska. I reckon I said Florida so many times it became so kind of magic place that would make me live happily ever after. Maybe if'n I had never met you, I'd be happy, but alls I think about is you."

He crossed the room and she was in his arms. "I'm here now, Rachael, so you better get happy."

"So, you mean yer not mad at me anymore?" she asked.

"No, I'm not mad at you. You're just too darn cute to stay mad at too long. I guess I was just surprised when I found out about you running the still. I tried to tell myself that I really didn't care about you, but after I left all I thought about was you. I've never stopped caring about you, Rachael."

"Thar you go agin, makin' me blush."

Marlene Mitchell

She awoke in the morning with a smile on her face. She rolled over and kissed Sam on his cheek. "Wake up sleepy head."

He groaned and pulled her close to him. "You know, I was thinking. Why don't we take a road trip? I'd like to find a place to open a small hardware store. I'm not sure it has to be here in Florida; maybe we could go further north, say… to Kentucky. Ever heard of that place. I hear there used to be a girl there that ran moonshine but she moved away."

Rachael grinned. "I reckon I have heard of Kentucky. Now that sounds like a right nice place to live."

The End